ESCAPE

PX DUKE

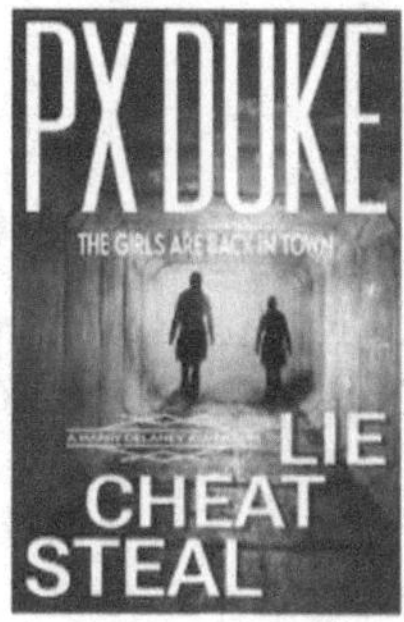

Find out why Harry makes his way from the North African desert to the Mexican Baja. Discover how he ends up having a triumphal return to the deserts of North Africa. Check out all six books of the Harry Delaney Adventure series.

Publisher: P X Duke
E-mail: peterxduke@gmail.com
Web site: pxduke.com

10 9 8 7 6 5 4 3

Printed in the United States of America

JIM NASH

ESCAPE

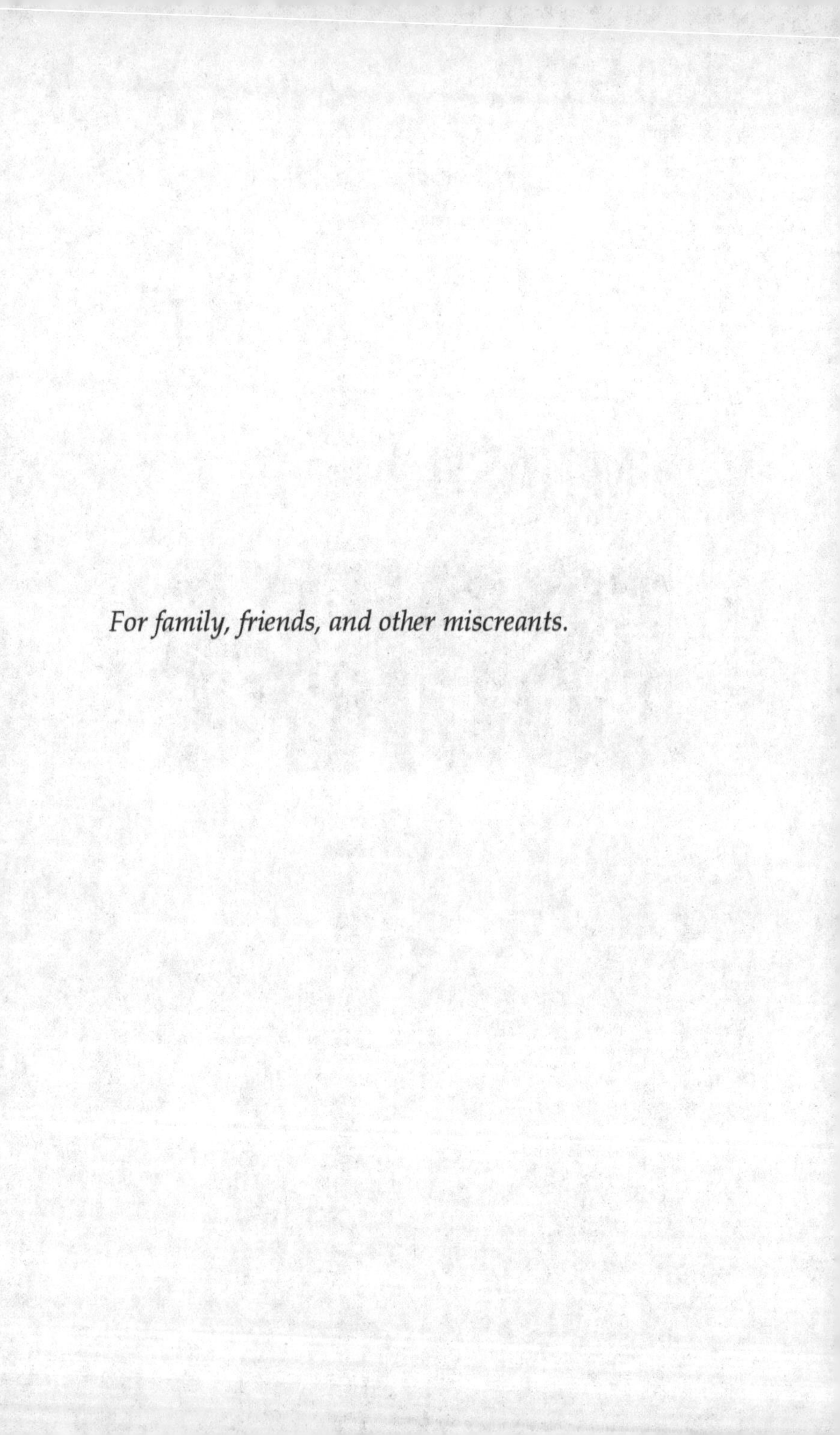

For family, friends, and other miscreants.

Chapter 1

Boots Mayberry suspected it was going to be a long night. The phone call with his supervisor, alerting him to the severe weather warning, only confirmed it. He turned on the radio and learned just how long. The public forecast called for extended blizzard conditions. Anywhere from ten inches to four feet of snow. In the high mountain passes, that meant four feet, easy. More, even. He knew, because he lived in the area all his life.

"The coffee's fresh, dad. I just made it."

Boots carefully filled his thermos half-full of his daughter Emma's special blend of steaming-hot coffee. Half-full because he liked to leave room for what he called the special sauce he kept in the truck. He started doing it a long time ago. It helped keep him going through the lengthy days and nights of constant plowing during a blizzard such as the one the weather forecasts promised to deliver.

"Don't forget your sandwiches. I don't know when you'll be back, so I made extras in case you have an extra-long night."

Emma handed over the carefully wrapped sandwiches she made especially for her father. They were his favorite, but she always included extras that would make him shake his head. She liked to make sure he kept awake, any way she could help him do it. She wouldn't see her father much while he ran the long shifts forced on him by the weather. She worried about him constantly.

She admonished her dad for throwing a pack of energy bars into his bag. "Do you really need those? Too many can cause problems. We've talked about that."

Boots blushed, guilty about being caught out. "I know, but judging by that last forecast, it's going to be a long time before I have time to sleep. Did you make the sandwiches I like?"

Emma grinned and gently chided her father. "Like you have to ask. Just like mom used to make." No way was she going to tell him about the others. Just like her mom did, she would let him find out for himself. Already she could see him shaking his head and smiling. "You might find some fresh cookies, too, but I never told you."

It wasn't unknown for a blizzard to take out the power. Just in case, she was baking up a storm. "Now get to work. I'll be here if you need me," she told her dad— just like her mom always told him when he went off to work during the worst weather.

Boots hugged his daughter before heading out the door. The mouthwash and aftershave wafted over both of them. It was an old habit hard to break. He liked to shower before heading out on these blizzard days. There was no telling when he'd get home if he became stranded at either end of his snow-clearing route.

He carefully closed the door and stepped out into gale-force winds driving snow and ice pellets. The hood on his parka flapped uselessly. Already the snow was piling up. In places it was already over the top of his winter boots. The fierce wind accompanying these storms always caused huge drifts across his sheltered property. He struggled to make his way to his four-by-four parked in the driveway.

Already he knew it was going to be a long night at the least, and even longer, according to the forecasts. He opened the door on the four-wheel-drive half-ton. He already installed the tire chains on all wheels when he suspected the storm could be worse than forecast.

Boots depended on the truck to take him to the maintenance garage and the powerful snow clearing machine that was his bread and butter. It was an older blower that was fobbed off, as they always were, when a new piece of equipment ended up assigned to interstate road maintenance.

It was the way things went, but he didn't mind. He liked the comfort and reliability of the older equipment. He was familiar with it. There were no fancy new GPS or computer-controlled power takeoffs or modern hydraulics problems the newer equipment experienced. They seemed to always be breaking down. With the older equipment, if it was maintained properly, it was *Drop the hammer and go.*

Boots started the half-ton and allowed it to warm. He got out and began clearing the snow and frost-covered windshield and side windows. He brushed away the snow covering the headlights and tail lights.

It was that kind of wind accompanied by snow that would clog everything. There'd be no respite for him tonight.

He honked the horn. Emma flashed the porch light in an off-again on-again goodbye.

He selected four-wheel drive, put the automatic transmission in low gear, and gently stepped on the gas. Four chain-covered tires spun and gained a measure of traction in the snow and ice-covered driveway.

A hundred feet down the lengthy drive, he was completely out of sight. He slowed and stopped in the middle of the roadway. The reduced visibility caused by the monster storm would make it too dangerous to pull over on the side of the main highway.

He heard stories of big-rig semis charging in off the

interstate to get to a hotel in storms such as this. Sometimes, they rear-ended whatever was in front of them, even if it was a blower equipped with high-visibility flashing lights and strobes.

Boots Mayberry would be damned if that would happen to him. So far, his record was spotless, but for that one incident. It was years ago. He put it out of his mind and opened the thermos. Hot steam greeted him by fogging the windshield. It temporarily obscured his view of the wall of wind-driven snow illuminated by the truck's high-beams.

He reached beneath the seat, feeling for the bottle. It was there somewhere. He came up empty-handed. Cursing, he opened the door. Immediately, icy wind inundated the warm cab with cold snow.

He cursed again and climbed out, slipping on the ice-covered step.

E mma worried about her father constantly when the snow fell during the winter months. Winter was the worst for him. It was years ago, but ever since the accident he was never the same. She wasn't so young when it happened that she would ever forget how devastated her dad became. It took him forever to come around.

Then her mom up and died. That right after the other had driven her dad to the bottle. She alone was left to look after him. By the time she turned a teenager, she was doing the cooking and the cleaning and the laundry. She drove into their small town to do the grocery shopping before she even had a license to drive.

Her father tried drying out time and again over the intervening years. Then he'd wake up screaming two or three nights in a row and back to drink he would go. It was particularly bad in the winter. That was when the accident occurred.

It wasn't any fault of her dad. Multiple inquiries all came up with the same answers. It was a fifty-year snow event. It was coming down too thick. The wind was too strong. The valley was so deep it created a huge funnel for the wind and the snow that obscured and covered everything on the roadway that night.

She turned away from the window and put it out of her mind as best she could by making extra sandwiches from the roast she prepared that morning. Sometimes, when it got real bad, her dad did their long driveway early. When he did, she'd run out and take him some extra for the long night they both knew would be coming up.

It wasn't like he was doing something he shouldn't by doing their road. He had to get back and forth to work. He had permission from the state, since in the winter his job was declared essential to keeping the roads open.

Judging by what had come up early in the day, this would be one of those times when he showed up to do the driveway clearing. Already it was piling up. She knew he would be on his way just in time.

She took out the extra thermos and set it on the counter. She went back to the window, now almost frosted over as the wind sucked the heat out of the old stone house. She threw a fresh log on the fireplace. Sparks flew and the orange glow filled the living room. She stretched out on the sofa and relaxed.

She would be able to hear the blower better from there when her dad powered up their road. She liked to have plenty of notice so she could flash the porch light and bring her dad a fresh-made lunch before he turned around for another run down the isolated two-lane highway to town.

Chapter 2

Miami

I turned on the television to watch another news story about a huge blizzard out west. The storm's fierceness announced by the news anchor was lost on me, living as I did in a weather paradise. Sure, it rained. No one was forced to shovel it to get to work. It got cold. Not like snow cold, but cool and frosty enough to damage crops. The roads were always clear. Well, okay, but for a temperamental alligator on I75 or the Tamiami Trail, but that was it.

I counted my blessings and concluded things were going well. I ordered and paid for the installation of a new neon shingle signifying I was the sole entrepreneur in the detective business. The gold lettering on the door glass resembled that of an old-time detective agency. It mirrored the neon hanging in the window.

Jim Nash - Investigator

I was happy with it.

In the interim, I took a few cases. Nothing earth shattering. Nothing to test my abilities to the limit. Simple cases. The usual hearts and daggers stuff. Wives wanting to chase down evidence against philandering husbands. Husbands wanting to test whether their wives were cheating. I didn't do divorce, but I did all that. And then some.

It was starting to pay off. Word of mouth business began to build. It got to a point where I needed something more than a phone in my pocket and a briefcase in the trunk of my new car.

It was a nice car, too. Not too modern. Ancient by most standards. A convertible. Not flashy. A light blue on white shade, just enough to mitigate the harsh Florida sun, complete with the factory air. A genuine leather interior, tucked and rolled.

I used some of my money to bring it up to date just a little. I found a custom car shop that came highly recommended. Call me a philistine if you must, but a modern suspension, disc brakes, and seat belts went a long way toward safety in the event of a car chase with the reinvigorated engine. Or a run from the police.

So far, I was good. No car chases to speak of.

I ended up taking the 1956 Packard out to the track. The old girl easily sat at 120 miles per all day. When I finished, I popped the hood for a look topside and then rolled underneath to check for leaks. When I rolled out, I was happy. I checked the oil and bought gas and was good to go. I even forked out cash to the city for a parking spot out front of the office, beneath the window.

The Packard Caribbean turned out to be good advertising. It got me more than a few customers that ordinarily I wouldn't have encountered. Most were wealthy, middle-aged women. Socialites, you could call them. Looking for information on husbands suspected of cheating. The first was so grateful for the evidence, she paid double my accounting. As thanks, I threw caution to the winds and took her for a drive.

I ended up bedding the second, but it was a short-lived affair on both our parts once she had the evidence in hand. By the time I was ready to say goodbye, she was, too. Strangely, I had to encourage her to pay the bill.

Perhaps I should have expected it. The excuses these moneyed Magic City women came up with to try and wriggle out of a final accounting was something I wasn't prepared for. Sleeping with them didn't help in the slightest.

I suppose you could say my office was located in the tony retro area of Magic City. The neighborhood bars catered to the locals during the day. In the late afternoons and evenings, the tourists moved in, full speed ahead, thanks to the nearby boutique hotels.

Spring break was coming up next. Soon everything would be filled with teenagers with fake IDs and hard bodies. I wanted nothing to do with that, although I appreciated the occasional hard body.

I liked my long days and short nights. I mostly stayed out of the bars. I didn't miss them. I didn't drink, anyway. Occasionally, I'd pop in to one close to the office to collect the local scuttlebutt and rumors. Mostly, I kibitzed with the bartender and vacated my seat when the place got busy and she had to get back to work.

The servers liked the locals, especially the ones that didn't drink who came in to shoot the breeze, drink ginger ale, and leave tips. I ended up taking more than one or two home on a semi-regular basis.

Mostly, I stayed friends with the lot of them. I even offered to take a case for gratis if the sob-story was memorable. I didn't mind. They were personable, and I mostly liked them.

Cheating husbands and boyfriends, as usual. Same old. It never ended. It paid bills when I sent my own out. Except for that one time, no one tried to stiff me.

So, like I said, I was getting busy. Too busy for a solo operation. I needed someone to run the office. I'd consider a man if I thought he could do the job.

I powered up the laptop and pulled up an old help wanted poster. For shits and giggles, I added a couple of requirements in the fine print. I figured it to be more of a joke than anything else. I deleted a couple of others and printed it out on cardboard stock. I taped it to the outside of the downstairs door and hoped for the best.

That's right. On the outside of the door. I wasn't accustomed to Help Wanted posters, obviously.

As it had the first time, the sign ended up stolen. I was beyond hoping that a viable applicant took it and would show up real soon now. Maybe it was the joke I made of the requirements. Maybe the wind blew it off. Each time, I ended up replacing it.

Still, there were no takers. Hell, I couldn't even talk one of the barkeeps into part-timing for me. They all heard about my previous escapade where one of their own, an assistant I hired away from a bar, ended up murdered. Thanks, but no thanks, basically.

I couldn't blame them.

After a while, I gave up. The help wanted poster disappeared a last time, and I only bothered to replace it when I was reminded, which wasn't often. I continued working out of the trunk of my car when the office wouldn't do. That's the beauty of a modern cellphone.

No mess. No fuss. No bother. When it rings, answer it. When it buzzes, read the text.

Nothing complicated there. So I dumped the girl-Friday search thing and settled in to look after my business all by myself.

How hard could it be?

It turned out to be a lot more difficult the busier I got. I managed to work around most of it with careful monitoring of the phone and texts and even some emails when someone discovered me on the web.

The old Packard wasn't built to have integrated Bluetooth, so I was out that. I rigged something temporarily. It worked most of the time to my satisfaction, and when I had time, I'd pay someone to install it.

Spring break was coming up. While ordinarily I didn't mind, the office was smack dab in the middle of things—bars, mostly—and I knew for certain that leaving the car out would be a mistake.

Fighting. Crying. Puking. Pissing. College and university types and pretenders would be everywhere on the local pub crawls. I wasn't one for spanking anyone, but I knew better than to leave a convertible out in the open—even one that no one had ever seen in this century.

Resigned, I sighed and printed out another help wanted sign. It was the least I could do. I got out a map and considered a road trip for a week. I could afford it.

Whether the business could, was another matter.

Chapter 3

Maddie Spence cursed and pulled the jacket over her head. She had been camped out in the city for days, switching out her parking spots so she wouldn't get discovered and ticketed. Her problem was the damned dog—not that he was a bad old dog. He needed to be walked. Trouble was, he constantly wanted to tug her in the direction of Jim Nash's old office.

So far, she managed to resist the pull.

"Friday. What's that in your mouth? Spit it out. It can't be any good for you. Spit it out now," she commanded She reached for the cardboard.

The black Lab wouldn't let go. Instead, he tugged the leash from her hand and ran down the street. At a suitable distance, the dog turned around, sat down, and waited expectantly. When his mistress didn't follow, he ran back, furiously wagging his tail.

"Friday, you are not being a good dog. What's going on?"

He ignored the scolding and bounded off, with tail held high in the air like a flag. He had a bit of a swagger as he searched for the familiar door.

She followed after the dog when he ran ahead and rounded a corner.

Maddie lost sight of Friday, gave up, and returned to the car. She stretched out in the back seat. Shortly, she pulled a jacket over her head and promptly fell asleep.

Friday found what he was searching for. He sat down and waited patiently. His vigilance was rewarded when the familiar man came out the door and recognized him right off.

The man reached for the sign, scratched the dog behind a familiar ear, and pulled the sign from the dog's mouth.

"Good dog, Friday. Take me to sleeping beauty."

Friday barked and bounded off down the sidewalk.

Jim followed.

He called to the dog and picked up the leash.

Six blocks later, he was standing beside a familiar yellow car. It was parked on the side of the street with the most shade. He tried a door handle. The doors were locked and the windows were rolled up to an inch of the top.

Friday barked. His new master kicked soundly at a door.

A disembodied voice scolded the dog. "Bugger off, Friday. It's time for your mistress to have some nappage. Go find one of your own kind to annoy while I rest up."

Maddie recognized a pair of familiar eyes looking at her through the window. A tilted head, questioning. The eyes weren't brown. They weren't even Friday's. Disbelieving, she pulled the jacket over her head. Then thought better of it. She perked up, sat up, and banged her head on the roof with a solid smack.

"Nash. Where did you come from?"

Confused, she rubbed at her hurting head.

"It looks like Friday found one of his own kind to annoy. Me," Jim said, loud enough to be heard in the car.

Maddie's eyes watered and overflowed. It couldn't be because of Jim, could it? She rubbed the bump on her head again and groaned. Nope. Not Jim. "What are you doing here? How did you find me?"

"I'm a detective, remember? Where have you been? I need an assistant. You're qualified. Your dog has already filled out the application on your behalf. At least he's the smart one. You get the job. I'll take the chance."

Maddie resisted getting out of the car. She was in a state. Wrinkled clothes. Bedhead. She raised an elbow and checked her pits. She needed a shower.

"Get your ass out of the back of that car and follow me. Now! You can park across the street from my car. You remember where I park, right? In front of the office you deserted?"

Friday whined and gave up. He shook his head and his entire body followed suit to the very end of his tail.

Jim called to the dog.

"Come along, Friday. If you know who butters your dog food, you'll follow me. This slacker of a mistress you have needs time to get her shit together for some reason."

Dog followed man down the sidewalk, tail raised and wagging fiercely.

Maddie looked after the pair out the front window. It was a familiar sight, and she couldn't halt the smile that took over her face as dog and man disappeared around a corner.

She splashed water on her face from a bottle.

Swiped at her pits.

Applied a bit of lip gloss.

She wriggled into a skirt.

Ran fingers through her hair.

Checked her reflection in the mirror and hoped for the best.

She got out of the car and walked around to the trunk. Rummaged for a blouse that wasn't wrinkled. Found one and traded old for new to confused glances from passersby.

Finally dressed to her satisfaction, she slammed the trunk closed and straightened her shoulders.

She was ready to face the day as best she could.

She wasn't so certain about facing Jim Nash.

Chapter 4

Boots Mayberry's search wasn't going well. From behind the wheel, he tried fishing beneath the front seats as best he could. Found nothing. It wasn't there.

He opened the door to get a better look. He wasn't prepared for the icy step. He slipped and almost fell as he made to grab the steering wheel. He let go and slid the rest of the way to the ground.

He pulled himself up and trudged through the snow to the other side of his four-by-four. He pulled open the door but the roof light was too dim. He reached beneath the seat, trying to feel for the bottle.

The half-ton inched forward. Panicked, Boots jumped in and slid across the seat. He pressed a hand to the brake and reached to wrestle the gearshift from neutral into Park. He squinted at the indicator, unsure if he had it locked. The indicator had been broken for months. He meant to replace it, but the parts still hadn't arrived. One more thing for him to get Emma to check on.

For backup, he stomped on the parking brake and the truck shuddered and then halted. He opened the door and made to get out. This time, it was the seat belt that held him in. When had he put that on? He unfastened it and slid down into deep snow.

He located what he was looking for in the back seat, wrapped in an old sleeping bag. He climbed back into the truck. Wrestled with the backpack until he found the thermos. Opened the half-full container he brought from the house. He emptied the bottle into the huge thermos and capped it.

At first, he told himself he would only take one drink at the end of his driveway. He put the truck in gear and eased his foot down on the accelerator. It took him a few moments in the blowing snow to realize the truck wasn't moving.

He fumbled with the parking brake until it released. The truck began to move. He cranked up the heat against the cold air and then realized his door was still open. He closed it and carried on down the driveway. He hesitated before turning right to make his way through town to the maintenance garage and the snowplow.

He made it to the empty parking lot through the blowing wind and snow. The snow hadn't started to pile up yet, but it was well on its way. He left the engine running and turned out the lights while he finished his second drink before beginning his shift. He struggled through the snow to make his way into the garage, where he climbed up on the huge blower and started the engine.

Boots realized he hadn't opened the garage door.

He got out, stumbled on his way to the switch, and punched the button. The huge door groaned in the wind and slid to the side.

He rejoined the idling snow blower and the powerful engine roared to life as he exited the garage. Reluctantly, he got out to close the door before climbing back in to the warmth of the cabin.

Boots released the huge curved vee-shaped plow. The blower shuddered as it crashed to the ground with a thump. He engaged the blower and eased down on the throttle. He pulled out onto the highway.

He was on his way to completing his first run.

Chapter 5

Miami

Maddie Spence climbed the familiar staircase two steps at a time on her way to the second-floor landing.

Friday, her black Labrador, scrambled up the stairs ahead of her to the second floor and waited patiently at the top. He seemed almost smiling. His tail wagged furiously.

Maddie scratched at an ear before halting at the closed office door.

The gold lettering was different. There was no longer a second name. His partner, Bobbie, must have departed. She'd wait for an update, if it ever came. Jim wasn't so forthcoming as some other men in her life.

She pushed open the door and walked into the office. It was all familiar.

Same furniture.

Andrea's mural on the wall.

A round-faced clock ticking away on a file cabinet.

She opened several of the drawers and checked out the files.

"You've been busy. The cabinets are filling up. Whatcha been up to while I was on vacay?"

She wanted to keep it light. Maybe he wouldn't really take her back. She'd seen him once, looking out over the ocean. He'd seen her exercising Friday. Her dog noticed him. Before she even thought about it, she ignored him, and never returned to that stretch of beach again.

Her loss, she guessed.

In any case, it was too late now.

Jim kept his head down. Pretended to be busy writing notes in a file folder.

She observed him pretend-finish before he looked up.

She went through the motions, as though it was their first time.

He saw fit to remind her. "Your desk is in its usual spot. You'll have to replace Friday's bed and bowls. Kitty money is taped to the underside of the top drawer. If you replace what you spend, the envelope will keep being useful."

Maddie turned and walked out of the office.

Friday accompanied her. At the door, he turned with a hangdog look and was about to sit down when his mistress called to him. The dog hesitated and then gave Jim the look before bounding after his mistress.

She figured Jim would give her an hour, no longer, on the old clock on the file cabinet. Then he would get up and lock the office door behind him. He'd head upstairs to the small apartment and kill another hour before going back downstairs.

Thus, she waited with her back propped against the office door. Faithful Friday waited by her side until Jim appeared.

"I need a shower," she told him.

He pointed up the stairs. "It's all laid out for you. Breakfast is warming in the oven." He walked past her down the stairs.

"Where are you going?"

"I have a case and I'm late. Come with if you want to be on the clock."

The shower could wait. Maddie and the dog tromped down the stairs.

He opened the passenger door of the convertible and went around to the other side.

"You putting the top down?" she wanted to know.

"Is that your way of telling me you smell like someone who's been sleeping in her car?"

Maddie was too embarrassed to look at the man.

Friday wasn't. He woofed.

"A girl's gotta keep living expenses under control. Right, Friday?"

The dog wasn't so sure. He refused to woof any form of encouragement.

"Well hell, even Friday knows when he's well off. You probably didn't have to drag him away from my car."

"It only took a little convincing," he said.

She reached back to scratch at her dog. He was too far away in the back seat. He was on the seat behind Jim. He had already nudged the man's neck with a cold nose in seeming gratitude.

"What're you smiling at, detective?"

"You do have a way with words, woman. It would seem Friday does, too, in his own way."

He pulled the car into a parking lot and got out. Dog and woman followed him to a sidewalk café cloned from all the others along the street.

"We're looking at a man reading a paper and drinking a never-ending coffee refill," Jim said. "His wife thinks he's out screwing around, but he only sits there and reads. Enjoys the ambiance. Does a little mild flirting with the server."

Which was true. The man had gotten his latest refill as the trio picked a street-side table in plain view.

"Why don't you amble over and take a table of your own? Friday might be a draw, too. Take him with you."

Maddie hesitated. She didn't look her best. A mere

three hours ago, she was sleeping in her car. Her blouse was wrinkled—not so much if she chose to look at it through her reflection in the coffee shop window.

She reached into her pocket for gloss and faced the reflection. She smoothed the gloss over her lips without looking. Finished with that and ran her fingers through her hair. Shook her head rapidly. It fluffed into a semblance of rational being.

"That's it. You almost look like you didn't sleep in your car last night. Right Friday?"

She gave him a dirty look before getting up. It changed into a broad smile. She knew he couldn't figure if she meant it for him, or if it was practice for the man across the street.

"I'll be back in a jiff."

She stood up and motioned to the dog before holding up her hand. She got down at his level and raised the flat of her hand. "Friday." The dog looked up at her expectantly. His tail halted its wagging. "Stay."

Maddie swished across the street in her schoolgirl-length tweed skirt complete with pleating. It was perfect for the spur-of-the-moment assignment. If the man passed the test, he'd send his wife a final bill and close the case.

Maddie caught him with the phone out, capturing the encounter.

She smiled and grinned and talked and chattered. The man nodded. Shook his head. Shook his head again. Finally, he held up his hand much the same way Maddie had commanded Friday. The subject slapped some money on the table, got up, and stormed off, obviously annoyed at being disturbed.

Maddie looked across the street and shrugged. In that instant he snapped her picture. She looked pretty good, even if she spent last night sleeping in her car.

The motorcycle and its rider was only partly in the frame of the photo when the rider took aim with a pistol. Shots rang out. The bike sped off.

He dropped the phone in time to see Maddie on the ground across the street.

Friday was on his way.

He panicked. Dodged cars and honking horns and people.

The dog beat him to his mistress. He tensed and crouched, standing guard over Maddie. He only relented when he approached.

"Are you all right?" He held out a hand and helped her up.

"Did you see who the shooter was aiming at?" she asked.

"If it was our subject, it was a miss. He's already in his car on his way to the office. It's where he always goes after his morning coffee and newspaper routine."

"Who would want to kill him?"

"I'm betting on the wife. Come on. Get it in gear. I need to let Boyle know I'm on the clock with this. He'll need to know about the man's wife, too. And get out of that schoolgirl outfit. If Boyle spots you in that, I'll never hear the end of it."

"Are you saying you missed me?

Jim fumbled my words, unable to admit to anything. "No. Yes. Well. Maybe."He had to grin. "I'm saying you look pretty good in that short skirt. You've kept the weight on."

"So now I'm fat?" Maddie's hands went to her hips. A knee angled out. A toe tapped the sidewalk.

Maybe she was faking the indignation. He wasn't about to chance it. "Oh for crying out loud. I hand you a compliment and you turn it into getting fat." He made a grab for Maddie's hand and pulled her across the street.

"You too, Friday. It's a losing battle around here as far as women go, isn't it?"

The dog didn't make a sound.

Unlike me, he knew when to keep quiet.

Chapter 6

Miami

Breakfast was more than a bit late and dried out by the time we made it to the apartment. Maddie headed for the shower. Friday stood guard at the door. I don't know if it was on purpose, ordered by Maddie, or if the dog decided on his own to be on the cautious side.

I tried a bit of bacon. That didn't budge him one bit, either, until I called to him. "Last call, Friday. You want bacon or not?"

He broke down and deserted his post. He chomped on the bacon and waddled back in a hurry to carry on where he left off with his mistress. She was none the wiser behind the closed door.

"You're a good boy, Friday. I won't tell on you. You are getting a bit broad in the beam, though. You need to get some exercise."

Maddie chose that exact moment to exit the bathroom. "Who's broad in the beam? Are you still on that fat thing? Give it up. I can be any weight I want to be."

"No, silly. I was just telling Friday—" She wouldn't let me finish.

"How fat I was."

It wasn't even a question. "I was not. I was telling him—"

"That I was getting broad in the beam," she went on.

"Oh for crying out loud. Give it a rest, woman."

I changed my tack.

"Friday, you're too fat. You need exercise."

The dog ambled over to stand by his mistress.

Maddie reached down for him.

"That's it, Friday. Good boy. I'll protect you. That man over there is calling us tubby."

Discretion being the better part of valor, I pulled the ringing phone out of my pocket. It was the café victim's wife asking about her husband. Immediately I had more than a strong suspicion she was the one responsible for the motorcycle shooter. I hit the record button. It wasn't for evidence. I wanted the recording for my records.

"Your husband is fine," I told her. "He had his usual coffee at the same sidewalk café, followed by a couple of refills. Then he went off to work."

I left decoy Maddie out of it and instead pretended I didn't see anything untoward happen. I made no mention of the attempted shooting, either.

"Nothing else?" the man's wife asked.

"No. Nothing."

"Shit. I paid—"

The phone went dead.

Maddie looked at me expectantly. I knew right off by her condition she was waiting for more than an explanation. "It's the wife. I need to go downstairs and sign off on this one. I don't want to be held responsible for the man's death if she gets lucky. I have to get in touch with Boyle, too. He needs to know."

"I'll be down after I get dressed."

"Good. As it stands now, you're covered in goosebumps. A couple of them are big and perky, and they don't look fat to me."

"Friday." The dog looked up at his naked mistress. "Go with Jim. Bite his ass off at the first opportunity."

"Come on, Friday. Maybe we'll take your mistress out for dinner tonight to celebrate everyone's return. I might even pay."

I put in the call to Detective Boyle and left a message. He would get back to me, and I'd be happy to let him take my latest case off my hands. Once I explained the phone call from the man's wife following the failed assassination attempt, he'd owe me one. In my book, that was a good thing. I might even play the recording for him, although strictly speaking, it wasn't made with consent.

Police Lieutenant Don Boyle had been the one to encourage me to get my private detective license. As an ex-cop, it wasn't difficult. He also turned me on to fishing, but lately I hadn't been doing much of that.

While I waited, I rearranged some of the office furniture that ended up being displaced when Maddie last took off. I stood back and admired my handiwork, hoping Friday would be happy too. His mistress had her desk back. He had room for his bed and bowl as well.

While I was at it, I located the old holster I loaned Maddie for the legal five-shot she owned. The note she left behind peeked out from within the holster. I forgot all about it when she left it on my desk months ago.

Jim
Thank you for everything. Friday thanks you, too. He wants to do it in person, but I just can't allow him to. It would be too hard on me. Maybe we'll see you again one day.
Maddie

I folded it and replaced it within the holster. Maddie chose that instant to walk in.

"Oh. You remembered." She picked up the familiar holster and tucked it into her bag. She opened the note, glanced at it, and folded it.

"Did you look at it?"

I nodded. "Yes I did."

"I guess this is the day, then."

"Seems to be. If it is, it's a good day, wouldn't you say?" I asked.

She kept her eyes on me.

I had to ask. "Is it going to be for longer than a day? If it isn't, you better clear out right now."

Maddie called for her dog.

Friday appeared and walked over to sit beside me. His tail swabbed the floor like he didn't want to ever get up again. He looked up at me and then at Maddie.

"I guess that's our answer."

I doubled down.

"Well, Friday can't speak, and you don't have a tail to wag—at least, not the way he can. What's it going to be?"

Friday woofed and looked at his mistress.

She looked back at both of us.

"We want to stay."

"Good. When you and Friday are finished wagging your tails, do you think you could write something up about what happened this morning? Boyle will probably stop by later. He'll want something from us."

Maddie located a legal pad and a pen and went to work.

While she was doing that, I grabbed Friday's leash and convinced him he needed to walk off the café's breakfast.

Come to think of it, so did I.

Friday and I did a circle tour to Maddie's car. We intended to turn around and haul our fatigued rear ends back to the office until I spotted a man and a woman giving her car the once-over. I took the opportunity for a well-needed break from our calorie-busting exercise in futility.

In truth, I was the one completely winded. We watched silently as the couple circled the car and pointed to the plate. They bent to shield the glass for a look inside and then walked on, mumbling to one another.

We followed at a distance until they got into a dark blue, four-door beater. It chugged off noisily in a cloud of exhaust. The plate number was obscured. We were too far from the office to get to my car to give chase.

"Well, Friday, it looks like your mistress knows people. Any idea what kind of trouble she brought with her?"

He didn't know anything.

I could tell, because he didn't answer.

We beat it back to the office for shade and water. By the time we arrived, it was a tossup as to who needed it more.

I left a note for Maddie to move the car as soon as she could because of her stalkers.

A quick look at my calendar told me I needed to get it in gear. I'd already booked a flight to Utah for a skiing vacation during Florida's spring break fiasco. Don't ask me why. I had never seen snow and perhaps thought the trip would be an excuse for a change in my life.

I called a garage and booked two spaces for our cars. I was tempted to call a pet hotel. Instead, I dialed the airline, asked a couple of questions, and completed a reservation for Friday.

I knew better than to do that for Maddie without first bringing it up. Instead, I called a florist and asked for flowers to be delivered to the office. When they arrived, I left them on Maddie's desk and waited.

Even Friday didn't seem to know what to do while we killed time. He ignored the flowers. He couldn't ignore the sunbeam streaming through the window. It landed on the floor between the two desks. It convinced Friday to take up the position and do what he did best. He snoozed with chin on crossed paws.

I wanted to be right there with him after our walk, but the doggie bed wasn't near big enough for two.

I put my feet up on my desk and leaned back in the chair instead.

Chapter 7

Like her father before her, Boots Mayberry's daughter Emma was a local. She was raised and grew up in the small mountain town. Went to the single-room school, where the older students helped the younger ones. She was later bussed to a high school, deeper in the mountains in a larger community. She graduated and remained behind, living alone with her father. Her mother had died when she was young.

She didn't mind the isolation the small town provided. She liked to read. She had plenty of choice with an internet connection and an e-reader, and wasn't disappointed. She worked part time in the small café in town, putting in hours serving coffee and donuts and sandwiches and holiday-baked dinners to the locals.

The job paid for everything she needed. What it didn't pay for was a life. She hadn't told her father yet, but she had applied to a college in Denver, thanks to her high marks and a scholarship grant because of them. The EMT course started in the spring, which meant she'd be able to return for the winter to look after her father.

Once she graduated, she'd be able to apply for a local EMT job, if any came up in the local volunteer fire department. That's what she hoped for. She couldn't bring herself to completely break with her dad. It was too ingrained in her over the years to look out for him.

She knew about his drinking in those early years. She had looked the other way. She couldn't help it. Especially in the winter, when he was most needed to keep the highway open.

When she was younger, he often took her with him on his snow clearing machine. She'd sit beside him and look on in wonder as the gigantic machine gulped and then spit out the huge loads of snow that drifted and built up on the roadway. She was proud of father and his abilities to keep the roads open.

When she was older and taller, he showed her how to operate the machine. She took some pride in being able to learn to do it. It didn't happen overnight, but in time she learned to operate the machine and clear the highway almost as good as her dad.

She knew, because he often told her so. Her reward was the huge smile on her father's face as her look of incredulity turned into a matching smile.

Of course, it was all on the QT. If anyone in the department found out about it, her dad would get fired.

Boots Mayberry leaned forward and squinted over the brightly lit dashboard panel. The snow blower's powerful bank of lights reflected off the wall of fierce, wind-driven snow drifting across the highway.

Already he was behind schedule.

The storm was slowly beginning to shape up as one of the worst in over twenty years of operating a blower, if not the worst. He wasn't too concerned. He had been born in the area, and knew the roads well, learning first on a bicycle and then later as a teenager in his beater of a car.

Boots unscrewed the cap on the thermos and tipped another gulp of his fortified coffee. He returned to leaning over the dash and soldiered on, oblivious to the dials and gauges in front of him as he concentrated on looking out the windshield.

The cabin was almost too hot to be comfortable. He had cranked the heat up high to help keep the front windows clear. The wipers beat a reliable pattern on the window. He switched their speed to high, but they continued to fall behind the buildup of snow on the windshield. The snow began taking over the side windows, too.

He took comfort in the sound of the powerful, reliable diesel groaning on, never once missing a beat. Isolated as he was in the cabin's warmth, he could only blink his eyes and squint out into the brightly illuminated white fog of snow surrounding him.

The thermos cup was getting in the way of his refreshment. He discarded it and drank straight from the container. He moved the plow over slightly and slowed for the compact car approaching from the west on the single-lane trail he had cleared earlier. There was no telling how many people were inside, but it pleased him to know they would soon be in town on the path he had cleared.

Boots approached the intersection with the interstate and halted. The entrance was still open. The upright gate waved and shook in the wind. It wouldn't be long before the Highway Patrol would arrive to close the snow-covered highway to all traffic.

Except for him.

When the road was finally closed, cars wanting to come through would have to cheat the barrier. He'd seen it done. The chain wasn't locked for a reason, but still, it would be dangerous on the ice-covered roadway.

He sipped at the open thermos and swallowed, knowing that his job would be a lot safer and less worrisome with the road closed. He backed up, turned around, and engaged the blades. He squinted out the windshield, shaking his head at the renewed vigor of the wind and the drifting snow.

Boots began a return run to widen the path he had just cleared. The intensity of the storm was increasing. The hurricane-like wind was driving the snow into parts of the highway he had cleared only an hour before.

It was looking like keeping the road open would be a losing battle.

Chapter 8

Denver

Maddie and I boarded the airplane and left warm, sultry south Florida behind. The flight to mile-high Denver was uneventful but for the fact it arrived late in the day. Friday survived the ride in his cage in the back of the cabin. He did the happy, tail-waving wriggle when he saw daylight and his mistress in the baggage area.

The dog left no doubt he was miffed at me. After all, I was the one who had sentenced him to the back of the bus. I couldn't figure it. With all the attention he received from the cabin crew, he ought to have been pleased as punch. I even heard an enthusiastic *Puppy!* When someone's kid got free and wandered to the back of the plane.

In the terminal, he got to meet a drug-sniffing dog, whereupon they both sniffed and snuffled until the drug dog's handler led him away.

Maddie kept him by her side while I retrieved our luggage and loaded up a cart with our bags. Tired wheels squeaked on our way to the rental office.

The agent checked the reservation and handed over the keys. "I see you're heading up to a lodge. There's a storm moving in that direction. Your stay should be a good one. Lots of skiing on fresh powder. Plenty of hot tub time. I wish I was going."

Outside, Friday treated the bit of freshly fallen snow as a treat. He'd never seen anything like it as he got down on his stomach and rolled around. His head shook. His tail waggled. Curiosity sated, he was ready for the car.

The route to Interstate 70 was well-marked, making it simple to get on our way. The roadway was wet, but clear of snow. Unfamiliar with driving in near freezing conditions, I kept below the speed limit and left the cruise control in the off position. Cars and heavy trucks all passed us, kicking up a mist of dirty spray that needed wipers and washer fluid to clear.

No doubt exhausted by his ordeal in the rear of the plane's cabin, Friday stretched out on the back set and snoozed away the drive.

Maddie worried about the lodge and Friday in unfamiliar grounds. "Are you sure they take dogs? What if he's too big? Did you call ahead to check? There'll be plenty of strangers. What if the other dogs don't like him? What if the people don't?" she worried.

"Yes, I called," I assured her. "The lodge takes dogs. The person I talked to has a Labrador just like Friday. Except he's a Golden."

That appeared to satisfy her.

"Did I mention the ski lessons? They have snowboard lessons, too," I added. "From beginner to experienced."

"How big is the room?" she asked.

I wanted to say it was a heck of a lot bigger than the car she and Friday had been living in, but I bit my tongue and smiled. "It's a suite. Big enough for five or six. It has a balcony, which will probably need to be shoveled by the time we get there."

I even packed a bag for Friday. While it didn't impress him all that much, it certainly impressed his mistress that I could be so thorough.

That was all right with me.

Not that I was trying to score points, but, well, I know how it goes sometimes.

I was feeling pretty good about it all.

Even the light snow falling into the evening darkness didn't faze me.

Chapter 9

I pulled into a gas'n'go on the city's outskirts and left the car running. I stepped out into an icy wind and light blowing snow. It didn't feel so bad when I closed the door behind it and took shelter in the welcome warmth of the store. I was on the lookout for road snacks. I loaded up and headed for the register.

The gas bar clerk asked if I had change.

"Change?" I rummaged through my pockets. Loose change rattled. "Sure. I have a little. How much do you need?"

"No, no, *tar change*."

I pulled a hand filled with what passed for silver out of my pocket. The clerk looked at me like I was an idiot and shook his head. "Tar change. Change for your tars."

I wondered why he would ask for change and not take any. Then, suddenly, I was struck by a lightbulb moment. "Oh. Chains. You mean tire chains. Sorry. No. I don't have tire chains."

I looked out at the big flakes of snow that followed us all the way from the airport. Being from the sunny south, it never occurred to me it might snow in the mountains, even though I was bound for a ski resort.

"Do you think we'll need them? The rental agency—"

"Whare ya frum?"

"Miami," I said.

The clerk's eyes appeared as though they were about to roll into the back of his head. "Figgered as much. There's a storm brewin'. Have a nice trip."

In the short time I spent in the store, the snow began coming down a lot heavier. The wind picked up, too, driving even more snow with it. It swirled around the building and the car. The icy wind followed me to the car. I opened the door and hung on. I had to force it closed.

Sticky, blowing snow covered the front and rear windows and was beginning to accumulate on the sides, too. I got out and brushed off the tail lights and checked the headlights before getting back into the running car.

"The clerk said there's a storm coming."

Maddie checked the map with a nervous shuffle of paper. "Maybe you should pick up a brush. You know, for the snow."

I fought the wind all the way back to make the purchase. For luck, I grabbed a gallon of washer fluid from the stack by the register. The clerk shook his head one more time, and I paid and left.

"Did the clerk say anything about closing roads?"

"We'll be on an interstate. Do you think they'd close it?"

She looked at me like I was nuts.

Nothing unusual there, but what the hell was I supposed to know about snow? Most of my life was spent under blue sky and warm sunshine thousands of miles away. "It's only another fifty or sixty miles. How bad can it get?"

I forged on into the blackness and blowing snow. The thick wall of snow diminished the headlights reflecting off of the tunnel of light. Forward visibility was reduced. It was even worse on high beam. The snow returned even more of the bright glare through the windshield.

I moved the seat up. Leaned over the steering wheel. Switched off cruise control again when I felt the tires spin out more than once.

I concentrated on driving in the unfamiliar conditions.

During a brief break in the wind, I started paying attention to the tall, vertical snowbanks on either side of the Interstate's westbound lanes.

"Maddie. Look."

I flipped on the brights, hoping to make the tops of the banks visible. A solid wall of snow was marked only by uneven ridges some kind of equipment must have left behind. The towering snowbanks enveloped the highway on both sides. It appeared as though we were in a toy car in the middle of a white blanket.

I cranked up the heat with the perverse idea that it would clear a path for us in the ever-worsening storm.

The wind increased. Powerful gusts buffeted the car.

I slowed, not so confident in my abilities as I had been on leaving the brightly lit outskirts of Denver's light snowfall behind.

"I think we need to get off the road. Help me find an exit, please."

My lack of winter driving skills became even more evident. The terrifying high wall of snow on both sides of the highway didn't help to cement my hope that we'd cross paths with a turnoff.

I chanced a quick look at the trip meter. It was at least another twenty or thirty miles to the lodge.

How much worse could it get? Asked and answered the first time. Except it got worse. The passenger-side wiper decided to freeze. Snow accumulated on Maddie's side. I thought about pulling over and then thought I better not.

"Your wiper isn't working very well. Do you think you could clear it? I don't want to stop in this weather."

Maddie powered down the window and made an attempt at reaching for the stalled wiper.

Couldn't quite catch it.

She unfastened her seatbelt and leaned into the back for the snow brush. "This should do it."

Maddie gripped the brush and leaned out the open

window. She struggled to hang onto the brush.

Banged at the barely moving wiper.

Missed and tried again.

Agitated by his mistress's apparent attempt to exit the car, Friday jumped into the front seat. He barked once and fastened his teeth onto Maddie's parka. He braced for all he was worth and went to work with all his might to pull his mistress back into the car.

"Friday. It's all right. Maddie is fine."

The dog wasn't about giving up. He wasn't about listening to me, either. He only tried harder.

His feet lost their grip on the seat. He doubled down, first releasing his grip and then going for a bigger piece of Maddie's parka. He wasn't having much success.

Maddie was laughing too hard.

Finally, she gave up trying to clear the windshield and sat back in her seat.Friday relaxed his grip.

"Good boy, Friday. You saved me."

He barked, admonishing her.

I'm sure he must have thought she was trying to abandon ship via the window, and he wasn't about to have any of it unless he was going with her.

She ruffled his ears and he licked her face.

He finally looked at me with a *Well, you were useless* look, and then looked away.

I immediately felt guilty, even though I had no reason to.

"That dog of yours—"

Maddie slapped the dash. "There. There's one. I can't read it. The sign is covered in snow."

I flicked my eyes from road to sign. It was impossible to read. All that was left of the green and white sign was the very top. I hit the brakes and almost slid past the turnoff. Wheels bumped as the anti-skid took over on the soupy, wet, snow-covered road.

The car skidded past the barrier and missed by inches.

Chapter 10

The flashing blue and red lights were only just visible through the blinding snow. A lone trooper wearing a bright reflective parka waved us over. We had two just like it in the trunk, but they weren't a bright yellow like his.

I rolled down the window and blowing snow infiltrated the car.

"The interstate is closed. Your only choice is straight ahead to the exit. Escape is about five miles down. Take your time and you'll make it all right. The plow just went through.

"Thanks, officer. We'll do that."

He looked us over before going on. Evidently, we were rubes, sitting ducks from a foreign land. The gas station clerk had recognized it, too.

"The road is down to a single lane," the trooper went on. "There are reflectors on both sides. Don't speed. The road is icy and slippery. Stick to the middle and you'll be fine. Leave the cruise control off."

I thanked him again, and he mentioned he'd be making one last patrol of the interstate. "Don't even think of trying it until the storm passes and the roads get plowed."

I nodded in agreement, and the trooper waved us past.

I clenched the wheel and eased my foot onto the gas

pedal. The storm seemed to worsen even in the short time we were stopped.

Wind funneled between the high banks, buffeting and shaking the car.

I kept a light touch on the gas pedal. Inside the car, we were safe and warm. If worse came to worse, the winter clothes we had outfitted ourselves with were in the trunk. I wasn't so sure how long the snacks might last with three of us.

"Maddie."

She kept on staring intently out the front window, as though with both of us concentrating, everything would be all right.

"If it gets really bad, we have Friday," I said.

Maddie smacked the back of my head.

Taking his lead from his mistress, Friday bumped the back of my neck with a cold nose.

We laughed only a little.

Nervous laughter.

I did as the trooper said and turned off at a snowed-in exit to leave the interstate. The back wheels slipped and straightened. I didn't have time to counter-steer.

After a couple of snow-bound miles, we rounded a corner and the not so bright lights of a small town winked through the wall of blowing snow. Faint lights shrouded in snow began appearing as we passed the occasional driveway on the outskirts. The intensity of the lights grew as the distance closed.

"A town. Can you read the sign? What's it called?"

Whatever it was called, it was a welcome respite from what we had driven through on the interstate. The place wasn't so big that it lit up the sky. What there was of it was more welcoming than continuing our road trip in the dark.

My tight grip on the wheel relaxed only a bit knowing we were finally safe and sound.

"We're going to miss a day on the slopes, Maddie. I hope you aren't too disappointed."

"I'm glad we're off the road. Let's stop at that place up ahead."

A neon sign whipping in the wind advertised a coffee shop. White snow drifted around the white building, giving it an eerie glow in the weak street lighting.

"A hotel wouldn't be a bad idea. I can't see worth a damn any more." I was tired of squinting into the snow.

I parked and Friday jumped out with us, eager to stretch his legs. The dog ran back and forth and rolled and woofed and rolled again, running and stopping and pushing himself around in the snow. When he had enough, he trotted back to the car. I opened the door. He shook himself off and jumped in as fast as he could.

"Even Friday has had enough. I'll get our coats out of the trunk."

We fought to don the parkas in the fierce wind and then struggled to make our way through the snow to the diner.

The wind died the instant the diner door closed behind us.

Someone yelled *Door!*

I reached back and gave it a tug to force it closed.

Warm, humid air and inquisitive looks greeted us. Locals, I presumed, intent on checking out the steady stream of arriving storm refugees.

An overtaxed ceiling fan barely kept the windows clear. Rain-like humidity leaked down the foggy glass. The drops grew in size until they dripped onto the sill into a growing puddle.

The welcome smell of hot coffee lingered in the air, almost overpowered by the odor of cooked food wafting from the grill.

A busy, solitary server waved an arm that said sit anywhere. After dropping plastic-covered menus on the table, the older woman with a tag that said she was Janine kindly provided a weather briefing.

She convinced us of something we already knew. We were smart for getting off the road.

"We stay open 24 hours in storms like this for people such as yourself. You can come back any time."

Janine informed us the small hotel a couple of streets over was filling up fast. She offered to call them for us, and Maddie accepted.

"Be sure to tell them we have a dog."

We were awarded the hotel's last room, in back of the building.

Janine handed off a cooked burger patty wrapped in foil. "I noticed your dog frolicking in the snow. I hope he likes it. Come this time tomorrow, burgers will be in short supply if the storm keeps up."

Friday didn't know it, but he would be in burger heaven when we hit the motel.

"What's the name of this place, Janine?"

"Escape." Janine wandered off to top up coffee cups.

I looked at Maddie. "I thought the cop meant escape, as in escape the storm."

"Poetic justice, dear. We made good our escape. We're safe now."

Chapter 11

A compact car turned off the interstate and halted at the closed and chained barrier. A man got out and wrestled with the ice-covered hasp. The chain swung free. He pushed the barrier up, waved the car through, and got back in without closing the barrier behind him.

The driver gunned it and wrestled with the steering wheel as the car fishtailed uncontrollably. It bumped a front corner into a snowbank, straightened, and continued toward town. A single headlight survived to illuminate the way.

It became obvious to the occupants that neither was familiar with the road nor the driving conditions. Constant speeding up on straight stretches followed by sudden braking and skidding in turns caused the car to slip and slide on its way toward town. The twisting, icy roadway did the driver no favors. The car skidded and corrected itself and skidded again, no thanks to the careless driver.

Lessons went unlearned. Slowing down apparently wasn't an option. The process repeated itself around every corner until the town's lights appeared. The driver turned to the passenger and lost control of the car again.

"Christ, will you watch the road? I could do better than whatever it is you're doing."

"You're too late. We're here."

The car skidded to a halt in the snowed-in driveway leading to the coffee shop. A hasty foot on the accelerator powered the vehicle over the low snowbank piled up by the plow.

The car skidded to a halt.

A man and a woman got out.

Feet slipped on the icy ground as they made their way to the warmth of the interior.

The woman halted, dropped on her back in the deepening snow, and waved her arms and legs. When she got up, a snow angel appeared.

"Bitch, get your shit together."

She giggled and chased the man into the restaurant, throwing snow and weak punches that did no harm.

She reached beneath her jacket absentmindedly.

Couldn't find what she was looking for.

Startled, she retraced her steps.

Cursing her stupidity, Fiona Lubinski kicked and scratched and dug and finally located the pistol. With a wet, freezing hand, she tucked it into the waistband of her jeans beneath the thick parka. The freezing steel contacted her bare midriff, forcing a grimace. The look remained all the way to the restaurant.

"Well don't you look so menacing. Who crapped in your breakfast cereal?"

"The gun is cold. I lost it in the snow when I was making the angel."

"Well for Christ's sake, Fiona, will you stop screwing around? It's the only one we have. Give it to me."

A couple got up to leave.

The duo raced to the table and moved dishes aside to make room for elbows and forearms.

Fiona looked around. There were too many people looking at them.

"No. Not here. Order something. I'm hungry."

She got up and made her way to the restroom. She

washed her hands. Splashed water on her face. Ran fingers through her hair in a vain attempt to improve her look. With nothing left for her to do, she regarded herself in the mirror. A cold-eyed reflection stared back.

She was a mess. Dark circles surrounded her eyes from sleepless worrying. The deal with the credit union hadn't gone so well. An off-duty cop happened to drive by while they were liberating travel expenses.

Her boyfriend had been shot in a gunfight while exiting the building.

She returned fire. She wasn't so certain she hit anything, but the gunfire died and they were able to make it to the car unopposed.

Minus her boyfriend.

Disgusted with herself for leaving him behind, she made her way to the table in time to remind Lucky, her companion, what a loser he was. He hadn't been so lucky, either. "We could have saved him. You're such a useless chicken-shit. If I ever get out of here—"

The server appeared, and Fiona was forced to halt her fierce whispering.

"You folks want coffee?" Janine asked.

"Sure. Thanks."

"The troopers closed the roads. How did you get here?" Janine asked.

"We came the other way. I guess he hasn't got that far yet."

Janine shrugged. She knew the east end of the state highway was always the first closed. The interstate exit was last in case stragglers came along. She wondered if they were lying or didn't know any better. "You just passing through?"

"Who wants to know?"

Fiona's hand moved to the pistol beneath her jacket. She fumbled her attempt beneath the thick layers of clothing.

Janine said, "No big deal. I'm glad you could make it off the road and out of the storm. You want something to go with the coffee?"

Fiona ordered and then asked about a place to stay. Janine waved her hand in the general direction of the town. "There's a hotel over yonder. The couple sitting at that table got the last room."

She tilted her head at Jim and Maddie.

Fiona chose that moment to take out her phone. There was no signal.

Janine said, "You might as well know. The phone tower is down."

So that's why there were no texts. The agreement was to switch out cars here. The bullet holes in the one they were driving were a dead giveaway. So was the broken side window.

"How about that phone on the wall?" Fiona said.

"It's a landline. It'll work."

"You got a phone book?" Fiona asked.

Janine brought it over. "I'll bring your orders when they're ready."

Fiona absentmindedly flipped through the book. "Where the hell are we, anyway?"

When no one answered, a man volunteered. He was half of the couple with the last room. "Best I can do is tell you you're in Escape, Colorado. No idea about the highway number. All the signs are covered in snow."

"Yeah. Escape. Here it is." Fiona ran her finger over the hotel listing in the thin yellow page section. The wall phone rang and she jumped.

The server picked it up. She spent a long time listening before answering.

"Yeah. Yeah. Oh. Of course." Janine looked around the small diner before lowering her voice. "We have two couples matching that description. Both of them came in recently."

She hesitated. "Yes. No idea on the cars. I can't see out the window in the storm. The roads are closed."

She hung up, turned, and bumped into Fiona.

Janine rushed into the kitchen, unsure how much the woman had overheard.

Fiona thought maybe the server had been in too much of a hurry to get into the kitchen. She looked after her and then decided it was nothing.

She dialed the hotel. It rang and rang before it was finally picked up.

"Hello? Hello?"

"I'm looking for a Nash. He most likely checked in yesterday. Or today, maybe."

Fiona listened and hung up.

She walked back to the table, stood, and looked over the room before sitting down. "Two rooms are reserved at the hotel under Nash. How the hell are we supposed to know which one it is? Lucky, who the hell is your contact? What did you end up arranging for us?"

"Friend of a friend. Last name is Nash. That's all I know. He brought a car up. He'll take care of ours for a fee. What more do you need to know?"

Fiona's eyes narrowed as she regarded Lucky across the table. If she didn't need this loser—

She put the thought out of her mind, but not before feeling for the familiar gun tucked in her belt.

The strain was beginning to get to her. With the phones out, she couldn't call any hospitals to check on the condition of her boyfriend. Using the restaurant's landline in the open was out of the question.

"Pay the bill and let's get out of here. The hotel is over a couple of streets."

Fiona shook her head as she realized they'd ended up in the very town where the car switch was to take place. It was a miracle with all the road signs covered in snow.

Maybe Lucky wasn't so unlucky after all.

Chapter 12

Fiona made a grab for the car keys and took the wheel. She tromped on the accelerator. The car skidded out of the parking lot and fishtailed down the street. She turned left and spotted the two-story hotel. It was the tallest building in the town.

The pair glued their faces to the window, checking it out.

"So, what are we go going to do?"

"Well, you're going to ask at the front desk for Nash. When they ask you which one, ask for the single one."

"Why do I always have to be the one out in the cold?" Lucky whined. "Can't you go for a change?"

"Just do it, dammit."

Fiona fumbled to find a station that was anything but talk radio.

Tapped the steering wheel.

Adjusted the heat.

All she wanted was to change cars and get out of town. She wouldn't be happy until they were back on the road.

Lucky made for the motel office. Found out what he needed to know. Returned to the car and leaned in the broken back door's window. "There's nobody in the two rooms. They haven't checked in yet. The woman said it was probably because of the storm."

Now what? Park and wait? Get out of Dodge in a hurry?

She wasn't happy with what the storm was doing to the roads. Even if they could get to the interstate, she doubted they could make it back to Denver. She checked the gas gauge.

"Shit. Shit. Shit."

Fiona pounded the steering wheel in frustration. She should never have allowed her boyfriend to talk her into believing they needed Lucky for the robbery. Lucky was a fool.

She would live with it for now, but she would make sure he'd be gone at the first opportunity.

Chapter 13

I looked out across the diner's snow-covered parking lot in time to witness a woman throw herself into the snow on her back. Arms and legs flapped and waved and she stood up, looked down at her handiwork, and grinned. Whatever it was made her happy.

The man looking on said something.

She rewarded him with a punch in the back. It appeared as though they were about to start an argument. Instead, she punched him again and followed him into the diner.

The door closed and I kept my eyes on her for an instant too long. A hand moved to feel around her waist. A look of panic appeared. She hurried out into the blowing snow, careful to put her back to the window.

She bent over whatever it was she made in the snow. She kicked at it and began fishing for something. She dropped to her knees.

Maybe she was looking for a missing phone. She must have found whatever it was, because she straightened and walked back to the diner.

The duo rushed to a recently deserted table. Leftover dishes scattered to be replaced with arms and elbows. They kept their parkas on. They appeared anxious, but I figured it was only what we too had experienced on the icy, wind-swept highway.

The couple kept looking around, as though searching for someone. The woman asked for a phone book. She scoured it, stood up, and went to the wall phone. She dialed a number and waited.

Maddie noticed my curiosity about the couple. "Well, detective, what have you determined?"

The woman hung up and returned to the table. Her hand went beneath her parka and adjusted something. I didn't think it was her waistband. I lowered my voice to a whisper.

"She's packing. That's what she was doing out in the snow. She was looking for her handgun. She must have dropped it when she made whatever it is she's so proud of."

"A snow angel, Jim. She was making a snow angel."

A snow angel? What the hell was a snow angel?

"In any case, remind me to keep a wide berth, would you? We're here in a winter wonderland. Let's enjoy ourselves and sit in front of a warm fireplace and take selfies to show everyone back home how much fun we're having."

I grinned and looked across the table at Maddie. "Are you having fun yet?"

She smiled coyly. "I will be when I get you out of here and into that motel room."

"I don't think we should be sending anyone selfies of that."

I returned my attention to the couple across the room. "She just handed off the handgun beneath the table to her boyfriend. The entire room would know it if they were looking."

Maddie didn't look. "Well, so much for my idea. What's yours?"

"Let's pay and get out of here. Snow angel be damned. I don't like the looks of those two, Maddie."

"Cozy hotel room, here we come."

Maddie grabbed Jim's arm and followed him to their snow-covered car.

Chapter 14

Lucky walked out of the diner with Fiona and immediately began complaining about the cold. His open parka flapped in the wind. Fiona only looked at him and shook her head. How had she been so stupid to get herself tangled up with this loser? Complain was all he had done since the robbery.

"Clean off your side of the windshield," Fiona told him. "I can't see a damned thing."

Reluctantly, Lucky ran a bare hand over the freezing cold glass, sweeping the snow away.

The wipers stopped working.

Fiona started the car and rolled down her window. She stuck her head out to find the way to the hotel.

She gunned the engine to clear the low snowbank and skidded to a stop in front of the motel lobby. She left the engine running and got out. She thought she shouldn't leave the keys in the ignition, but the car was cold and covered in snow. She wanted the heater to take care of it.

The clerk took pity on the frozen-looking young woman the instant she opened the door. The wind whipped and almost dragged it out of her hand.

Fiona wrestled it shut and the older woman smiled.

"Thanks for saving my door."

"No prob," Fiona said. "We're supposed to be meeting with a man named Nash. Has he checked in yet?

It's important that I get to see him. The phones are down and I can't get in touch."

"There's a Nash registered. He's with his wife in a double. Or maybe it's his girlfriend. They're parked out back. The single by that name hasn't checked in yet."

"All right. Thanks."

Fiona pulled the car around to the hotel's back lot. She parked and rolled down her window enough to keep an eye on the entire lot. A single car had a rental sticker partly visible on the snow-covered bumper.

If that dumb bastard brought her a rental—

The couple came out of their room and she forgot about it. A black dog bounded ahead of them. They had to be taking it for a walk. Busy with the dog and fighting the wind and snow, the couple didn't appear to notice the idling car.

Fiona recognized them as the couple from the diner. The man had been watching her, pretending not to look when she handled the gun tucked into her belt. He knew. Maybe he was a cop. Or military.

The couple disappeared around the corner of the building.

Lucky started all over with non-stop complaining.

She regarded him coldly in the dim light of the car's interior

"Lucky, if you don't like it here, go someplace else," she told him.

He looked at her incredulously. "Where am I going to go?"

Whiny. He was always whining about something. Damn her boyfriend for getting her hooked up with this one. He was useless. In the firefight outside the credit union, he'd been useless, too. Hadn't fired a single round.

Lucky exited the car and walked behind it, finished what he was doing, and climbed in. The interior light came on, illuminating the dark stain on both pant legs.

"For Christ's sake, Lucky. You can't even take a leak."

"The wind—"

"Yeah yeah. The wind."

His dick had to be so short that even she wouldn't be able to find it. She laughed at the image.

"What?"

"Nothing. I was thinking about what we need to do."

She had to do something.

If their contact wasn't going to make it in this weather, they needed somewhere to stay. So far, it looked like the hotel was the only place. They couldn't hang out at the diner. Lucky was too stupid. He'd probably get them caught.

"Lucky?"

He looked across the seat.

"Walk around to the front and ask the clerk if we can borrow the key to our friend's room. Tell her it's too cold to wait out in this blizzard. Tell her we're getting low on gas. Tell her anything."

Lucky opened the car door to get out.

"And don't let her front door blow off in this wind, okay?"

Chapter 15

I put the woman and the handgun out of my mind to concentrate on driving in the slippery snow. I skidded onto the main drag. I turned off into the two-story hotel, parked, and entered the lobby. I caught the wind-blown door at the last second.

A lobby filled with antiques dating back to the early twentieth century greeted me. An old cigar store Indian did double duty as a silent sentry.

I rang the bell. An elderly woman came out to greet me.

"Janine, the server at the coffee shop told us about your place. She called to reserve a room. Nash. With the dog."

"Oh, yes. Someone else called, too. She asked about a Nash. She wouldn't leave a message. Perhaps she'll call again."

That was strange. No one knew we were here. It had to be a miscommunication. With all the strangers taking refuge from the main roads, it was bound to happen.

I took the proffered key and fought the snow to get to the back and the parking spot in front of the room.

Maddie brought the car around.

Friday was happy to be let loose. He bounded out and ran and jumped and rolled like he was happy to be here.

Maddie and I wished we were someplace else when we

saw the room. Were it not for the blizzard—

"We'll make the best of it. I'll get our winter gear out of the trunk and we can take Friday for a walk."

"Good thinking, detective. If we get lost in this maelstrom, he can lead us ashore."

Friday tired of the snow at the same time I finished unloading the trunk.

I carried in our parkas and boots.

Friday was right behind me.

By the time we dressed for the weather, he was up on the bed, looking disgusted.

"I don't think he's too keen for a walk, Jim."

"It'll build his character. He'll be so happy when we get him back to Miami he'll love you forever."

"He already does that. You're thinking he might love you forever," Maddie said.

"Maybe. But he's going to have to show he cares by coming along on our walk. Where's the leash?"

On hearing the word leash, Friday jumped off the bed and retreated as far away from the door as he could get. He plopped down on the floor, closed his eyes, and pretended to sleep in front of the radiator.

"Gosh, I wonder where he learned that? I seem to recall a woman asleep in a car—"

Maddie ignored me and called to her dog. "Come, Friday. It's time for our walk."

Friday reluctantly roused himself from his pretend sleep and waddled unenthusiastically to the door.

An idling car confronted us as we exited the room. It didn't seem all that unusual with the blizzard raging and the snow swirling around the old hotel. The window went up and the car disappeared around the front of the building.

"It must be more people looking for relief from the storm. Come on, Friday, it's time to walk off some muffin top."

It wasn't pleasant. The wind huffed and puffed and picked up snow already fallen to add to the fresh stuff blowing in. Ice pellets blasted our bare faces. I gave Friday free rein and he tugged the leash out as far as he could before rushing back. Like his human companions, he wasn't accustomed to the weather abuse.

"All right, Friday, we'll go back."

Maddie turned almost as fast as her dog. "I thought you'd never give up, Nash."

"What? Friday? Is that you? You've been holding out on me. You can talk after all."

She dug fingers into my side and I pulled her down into the snow.

Friday snuffled snow and his warm breath over our faces and pretended he was enjoying it, too. Undecided, he gave up and sat down in the snow.

When he figured out his rear was getting cold, he jumped up and made a fast dash for the room until he caught up to the end of his leash.

Chapter 16

The car had moved to a spot beside ours in front of the adjacent room. I tried to look through the frost-covered windows. It was an impossible task, and I didn't want to disturb the buildup of snow.

I handed over the leash to Maddie and walked between the cars. I brushed at the license plate with a gloved hand. Snow slid off. Holes in the trunk lid appeared above the plate.

Bullet holes. I didn't need to look twice. And a broken rear window on the passenger side. Stolen? What the hell? This couldn't be good. I checked the room window. No curtain parted. Maybe they were asleep in the room next to ours.

I closed the door to our room and left the fierce storm. Inside, the wind only whistled around the spaces between the door and the frame.

"Maddie?"

She kept drying Friday with a towel.

"That couple from the diner. The car that was parked when we left with Friday?"

The couple in the room next door definitely wasn't asleep. Moans and groans said they were doing anything but sleeping.

"What about it?"

"It's parked beside us."

"No big deal. They must have reserved a room the same way we did."

"Yeah, but—"

"You're on a winter wonderland holiday. Give up being the detective and enjoy it."

"Ordinarily I would."

Was there any need to tell her? We'd be out of here tomorrow. But would we? Janine in the diner mentioned the storm was settling in for a good blow. It could be days before anyone got out. If that was the case, so much for the waiting lodge.

They would be trapped with the people in the room next to them. They'd see them in the lobby. The café. They'd be looking for a car if experience told him anything. Maybe even a hostage if they were desperate.

The State Police would no doubt arrive when the roads were finally open. Maybe even before that by helicopter. How desperate would the couple be if that was the case?

"Bullet holes are plastered all over our neighbor's trunk."

Maddie halted her rubbing and dropped the towel. She seemed to be considering how she might talk me out of having witnessed the holes.

Friday scurried off to lie down by the radiator.

"Well—" She drifted into silence before getting up to part the curtain to stare absent-minded into the night's raging blizzard. "The cell phone towers are down. We can't call anyone."

She dropped the curtain and picked up the room phone. She shook her head. The phone was dead. She dialed but the switchboard wasn't available, either.

"You could go to the lobby and ask to use theirs."

With the roads closed, the state police wouldn't be anywhere close to here. The lone officer who greeted us at the barrier would be long gone. I doubted they would be patrolling the interstate in this weather. With all roads closed, we'd be on our own.

"I'm good. There's no reason to concern ourselves. We haven't had anything to do with the pair outside of seeing them in the diner."

Yet.

Unable to think about anything else, I waited until Maddie went for her shower. I pulled on my boots and parka and made sure to check the locked door before heading for the lobby. I opened the door and kicked my boots free of snow as best I could.

The woman from the diner was there. Like she was waiting. Had she seen me checking out the car?

The clerk was there, too.

"Here's Mr. Nash now. Mr. Nash, this young woman is looking for a gentleman with the same name. He's supposed to be staying in our hotel. Are you the man she's looking for?"

I took a good look at the woman in a black parka and long leather boots. She smiled back with a doubtful look. She was tall, with wild blonde hair cropped short. She had a haggard look about her. Dark circles rimmed her eyes. It was no wonder, considering the bullet holes in the back of their car.

"I couldn't be. I've never seen her before. What's your name?" There was a story here somewhere. Out in the wilds of Colorado in a blizzard with no police, no phones, and no escape. It wasn't for me to be asking the questions.

"Fiona. My name's Fiona. Are you Nash?"

"That's my name, all right. Jim Nash. My partner and I are here on a holiday. We were headed to a ski resort when we got caught up in the blizzard and forced to hole up in town. I think I saw you in the coffee shop earlier."

I smiled, and that seemed to placate her. I wondered if she noticed me looking when she handled the gun.

I tried putting the image out of my mind on the walk

back to the room as I fought to trudge through the deep, drifting snow. The wind wasn't letting up in the slightest.

Okay, so I forgot most of it. I couldn't forget those bullet holes.

Maddie was coming out of the bathroom when I closed the door.

I took off my parka and settled on the bed.

"Did you get any answers?"

"Her name's Fiona. She's looking for some guy named Nash. That's all she knows about him. The landlines are down now, too," I told her.

"So, we're stuck here for the foreseeable future. Did anyone know how long the storm was going to last?"

I patted the bed. "Come here and we'll talk about it."

Chapter 17

Fiona Lubinski took one look at Lucky in the shower and knew immediately that her earlier thoughts on the size of his dick were completely off-base. She tore her clothes off, pulled the curtain aside, and pushed him out of the way to make room in the tiny shower. Her error became even more apparent as Lucky rose to the occasion.

By the time the water turned cold, they were on their way to bed in a furious scramble of hands and mouths and naked bodies. The headboard took a beating the likes of which it had never seen in recent history. So did Fiona as she doubted the abilities of her longtime boyfriend, thanks to Lucky and his well-aimed and oversized appendage.

During a well-deserved break, Fiona scrambled out of bed. She searched for her panties and blouse she had so nimbly discarded on her way to the shower. She pulled on the blouse and buttoned up and slipped on her panties.

She climbed on the bed and began jumping up and down. Breasts bounced and shirt flopped as though she were on a trampoline.

Fiona said, "What are we going to do? The car guy isn't here. If he was close, he'd be here by now. He wasn't in the restaurant with the others. The guy next door is a Nash, but he's not the one we want."

"How do you know?"

Lucky's wide eyes followed Fiona's ass as the shirt rose and fell. She was a little skinnier than he liked them, but that only meant everything stayed in the right place, whether she was standing up or laying down.

"I talked to him in the lobby," she said. "They're headed for a ski lodge. They ended up stranded just like we did before the roads closed."

Buttons popped, exposing Fiona's breasts.

Lucky's eyes followed them. "I don't remember seeing them in the café." He wanted another feast.

"Yeah. They were there. I caught him checking me out."

Lucky made a grab.

Fiona's squeal turned to laughter and she tumbled willingly onto the bed.

She rolled onto her back and yanked her panties off in one practiced motion. She wasn't about saying no now.

For act two, she threw a leg over. When she finished, the bed had shifted almost to the middle of the small room. She lost her head twice for her troubles before collapsing on top of a thoroughly exhausted and sweat-covered Lucky. She wasn't so wide-awake either.

"I apologize for calling your dick tiny. Are we okay now?"

She remembered she hadn't actually said it. She'd have to make it up to him later, after she allowed him to rest.

Lucky's smug self-satisfied look said it before he voiced it. "Of course we're okay."

He absentmindedly touched a breast before rolling over as if to sleep.

The passion she'd put into their fevered lovemaking disgusted her. Not once had she thought of her missing boyfriend.

Fiona climbed out of bed and headed for the shower to wash away the sins of her willful escapade.

She dried off and pulled on jeans and a t-shirt. She tucked in her shirt before climbing back into bed.

She tossed and turned.

Sleep refused to come.

She was stranded.

Worse, she willingly cheated on her boyfriend. It had been good, but she was furious with herself for allowing it in the first place.

If she knew anything, when the blizzard cleared, cops would be first on the scene, concerned for the wellbeing of the town. They might even come by helicopter.

She had to get out, one way or the other.

Where the hell was the car?

Chapter 18

The reflection on the growing snowbank outside our window went dark. I let the curtain close and pulled on my clothes and opened the door.

I left Maddie sleeping.

Friday didn't bother to look up. He was content to remain inside after his last foray into the snowy cold and his frozen rear end.

It seemed like the wind was dying. The snow appeared to be coming down a lot lighter. I couldn't be sure, of course. This was the first blizzard I ever witnessed in my life.

I opened the driver's door on Fiona's car and searched for the trunk latch. I pulled the handle. The lid popped without a sound, held down by the weight of the snow.

I went through the front and the back seats and came up with nothing. A couple of elastic bands. For the woman's hair, probably. And plenty of snow in the back through the broken rear window. Most likely to steal the car.

Satisfied, I eased the doors closed and went to lift the trunk lid. Snow slipped off, revealing the bullet holes.

The light came on and I was treated to a couple of bags and some empty cash wrappers. They hadn't taken all of it inside. A small amount appeared to be missing.

What for? Takeout? Unlikely. Since the woman was

looking for someone, it had to be about a payoff of some sort. Going by the bullet holes, perhaps the car had been used in a robbery. Without a working cell tower, more information was off the table.

The cash wrappers would explain the woman's gun. That had to be the reason for the elastics in the front. Had they been on the road since Denver, as Maddie and I had been? The answer was a probable yes.

Okay, so we had a couple of desperadoes looking for a man named Nash. More than likely, he hadn't appeared, thus the woman's query at the front desk. Like everyone else, he too had been delayed by the storm and the road closings. If he would show at all now.

I wondered if Maddie would be in danger because of the name mix up. I'd seen Fiona in the hotel lobby. She looked disheveled and confused. If she was lucky, her boyfriend would screw some sense into her before she made a serious mistake and came for our car.

I eased the trunk lid down and leaned on it. It snapped shut, and I went inside.

Beneath the sheets, Maddie shivered and moved to the edge of the bed. I undressed and pulled up the covers and moved to snuggle against her in an attempt to gain a respite from the cold air I'd been bathing in.

"Well, Detective Nash? What did you discover?"

There was no fooling Maddie.

Good boy Friday, didn't care in the slightest. He was happily asleep next to the radiator.

Chapter 19

It **was Maddie's turn** to take Friday for his walk first thing in the snowy morning. She knew it was still snowing because she'd already looked out the window. Several times. The view didn't improve each time.

She dressed reluctantly, getting up and sitting back down.

Pretended to look for articles of clothing discarded and scattered during last night's lovemaking.

"You could just shoo him out the door, you know. Just like us, he won't wander too far. He learned his lesson when his cold backside connected with the snow," I told her. "Especially if you leave the door open for him."

She continued pulling on layers of clothing to protect against the intense cold and wind.

"Easy for you to say."

"Just like real life, isn't it?"

"All right, we're going. Aren't we, Friday? Come along. I won't leave you alone out there, unlike your master still in his warm bed."

Friday couldn't hold it any longer. Already he was by the door, impatient, begging to go.

Outside, Friday tugged at Maddie and the leash for two circuits of the hotel before halting at their room.

Maddie's cheeks were a chill pink, thanks to the brisk wind.

Snow-covered Friday only looked disgruntled to be outside in weather that definitely wasn't home by any stretch of memory.

The door opened and a cold wind blew in.

"You're back already? That didn't take long."

I raised the blankets to welcome a disrobing Maddie and moved to make room.

I didn't get Maddie fresh and cool from her winter excursion.

An over-eager Friday's ice-cold nose, frosty feet and snow-covered body jumped in beside me and stretched out in the warm spot I left behind.

"Friday. Bad dog. Shame on you. Shame. On. You."

Maddie giggled.

I slithered out as fast as I could on the opposite side of the bed.

Friday definitely wasn't about listening to me. He only looked across at his mistress and wagged his tail as her laughter went on and on.

"Good boy, Friday. You got that man out of bed, finally."

"So now I'm that man, am I? Don't encourage that dog."

I readied myself for the brisk walk to the café by dressing in easy to remove layers.

Friday thumped onto the floor by the radiator and refused to even look at his food bowl or his water. He wouldn't look at us, either, probably thinking that if he did, we'd take him with us. He appeared to welcome being a weather refugee safe and warm next to the radiator.

Clogged sidewalks forced us into the middle of the street. We had the café in sight when the car fishtailed past. I recognized Fiona's partner as he shifted in his seat and stared out a window partially covered in frost. Either he was looking for respite from last night's activities or he was checking out Maddie in her thick parka and loose wind pants.

"He wants you."

She only grinned.

"After last night's workout with that woman, he's in no mood to want anything. Trust me."

"Do you have any evidence to back that up?" I asked.

"Yeah. You. What we did last night. How soon you forget."

She ran ahead to the restaurant.

I followed her to the small counter. On the way, I passed Fiona and her partner at a four-top by themselves. The diner was too small for her not to notice. A chair scraped and she approached, smiling. I recognized it as a smile I didn't want anything to do with.

"You can join us if you want," she said. "We have room for two more at our table."

Maddie muttered a quiet Oh crap under her breath.

I ignored her and stood up and she followed me to join the couple.

After introductions, Lucky and Maddie sat quietly.

Fiona filled us in on how she'd been unable to find the man she mentioned in the lobby the previous evening.

"He's probably delayed by the storm, Fiona. We all are."

That smile again. I avoided it and instead looked around at the rapidly filling restaurant. Some were straggling in from the motel.

"You're the one waiting for him," Lucky said.

Fiona gave the man a look that should have sent him straight to hell. "We were supposed to pick him up and head for Denver. I guess he could be anywhere in this blizzard."

"The locals say it's a bad one. We made it through the barrier yesterday as the trooper was closing it. If your friend is stranded, I hope he's somewhere warm."

That sealed it.

Fiona deflated immediately.

Lucky didn't look so great either.

Fiona got up and went to the landline. She picked it up and listened before putting it down and returning to the table. "Now the phone is dead. Nothing works in this dump."

Maddie shifted her gaze from the window and the fiercely blowing snow to the woman across the table. "It's not so bad, Fiona. We're safe. We have food and a warm place to stay. We're the fortunate ones. We could be trapped somewhere on the highway with no food or heat and only the back of a car to sleep in."

As though not entirely convinced, Fiona turned her gaze to the window.

In the hours since daylight, the storm hadn't let up. If anything, it was worse. Wind-driven snow streaked across the window, obscuring the parking lot and everything beyond.

Fiona returned her gaze to Maddie. "I saw you walking your dog this morning. He's beautiful."

"He wasn't so keen on going outside. We're from Miami. None of us are used to snow and cold."

"What's his name?" she asked.

"Friday. He sat his butt down in the snow yesterday. It took him a couple of seconds to realize how cold he'd gotten all of a sudden."

Fiona laughed. "I can just see him doing that. It's great. Right, Lucky?"

The wind whistled past the door of the warm, cozy restaurant as another couple sought refuge and breakfast from the cold.

"It would be a lot greater if we were back in Denver," Lucky said.

Fiona gave him a hard look. "We can't go back to Denver."

She realized what she said. A dark look overtook her face and she corrected herself. "The storm. We can't go back because of the storm."

One look at Maddie fidgeting in her chair, and I could tell she wanted out of the diner.

"We can't get to our ski lodge, either. Maybe tomorrow. Come on, Jim. Friday needs another walk."

I moved to pick up the tab for the coffee.

Fiona reacted instantly to cover my hand with hers. "I'll get this one. You can get it next time." She smiled warmly before releasing my hand. "I'll see you back at the hotel."

Maddie walked toward the door, mumbling under her breath.

"What was that, sweetheart?"

"Oh no she won't. Not if I have anything to do with it."

"So then, it's okay if Lucky checks you out, but—"

"You know it, mister. He can look all he wants. If she tries anything with you, I'll scratch her eyes out after I beat her senseless."

Maddie ran ahead, laughing.

I caught up and pulled her down into a snow bank. "You're one tough hombre this morning. Let's get back to the hotel and see how tough you really are, woman."

"Promises. After the way you were snoring last night, I thought it would be me and Fiona for breakfast this morning, James."

"Given the woman's performance last night, I'm surprised poor Lucky is even alive."

Chapter 20

Boots **Mayberry ran out** of his fortified coffee hours ago. He unscrewed the top on his third or fourth energy drink. He brought it up to his lips and emptied the container in three giant gulps.

It had been a long, rough night.

He was forced to the depot for fuel, twice.

The noisy blower was starting go get to him, even with ear protectors. His entire body was numb from the vibrations of the powerful piece of road-clearing equipment and the hours he spent behind the controls.

He needed a break. He knew if he stopped at home for a coffee refill, Emma would demand he stop for food and a nap. She might even take over if she thought he was too exhausted to continue.

He couldn't take that chance.

He halted the gigantic machine on the street in front of the coffee shop and left it idling. He tipped his empty thermos in case there was a drop left before climbing down the slippery ladder.

His feet skidded on the ice-covered bottom rung and he ended up ass over teakettle in a snowbank on his hands and knees. He struggled to get up. Finally, he closed a bare hand on the cold steel of the machine for support.

Halfway to the restaurant, he turned back.

He went down on hands and knees once more, this

time on purpose. Bare hands flailed through the cold snow, searching for the thermos that slipped from his grip. Realizing where he was, he stood up and kicked at the snow. His foot connected with the metal container. He bent to pick it up and made his way into the restaurant.

Janine called out, taking pity on a frozen, shaking Boots standing at the counter. "You want something to eat, Boots?" She smiled warmly, immediately recognizing the picture of exhaustion before her. She patted his hand and hesitated before pulling away.

"No. Haf'ta go back. Work. Jus' coffee. No cream." The exhausted Boots could barely speak.

Janine shook her head as she took the thermos from Boots. She brought it to her nose and inhaled. She made a face and went into the kitchen to rinse it.

"Jus' half. Jus' half," Boots told her.

Janine knew better than to question Boots. Normally, she'd call Emma, his daughter, when this happened, but the phone towers were out. The restaurant's landline was down, too, courtesy of the fierce storm.

Fiona watched with amazement before casting a knowing look at Lucky. "He's drunk."

"How can you tell? Look at what he's driving."

"My old man was a drunk. And what he's driving leaves plenty of room for mistakes when you can power over everything blocking your way."

"Yeah, it's no good to us," Lucky said.

"Don't be so sure. I have an idea."

Chapter 21

Emma **finished up with** the cooking and baking she thought she needed to weather the storm. With time on her hands, she worried about her father. Usually, he returned for more coffee and the extra sandwiches she always prepared. With the phones down, there was no way to contact him. Their own road was piling up with snow to a level she never experienced.

It was getting to a point where she needed to go out and look for him for her own peace of mind. She packed her father's sandwiches and coffee in her backpack. She prepared for a camping expedition in a snowbank by pulling on thick winter gear, starting with wind pants over her insulated thermal bottoms.

The last item she donned was her helmet. Heated gloves followed. She walked out to start the snowmobile. It cranked, but it wouldn't turn over. She checked the tank. She found a half-full five-gallon fuel can in the garage. It would be more than enough to take her where she needed to be.

She allowed the snow machine to idle for a few minutes before rocking it from side to side to break the drive belt and the front skids free from the icy, frozen snow. She squeezed the throttle slowly and advanced toward the end of the driveway. It allowed the belt to warm and the speed to build up.

By the end of the long, familiar road, she was at full throttle.

The road would be blocked at the interstate ramp.

At the driveway's intersection with the highway, she slowed and leaned into the corner to bank the machine into the turn.

On the straightaway, she squeezed the throttle for full speed ahead.

Emma braked hard to end the ride at the interstate cut-off and the barrier. She completed the trip in record time, but she didn't cross paths with her father in the huge snow blower.

She got off and checked the barrier. Someone left the chain undone. She fastened it and returned to the machine for the ride to town.

It was obvious this section of the roadway hadn't been cleared recently. Where the snow-covered road was visible, it was polished to ice by the wind-driven snow. Only a narrow trail remained between the towering snowbanks on either side.

Either her father was in town taking a break at the restaurant, or he happened on something on the other side of town to cause delay. She knew that section of the highway to be treacherous, surrounded as it was by high valley walls that were almost vertical. It provided a funnel for the snow to build up and be forced through, driven into the widening valley that surrounded the town.

She charged down the snow-swept highway on the snowmobile. She squinted ahead, her vision obscured by the falling snow and the bright headlight reflecting into her eyes from the wall of blurry white. She wished she had changed out the white light for a yellow. It would have made the going a lot easier.

She relaxed her grip on the throttle in every blind corner. She didn't want to meet the blower coming the other way. Neither she nor her dad would get a lot of time to halt before encountering the metal on metal of the whirling rotors.

That's what happened years ago when her father came across a car buried in the snow. It was a family of three. He'd been unable to see the compact car in front of him. He powered through the drift. By the time the blower's whirling blades came to a standstill, it was too late.

The powerful blades chopped at the rear of the car and hadn't stopped until they reached the back seat. The bodies were found where they were sleeping, still wrapped in their sleeping bags. Neither the people in the car nor her father had seen any of it coming in the fierce blizzard that this one was beginning to resemble.

Her dad wasn't the same after that. How could he be? He turned to drink to forget.

It was on nights like these that she worried the most about him. It was on a night such as this when he'd destroyed the car and the people inside.

Emma braked to a halt in front of the restaurant.

The blower wasn't anywhere in sight.

She removed her helmet, walked inside, and looked around. Her father wasn't there.

Janine spotted her and called out. "He was in earlier, Emma. I filled a thermos for him and he headed back out right away. I offered, but he wouldn't take time to eat anything."

Emma always worried about her father during the worst storms, and this was definitely turning into one of the worst. Should she head north on the local highway to search for him, or should she stop worrying and go home to wait?

Janine waved her over and lowered her voice. "Your dad seemed drunk, Emma. I don't want to cause problems, but he shouldn't be out on the roads like that."

Emma looked doubtful. She knew her father had halted his drinking years ago. It was something they never talked about, but surely, she would know if he had taken it up again. "Did he ask for his usual half-thermos?"

"Yes, he did," Janine said.

"Normally he fills the rest with energy drinks. I keep telling him not to, but he won't listen."

"Typical of all the men around here, dearie. Don't worry about it." Janine lowered her voice to a conspiratorial pitch. "Maybe he wasn't drinking, but he left the machine running in the middle of the street. He almost tumbled out of it on his way in here. He even dropped his container in the snow and had to go back for it."

That wasn't like her father. Now she was worried. He was meticulous when it came to doing his job. He had been that way for years.

Emma returned to her snowmobile. She started it and turned for the part of the highway that ran north out of town. Before going any farther, she checked her gas gauge. She filled up at the local gas station and slid twenty dollars under the door of the closed and locked business.

Back on the highway, the single lane looked to have been recently cleared. That meant only one thing—her father was in front of her. She squeezed the throttle all the way to the handlebar and guided the machine easily along the snow-covered highway. The buildup of snowbanks on either side of the road helped her rocket through the turns at breakneck speeds.

Chapter 22

Boots Mayberry was almost certain he had spotted a faint glimmer of light somewhere in front of him in the drifting snow.

He slowed and disengaged the powerful blades on the noisy snow blower.

He backed up, stopped, and left the engine running.

He squinted harder, as though that would help him find it again.

He turned the bank of headlights off for a better look.

There was no debate about whether he should carry on, or get out and take a look.

He climbed down, put on his gloves, and walked in front of the idling machine.

A glimmer of light caught his eye.

He ran up to the wall of snow and began frantically digging with his hands. Frustrated at the lack of progress, he went back to the plow.

He unlatched the accessory box on the side of the machine, opened it, and took out the shovel.

He returned to the car covered in snow.

As he dug, the faint glow in the snowbank became brighter.

He dug faster until the shovel scraped against metal.

Perspiration ran down his face.

He blinked the sweat out of his eyes.

His breath came shorter and faster.

He needed a break from the effort, but he couldn't take the time. He couldn't let whoever might be in the car wait even a minute longer.

Boots' grip on the shovel slackened. He struggled to open the car door. It wouldn't budge. It was frozen shut or locked.

He raised the shovel and banged it against the window to smash it.

Weak and ineffectual blows bounced off the glass.

Shooting pain down his left arm brought him to his knees.

There was a pounding in his chest.

He released the shovel and doubled over.

He tried to stand up. He couldn't.

All he could manage to do was to lie on the ground beside the car buried in the snow.

With his right hand, he felt for the phone in his pocket. He fumbled to retrieve it and then remembered the towers had been affected by the storm. There wouldn't be a signal.

He gave up and resigned himself to freeze to death in the middle of the worst blizzard he'd ever experienced.

Boots was convinced this one would be his last.

He closed his eyes and tried not to think about leaving his daughter Emma all alone.

Chapter 23

Jim wasn't the only one uncomfortable with the bullet-riddled car parked next to theirs behind the motel. Maddie wasn't pleased with the situation either. The couple in the room next door would be bad luck during normal circumstances. It became even worse luck since becoming stranded and isolated in the small town in the middle of a fierce blizzard.

Fiona and Lucky were arguing again. The angry voices filtered through the thin walls as though through a door wide open. Last night, they argued about the woman's boyfriend back in Denver. Their fighting proved to be a temporary distraction, considering the never-ending sounds that went on for what seemed like most of the night.

More arguing began after Jim went out to walk Friday, although this time it wasn't anything she could make out. A loud discussion, perhaps. Then came a tap on the door and she opened it to Fiona staring back at her through the frost-covered screen door.

A huge dark circle surrounded the woman's right eye. A cut on the opposite cheek was bleeding.

Maddie didn't want to do it. She knew better. Then she considered the shape the woman was in and couldn't refuse. She opened the door for the battered woman to enter the room. "What happened to you?"

She knew the answer. It was patently obvious thanks to the paper-thin walls.

"It's Lucky. He's jealous."

He wasn't so jealous that it kept either of them from their crazed love-making most of the night and again this morning.

"There's not much to be jealous of out here in the wilderness unless he's not partial to snow and cold. What's wrong with him?"

Maddie thought of the car with the bullet holes in the trunk. She had gone out to take a look for herself, and not because she didn't believe Jim. They must have robbed someone. Or some place. Likely a bank. Was bank-robbing even a thing any more? Someone, more than likely the police, had peppered the fleeing car.

Maddie came to a realization as she listened to Fiona. The longer she and Jim remained, the more those two would go on insinuating themselves into their lives. They had to have something the pair needed. Or wanted. For whatever reason. The hand-patting in the restaurant was evidence of that.

"Like I told you earlier, we were supposed to be meeting up with someone out here," Fiona explained again. "He hasn't shown up. Now we're worried he isn't going to make it in this blizzard."

Yeah, and you're looking to us to provide you with a way out. She was glad Jim hadn't mentioned they owned a detective agency back in Miami.

She was doubly glad when Jim returned from his walk with Friday.

The dog sniffed the air through the open door before entering the room and recognizing Fiona. He stood off, waiting for Jim to come in behind him.

Fiona reached to pet Friday.

The dog dodged the outstretched hand and moved to stand beside his mistress.

Disappointed, Fiona smiled at Jim and squeezed past him to return to her room.

"What's with her?" Jim asked.

"Did you see her face?"

"I noticed. I don't want to get any more involved with those two than we already are."

"I know, Jim. I was thinking of the holes in the trunk of that car the whole time she was here. Even so, I couldn't turn her away looking the way she did. Lucky obviously did a number on her."

"And maybe it was a put-on to gain your trust. You never know with people like that."

He was right, of course. I had been on my own long enough. Still— "Let's go to the restaurant. Maybe the phone is working."

The ferocity of the blizzard hadn't lessened. If anything, it was worse.

We tripped and stumbled and struggled through blowing snow and deep snowdrifts. We recognized the foggy windows of the diner and readjusted our track to the door. The familiar rattle of the cowbell announced our arrival to those already settled in.

The diner was populated with snow-bound regulars seeking respite from the blizzard. We were welcomed as fellow stranded travelers with smiles and nods. We took seats at the counter and everyone carried on with their conversations.

Janine greeted us with a friendly smile before informing us the phone was still out.

We settled for ordering breakfast.

Listened to the stale rumors circulating around the room.

Some stories were on their third or fourth versions, but they were repeated like gospel. When more refugees came in, the talk of the storm of the century halted and then began all over again as new rumors flew.

"Oh shit. Here they come, Jim."

The car slid to a stop in front of the restaurant. Fiona looked even more haggard than she had earlier. Pale and with hair a mess, her parka was wide open and she was shivering.

Maddie only needed one look.

"She looks horrible, Jim. And dangerous."

"Could be withdrawal. I'm telling you, Maddie, be careful with that one. And her partner. Boyfriend or no back in Denver, they've bonded. If it's drugs, the pair of them will be getting desperate soon.

I hesitated before going on.

"There's no way out of here for any of us until the storm dies and the roads are cleared, drugs or no."

Chapter 24

An antsy, nervous Fiona dragged Lucky out of the diner and back to the room. The man had turned out to be a fantastic lover, rough around the edges, but controllable and eager to be on top of her. She liked that.

She tore at her clothes. Ripped at his. Finished with him and rushed out of bed. Kicked him. She kicked again before he snarled at her to quit.

"Come on, baby. I came up with something just now when you were on top of me."

That she might think of something else during their mindless screwing hadn't occurred to him. "What? So now it's my fault? If you'd ever learn to give a little—"

"Never mind that. I figured something out," Fiona said.

Going by how she behaved when he was on top of her, Lucky figured the only thing she'd come up with was satisfaction after his job well done. "Do I have to guess?"

"Hurry up. Get dressed. We're going for a drive. I'll tell you in the car."

"What about breakfast?" Lucky whined. "You yanked me out of the diner. I'm starving."

"I picked up some chocolate bars from the vending machine in the lobby. That should hold you until we get back."

Fiona pushed him out the door to the freezing-cold

car. They made feeble attempts to clear the buildup of snow and ice before giving up. Impatient to be gone, Fiona pulled out of the parking lot. Her head was partway out the open window so she could see where she was going.

She twisted the wheel to avoid the snowmobile screaming past her on the way to town.

The car fishtailed into the snowbank. She wrestled with the shift lever, moving it from reverse to drive and back in an attempt to rock the car back and forth to get unstuck.

The effort had little effect until suddenly the car rocked free of its own accord. She floored the pedal and accelerated down the highway, tires spinning, away from the town and the interstate.

Chapter 25

Emma **Mayberry came up** quickly on the turnaround at the end of her dad's route. It was barely recognizable in the blowing snow. She only saw it because of a break in the wind and the sudden flashing lights. The huge plow was parked and running. A partially snow-covered dark form lay on the ground in front of the plow.

She abandoned the snowmobile while it was still moving. It bumped gently to a stop against the enormous machine.

The tall bank of lights on the snow blower illuminated everything around it. It was plain that the body was that of her father. She tore off her helmet and gloves and tossed them aside. She knelt beside him, checking for a pulse.

She raced to the plow and climbed into the cabin to look for the sleeping bag he always carried. She found his gloves and wool hat. She spread the bag open and rolled her father into it after pulling on his gloves and hat.

She checked her phone in case there was a signal. There was none, and she replaced it in her pocket.

Emma climbed onto the snowmobile with a vengeance. She glued the throttle to the handlebar and sped down the road toward town.

She roared up to the door of the coffee shop, got off, and ran in. The door banged against the wall. The building shook from the door and another gust of wind.

All eyes turned to her. "I need help. My dad has had a heart attack. He's on the ground at the end of the road. I need help and a car to get him here."

Maddie looked at Jim. "Go."

The cook came out from behind the pass-thru window dragging his parka. "I was a medic in the military."

Jim followed Emma to the door. "My car is behind the hotel. Take me there."

Jim jumped onto the back of Emma's snow machine and fought to hold on to her as she scrambled over the snowdrifts to the hotel. It was the fastest Jim had made it since arriving by car.

"Help me clear it."

They rushed to clear the front window. Satisfied, Jim got in, slammed the door, started the car, and made for the café. It was tough going until he made the snow-swept main street blown clear and icy by the fierce wind.

"He's outside on the ground," Emma explained. I wrapped him in a sleeping bag and put on his hat and gloves. Do you think he'll be all right by the time we get there?"

Jim didn't know what to say. This was his first foray into freezing cold weather.

The cook seemed to be at a loss, too, but he at least offered some hope. "You did good, Emma. We'll get him back to town."

The cook climbed onto the back of the snow machine with Emma. Both vehicles made their way toward her dad. Jim raced the car as best he could down the icy road. The snowmobile passed him.

A car coming the opposite way sped past. It was impossible to see inside its snow-covered windows.

A familiar sight greeted him as soon as he slowed and turned onto the turnabout. The car usually parked beside their rental at the hotel was in front of him. The front end was smashed in. The doors were open. The car was empty.

He coasted up to the giant snow blower.

Slipped on the ice when he pumped the car's brakes. Pressed steady on the pedal again and the anti-skid came to life.

A black form lay on the ground in front of the machine. The cook medic jumped out and ran to Boots.

Boots tried to speak. His words slurred.

The medic announced that his pulse was strong. There was no smell of alcohol on his breath.

Emma comforted and soothed her father as the two men picked him up. "Don't worry, dad. We'll get you back to town as fast as we can."

They wrestled him into the back of the car. Boots tried to talk. His words made no sense. Emma and the cook stayed with him as Jim began the return trip over the snow and ice-covered narrow road.

"Where are we going to put him, Emma? Janine said your place is out in the boonies. You're going to need help until the storm eases."

"I don't know. I don't know," Emma worried.

"Then take our room at the hotel. Maddie and I can sleep in the lobby."

Jim checked the reflection in the mirror. Emma's look of relief stared back at him.

"You'll need to stay with him, Emma."

He motioned to the cook sitting beside him in the car. Medic or not, he was better than nothing. "Maddie can cook. So can I. We'll take over for the cook until we aren't needed."

"In that case, Emma, I can use the snowmobile to run back and forth around town to collect everything I'll need if Jim will take me back to it."

It would be faster than using a car.

The town's streets were clogged with snow and impassible.

Chapter 26

So much for the ski lodge vacay. Even so, this made for a better story to tell once he and Maddie could get themselves out of town. There was no way that was happening with the bank robbers in the room next to Emma and her father.

I skidded the car over the drift impeding access to the hotel parking lot and slid to a stop in front of our room. We opened the car doors and carried Boots into the room.

Maddie and Friday were inside.

Friday was almost smiling as Maddie ran the brush across his back for his daily brushing. His tail wagged when Jim appeared.

"What's happening? Who's that?" she asked.

"Emma's father runs the snow clearing equipment. He was on the ground in front of the plow when she found him. He's had a heart attack. I volunteered our room for him since this storm isn't going anywhere and they live too far out of town."

"All right. I'll pack up. Where are we going?"

"The lobby for now. It's the only place."

Tears of gratitude streamed down Emma's face. "You could stay at our place. It's out in the country. Once I get my dad comfortable and settled, I'll go back to the blower and work my way out so you can safely make the drive. I'll need a ride if you'll drive me."

Maddie looked at Emma. She'd seen the huge machine in action, and it didn't look to her like the girl was capable. "You can drive that thing?" She should have known better.

"Oh yeah. My dad showed me how when I was little. He'd let me sit in his lap and he'd teach me about all the controls. It's no big deal."

Emma fussed over her father as Maddie and Jim finished packing. She covered him in the sleeping bag and all the blankets she could find.

The cook was satisfied that Boots' condition was stable, as far as he could tell.

"I need a blood pressure cuff. We have to get the snowmobile back."

Jim and Maddie struggled through the snowdrifts, dragging their bags behind them to the lobby.

"I'm going to take Emma back to the snow blower after she gets her father settled in. Have you ever driven a snowmobile?"

It was needed to get around town to collect first aid gear for Emma's father.

"Uhh—" Maddie started and stopped.

"Well then, dress your warmest and bring your mittens. I wouldn't want you to freeze that little tush off."

Maddie began pulling on her trendy winter gear. "And here I thought we'd be at a ski lodge by now. I'd be styling out at the bar and flirting with the hottie ski instructors."

"Yeah, like I'd leave you alone long enough for that to happen. Are we bringing Friday?"

The animal looked up at Jim with a hang-dog look that said he wanted to stay where it was warm and cozy and dry until his mistress opened her mouth.

"I don't see why not. He's in this with the rest of us."

Friday let out a resigned snuffle and sat by the door to wait.

Jim took his time on the slippery road, not wanting to jeopardize the car by running it into the steep, icy banks. At the turnout it was obvious a car had been shoveled out of the huge snowbank in front of them. It had to be Fiona and Lucky. They'd passed a car, smashed into a snowbank, close to the turnaround.

Emma gave Maddie a crash course on how to operate the snowmobile. She climbed on behind the woman and guided her in a run up the road and back.

"Slow is better for a newbie," Emma told her.

Satisfied with Maddie's abilities, Emma climbed the ladder into the snow clearing machine and reversed it.

It was their clue to head for town.

Friday sat up in the car's back seat to keep an eye on his mistress.

Maddie struggled with the snowmobile at first, testing her abilities with the throttle. She slowed in the corners. As she became more familiar, she passed the car.

Friday jumped into the front too late to see Maddie disappear around a corner.

"Damn that women driver, Friday. You must be used to it by now."

Friday woofed his disapproval and settled back down in the seat to wait to catch up to his mistress.

It didn't take long.

I rounded a corner and witnessed the machine laying on its side, still running.

Maddie was attempting to wrestle it right-side up.

Friday jumped out of the open door behind me and nuzzled Maddie's hand.

Together we righted the unfamiliar machine after much huffing and puffing.

"What happened?"

Maddie grinned like a banshee. "I took the corner too fast and couldn't bank it properly. Can we get one of these?"

"I don't think it would be the same in Miami, but if you want one to sit on in the office and rev up—"

"Nah. It would be too noisy."

Maddie pushed me into the snowbank, jumped on the idling snowmobile, and roared off into the blizzard.

"Friday, you need to talk to that woman. The sooner, the better."

Friday seemed to know she wouldn't listen. He didn't make a sound.

The snowmobile wasn't at the hotel when I arrived.

I worried Maddie wasn't back until I spotted her walking around from the back of the building.

The cook had taken the machine to retrieve a blood pressure monitor and some aspirin.

"How's he doing?"

"He's sleeping. I came to check on you. I'm going back to stay with him. He shouldn't be alone. Come on, Friday, we have work to do."

Friday, ever eager to escape the snow and cold, jumped at the chance and followed his mistress into the room.

The huge snow blower piloted by Emma went by on the highway. A cloud of swirling snow enveloped it, swept up by the whirling blades. The air horn sounded as she slowed and waited.

I collected our bags from the lobby and followed Emma at a respectable distance to the turnoff. I parked and waited at the intersection until she finished clearing the road to the house.

Emma halted the machine and got out. "I'd have been back sooner but I put the coffee on for you. I really appreciate—"

I held up my hand. "It's the least we could do. It's too far from town for your dad to be out here. We can all take turns in the room. Even Friday will get a shot."

"Aww. He's a real cutie. Say now, whose car was that in the ditch?"

I wondered if I should take the time to explain, and then went full steam ahead. When I finished, Emma instructed me to follow her back to the house. It was an easy trip with the snow blower's blades disengaged. I only had to look out the windshield and keep the white and blue strobe lights in sight.

She halted and climbed down and waved me into the house. Inside, she walked to a gun safe and opened the combination lock before regarding me.

"You qualified?"

"I'm a retired cop, now a private detective back in Miami," I said.

"In that case, pick as many as you need. The ammo is there, too. I noticed the holes in that trunk. Couldn't miss them, in fact."

"Yeah, those two are in the room next to us. They've been fighting and arguing over her boyfriend back in Denver and screwing their brains out since they checked in."

Emma grinned. "Well, as long as they keep happy—"

"I don't think it's going to last much longer. I think she's an addict."

"In that case," Emma said, "we better hope this storm blows over soon."

"Not soon enough, Emma. Thanks for the protection. I'll leave it behind when we go. And remember, those two are dangerous. Keep a wide berth."

"I've got an excuse to make a run through town now. I'll clear a couple of streets so you all can get back and forth from the hotel to the restaurant a lot easier."

I almost forgot about our promise to cook in the snow-bound restaurant.

"That reminds me. I wonder how Maddie is making out on the cooking detail."

Emma called out as she left. "All hands on deck."

Chapter 27

Maddie didn't mind her new cook duties. In fact, she kind of enjoyed it. She got to meet everyone stranded by the weather as well as some of the more eccentric local regulars.

Janine kept the coffee pot full and the orders coming. When Maddie got overwhelmed, or didn't know how to cook something, she told the customer they were out. No one complained when she substituted eggs sunny-side.

Janine slipped her the eye once or twice over a couple of her subs, but all in all, it went pretty good until Jim showed up to take over.

It was a good thing, too, because this was all new to her. She was exhausted, more from nervousness and wanting to do a good job than fatigue.

"Emma is going to come by and show you where the turnoff is to her house," he told her.

One look told him Maddie wasn't going to last much longer, and by the time Emma showed up with the heavy equipment, she was dead on her feet.

"Come on, Maddie. I'll take you home in style." Emma gestured to the huge machine outside.

Maddie looked out the window and back at Jim. "Holy shit. Is she serious?"

"Get it together, girl. I'll keep Friday here with me while you two have all the fun in the blizzard. I already told her about Fiona and Lucky. She'll probably offer up a little something from the gun safe. Don't refuse it until we can get our asses out of here."

I made sure to let Emma know Maddie was qualified, too.

Maddie said, "Right now, I'm too tired to care."

I put my arms around Maddie and hugged her hard. She was on the verge of tears when the entire diner stood up and applauded.

Maddie took a bow and left the diner.

She struggled to make her way to the huge yellow snow machine without looking back.

Emma told her where to grip and where to step.

She climbed into the cramped quarters and waited for Emma to join her.

"Take me home, Clementine. I need rest and recuperation. My feet are killing me."

Emma handed over ear protectors and they were off.

It was rough and noisy. When Emma engaged the blower to widen the driveway, the blowing snow engulfed the machine, making visibility almost impossible.

Emma halted the machine at the house. She got out and Maddie followed, making sure to copy Emma's movements as she climbed down.

It was warm and cozy inside the house. A fire glowed in a wood stove in the kitchen. A propane stove started right up beneath the coffee pot.

"Jim told me those two in the room beside you are criminals of some kind. The gun safe is open. He already filled his pockets. He asked me if it was all right if you did the same."

The women studied each other.

"It's all right," Emma said. "Jim told me you were qualified. Close it and lock it when you find what you want."

Chapter 28

My plan to bring Maddie along on my ski lodge winter wonderland was fast going downhill—and I didn't mean the ski resort slopes. Getting caught in the blizzard nailed it. Now, with Boots' heart attack preventing anyone from running the plow, who knew how long it would take to make good our escape from Escape.

So much for planning. I waved to an exhausted Janine, and she picked up the coffee pot.

"Who's filling in for you?"

She only shook her head and returned to fill my mug.

"Maybe Maddie and I can help. What do you say? You want a break to go home and get caught up on your sleep?"

I thought Janine might fall to her knees and kiss my hand. "With you two lovebirds in charge I won't have to worry about payday, will I?"

"Nah. All tips are yours. I'll even pass on the bad-mouthing I get from my satisfied customers." I grinned up at her.

"I was afraid of that. In that case, you've got a deal," a grateful Janine said.

She flung her apron over the back of a counter stool, checked in with the cook, and double-timed it for the door, donning her parka on the way out.

She stepped into the snow, halted, and seemed to change her mind. She had left so fast she was forced to return for her winter boots. "I'll see you sometime tomorrow," were her last words.

I was good with that. It wasn't difficult to convince Maddie. We'd be slow, of course, but speed wouldn't be a necessity. All the coffee shop's customers were trapped. There was nowhere else to go.

Maddie volunteered to work the kitchen. While doubtful she was capable of doing the job to replace the cook and former medic who was now taking care of Emma's father, Boots, she thought she could fry eggs, cook bacon, and make toast.

She searched for and found a clean apron and went to work.

I smacked her behind and she waved a spatula at me. "Kiss the cook or be gone. I'll not be putting up with your sexual harassment on the job."

A loud voice broke through the chatter and boomed. "You tell 'em, girl."

Maddie grinned and called out. "Thank you, good sir."

I blushed and complied. I had no other options. I slunk away to the front of the house.

I tried hard not to screw up the orders, but details got the better of me. A forgiving crowd waited patiently to see what they would end up with. Where else could they go?

Already Maddie was helming the kitchen. Plates slammed onto the stainless pass-thru. The new cook was in high gear. "Order up!"

It was that way to the very end of the day.

I was ready to die from exhaustion. Okay, so maybe I wouldn't die, but my feet were killing me.

My back was complaining.

My fingers were stiff.

Worse, I didn't know a soul I could whine about it to.

Maddie refused to listen. She had her own problems as cook and chief bottle-washer.

Emma was out keeping the roads open.

Friday was ensconced at Emma's, too content to care about anything other than a snooze in front of a warm fire.

The restaurant door flew open and a familiar voice greeted me, one that Maddie wouldn't be happy to hear. Fortunately, she was busy in the kitchen making noises I didn't recognize.

"Jim? What the hell? What are you doing?"

"I'm filling in for Janine, the server. She needed a break. I told her to come back tomorrow."

Fiona Lubinski stripped off her parka and grabbed an apron. "I can help. Lucky can do the dishes."

She called out to her confused partner in crime. "I just volunteered you for kitchen duty."

Lucky, the new kitchen lackey, grumbled and donned a dirty apron before rounding the corner to the kitchen's business end.

Maddie was going to be a long way from happy when that one put his face past the door. And so she mumbled and cursed and finally accepted that we were in crisis mode until the blizzard ended and we could get ourselves out of town.

Maddie stuck her head out the pass-thru. "You didn't tell me Fiona was out front." She was just plain annoyed, judging by the look of incredulity on her face. She was wondering what she'd gotten herself into.

"I couldn't very well tell her no, could I? The cook is out indefinitely while he takes care of Emma's father. I couldn't stand around and let Janine collapse. Fiona caught sight of me and volunteered to help." I looked around for her, but she was missing.

Maddie caught her coming out of the woman's made up like a dance hall floozie. "For crying out loud. Look at that woman. She actually thinks she has a chance."

Idiot that I am, I couldn't keep my trap shut. "Well—"

Wrong word. Any word would be wrong.

Maddie kicked me in the shin before turning to the grill to strip it of food and load plates. "Order up. Get your ass in gear, mister. We have blizzard refugees to feed, and the cupboard is getting even more bare by the hour."

I made an executive decision. I printed a sign and hung it on the inside of the door. Customers would see it on their way out.

Diner closed 9 p.m. Open 9 a.m.

It was a long haul for the diner's neophyte staff, but closing time did finally roll around.

Sore feet.

Stiff fingers.

Burns.

Cuts.

Scrapes.

Bandages.

Backs and tired muscles ached in places we didn't know existed.

"Right now, I'm too tired to care. I just want to go to bed and sleep it off," Maddie said.

I put my arms around her and hugged. "You smell like bacon and eggs," I whispered in her ear—probably not the most romantic thing to say under present circumstances. She bent my ear to complain about her black and blue rear from Lucky's groping hands.

I wasn't faring any better. Fiona rubbed herself against me so many times I felt like a post getting scratched by a cat. I was certain if the day went on any longer, the woman would start to purr.

Discretion being the better part of valor, especially

where Maddie was concerned, I chose not to reciprocate my complaints about Fiona.

With the diner locked, I settled in with a coffee before helping with the dishes. Fiona rubbed my leg with her foot. I shifted uncomfortably on the counter stool and immediately wished for Maddie to hurry up.

"Who's locking up?" Fiona asked.

Lucky volunteered.

Fiona nodded agreement.

Maddie got busy counting out the day's receipts before slipping them into her purse.

She handed the keys over to Fiona.

A surprised look on Lucky's face told his story. It was all about the cash in the purse.

Had they robbed a bank and gotten away with anything at all?

Or were they two greedy people who wanted everything they could get their hands on?

"Come on, Maddie. It's time to go."

Chapter 29

While we were occupied and busy in the diner, Emma must have gone home. The driveway was freshly cleared. The bed in the spare room was made up. Thick, downy comforters piled on top of the bed greeted us. Towels and housecoats were laid out, too.

"It's like a hotel," Maddie said.

"Yeah, and Emma doesn't have time for this if she's clearing the roads and checking in on her father. You need to talk to her, Maddie. We're not guests for her to pamper."

"She's young. She'll get over it. And yes, I'll talk to her. I think she's stubborn, though. Maybe she won't listen."

I gave her a tired grin. "Well then, in that case, stubborn knows stubborn, doesn't it?"

I did my duty with Friday, taking him out for a quick run up and down the driveway. It didn't take him long now that he had a nice warm fire to sleep beside. He was out to do his business and back in a matter of minutes.

"Friday, you're a lazy lump," I told him. "While you've been lolly-gagging by the fire, we've been busting our rear ends and our feet."

He didn't care. His head went to the floor and he rolled onto his back like a content puppy in a sunbeam.

"So then, sailor, wanna share the shower?" Maddie's

voice drifted down the hall. Her clothes slipped to the floor.

Mine ended up in a pile.

I followed her into the warm water and let it wash away the smell of French fries and grease. In an hour we were buried under the covers and fast asleep.

Morning came too early.

"We didn't bring enough clothes for this, Jim. We're going to smell like French fries until we get back to Miami."

A voice called out from the kitchen. "You're my size, Maddie," Emma said. "And Jim looks to be almost the same as dad. You're welcome to go through the closets to find whatever you think is right."

"What are you doing? When did you come back? What are you doing here? Shouldn't you be with your dad?"

"I was until it was time to do the driveway to get you to the diner. You have to be back to work for nine. I made pancakes and bacon. Shut up, sit down, and eat," Emma commanded.

Emma's homemade pancakes were the best. Even Maddie had to give it up for them. The Canadian maple syrup killed it.

"How is your dad doing?" Maddie asked.

"He's all right. He's taking aspirin and drinking hot fluids. His blood pressure and pulse are good. It was more likely fatigue and that darned energy drink stuff he uses to keep awake. He keeps his thermos half-filled with that stuff during storms like this."

"Well, he needs to stop it right now before something serious does happen," Maddie said.

"He thinks I don't know. It's exactly what I've been telling him all winter. Maybe a little positive reinforcement from you two if you get a chance—" she halted.

"All right, peeps. Out to the car."

"Wait a sec. Did Fiona and Lucky show up last night at the hotel? They seemed awful disappointed they didn't get to cash out."

"Yeah, about that," Emma said.

Maddie gave Emma a questioning look.

"I went through your purse for the cash and locked it away in the gun safe. I hope you don't mind."

"That makes me feel better. I don't trust those two any more than I can make a snow angel," Maddie said.

"Hang around here long enough and I'll show you. Let's go. It's time."

Emma fired up the blower and lowered the blade to begin clearing a path to the highway and into town. In the car, Maddie rested her head on my shoulder and we held hands all the way.

The romantic mood lasted until we spotted the lineup waiting to get into the diner. Stiff muscles complained before we set foot in the place.

"Suck it up, buttercup," I told Maddie.

"Right backatcha, bay-bee," she said.

Chapter 30

Emma was busy keeping the highway and the road to the diner clear.

How Maddie and I were going to handle Lucky and Fiona would not be so straightforward.

"Did Emma open their gun safe for you?" I asked.

"She did. I picked up a nice little 8-shot revolver. It's only a .22, but it should do the job close-in."

"Those two should have had you on that bank job."

"Yeah, well, you're the one stuck with me now. Love it or leave it," Maddie grinned.

"I'm going for the first, but don't push it."

We sighed from exhaustion and carried on toward the diner and our new jobs. I wrestled the car over the low snowbank into the diner's lot.

Already people were starting to file in. Fiona must have opened early.

I spotted the woman decked out in a short skirt that an apron barely made legal. "What the hell?"

"Oh, she's gunning for you, detective. Strange that you didn't see her coming."

"Two nights ago, I heard her do exactly that. Again and again."

"Now I know why you had such a problem lasting."

She pulled open the door to the restaurant."

"Maddie—"

She held the restaurant door against the wind. "I'm not complaining. I want you to know that I know. Maybe I can borrow a skirt from Emma's closet." She stuck out her tongue before heading for the kitchen.

"Are you sure you don't want one from Fiona's closet?" I asked, as Fiona showed up.

Fiona greeted me like something long lost and only recently found. "Hi Jim. How are you this morning?" She waved and smiled.

Maddie didn't get so much as a glance from the woman. She was too busy pretending to ignore her presence until she couldn't.

"Oh hi, Maddie. You're here, too. You didn't have to come in. I can handle it."

Maddie gave me the look and headed straight for the kitchen.

Lucky, already busy burning eggs, greeted her like she was his favorite person.

"Hang it up, Lucky. You can't cook worth shit," I heard through the pass-thru. "The grill is too hot. You're wasting food. Move over and let me start fresh."

I poked my head around the corner to witness the destruction wreaked by Lucky.

Maddie busied herself scraping the grill of the burned eggs and home fries, greased it, and started from scratch.

Fiona sidled up to me in the doorway.

A warm breast caressed my upper arm. I noticed right off that she wasn't wearing a bra. I also noticed her breast was very firm.

"Jim? Could you come into the kitchen for a minute? I need something." Maddie grabbed me with both hands and pulled me into the cooler.

"If I see that woman rubbing her tits all over you again, I'll stab her in the front. After she falls down, I'll stab you in the back. Understood?"

"Hey now, I have no control—" I didn't get to finish.

"Once I'm finished stabbing you, I'll drag your warm body into the cooler and let it hang until it's cold. I'll throw your cold body out the back door into the snow. No one will find you until spring. How's that for control?"

I looked at her, shocked that she would say such a thing. There was no stopping her.

"Meanwhile, me and my good dog Friday will be sitting pretty in your Miami office, pretending to wonder what happened to you when Boyle comes by to ask how the vacation went."

"How long did it take you to come up with that?" I asked.

"Not long. Between the time I saw her rub you and when I called to you. I can take more time and come up with something more imaginative if you like."

I held up my hands and chanced a grin. "No, I'm good, thanks."

I was certain she was overstating it, but I wasn't about to take any chances. "It's good to know you and Friday will be coming back to Miami with me when we get out of here."

"So far. But don't push it," she grinned.

"I'll be over here with my back to you doing the dishes. Let me know if I need to sharpen a knife for you."

Fiona called through the pass-thru. "Jim, could you come out here? I need you to do something."

She disappeared and I looked at Maddie. Her lips were moving but I couldn't hear a word she was saying. "What's that, dear?"

"Look, I know we need to be careful. I also know you're not interested in the least. We need to figure out what we're going to do with those two," Maddie whispered.

Lucky presented his smiling face.

"Speak of the devil," Maddie said. "The same goes for you."

Maddie rolled her eyes and smiled back at him. "What can I do for you, Lucky?"

She looked at me and smiled sweetly. At least she wasn't throwing knives at poor Lucky. Yet.

Fiona wanted to adopt me. She smiled and purred and flirted and kept throwing her breasts at me like a porn star in a five-minute video.

During my break she brought me coffee and so much pie and ice cream I thought I'd explode.

Saying no didn't occur to me.

I thought Maddie would be glad I kept the woman out of the kitchen.

I couldn't fault the pie. The apples were firm. The amount of cinnamon was just right. The crust was nice and crisp and not overdone. Every bite was a sensation that needed to be taste-tested before swallowing.

I was on break at the counter, enjoying another fine slice.

Fiona leaned over the back counter, stretching on tiptoes to reach a shelf. She was looking for a plate.

I inhaled when I shouldn't have.

Tried to cough.

Couldn't.

Instead, I began choking on my pie.

Chapter 31

I never thought of Janine as a savior. Or my savior, at least.

She glanced and looked away and then, unbelieving, her head snapped back for another look.

My own glance resulted in a head-spin so fast I thought I might put my neck out.

Janine. When did she get here?

She back-slapped me like she wanted to send me into tomorrow.

I did some deep breathing while she quick-stepped to the end of the counter in record time.

Fiona settled back onto her heels. She didn't even try to pull down her skirt. Instead, she ended up swinging her bare ass in my direction.

If Maddie ever found out, the woman would be dead and I'd be on life support for looking by mistake.

"Fiona. Dear," Janine said

The woman turned to face her.

"We've limited the diner hours to get things back on track. I'm back from my break. Thank you for helping. You really did a great job. I don't think your services are needed any longer. If they are, I'll be sure to let you know."

Fiona looked from Janine to me and back. The disappointment was so real I almost felt sorry for her.

"Yes. I'm sorry. I was only—"

"Of course you were, dear. And Jim is grateful, I'm sure."

Talk about a diplomat. My lips moved and Janine held up a hand.

I shut my mouth so fast my teeth hurt.

Janine moved closer to Fiona and lowered her voice. She was just loud enough that I could hear what was being said.

"If his girl finds out what you did, she'll stick a dull knife in your back and twist it until it comes out the front."

Fiona looked skeptical.

That didn't halt Janine.

"I don't want anything like that to happen in my diner. I'd have to close it and then no one will have anywhere to come and spread gossip. Understood?"

Out of the corner of my eye, I saw Maddie coming out of the kitchen.

She spotted the threesome gathered at the end of the counter. "Are you guys having a staff meeting without me? What's going on?" she wanted to know.

Janine gave me a look that would have frozen a lesser man.

Strangely, I found it necessary to lock my jaw and seal my lips.

Janine said, "I was catching these two up on the condition of Emma's father. He's a lot better. He might be able to move home."

Maddie changed her look from one of concern to that of gratitude at hearing the news. "Jim, maybe we should prepare to move out of their house, just in case. What do you think?"

"I'm with you. I'll go pack us up and take Friday for a walk while I'm there."

I couldn't say no to that. Any excuse to get my ass out

of the diner was fine with me.

Fiona, never one to refuse an opportunity, brazenly asked to come along and see Friday.

Janine handled that, too. "You need to go home and get dressed, dear. It's time. Jim, why don't you take Maddie with you? I'm sure she could use the break."

I sighed with relief and silently thanked Janine for being on the lookout.

Janine's smile told me I should worry about her sticking the knife into Fiona.

I didn't give it another thought when the door to the diner closed behind me.

Fool that I am, I debated whether I should tell Maddie.

Not so big a fool as I first thought, I decided against it for my own good health.

Chapter 32

I drove down the recently cleared driveway to Emma's place in the country.

Emma had taped a note to the door to let us know her father was much better. He was anxious to get home. She would be bringing him from the hotel tonight.

"I don't know, Jim. What do you think?" Maddie asked. She was concerned about taking up space and being underfoot when Boots came home.

"There's no way Boots can go back to work. He needs his rest until a proper doctor can look at him. Emma will have to be the one to keep the roads cleared."

It was true. Emma was the only one capable of doing the job.

"Maybe we can take shifts with her dad while she's out clearing the roads. I'm sure that would put her mind at ease."

"That sounds good. We'll move back into our room next door to miss congeniality and her partner."

"Yeah. About that—" I almost bit my tongue off, but I'd be damned if I'd say another word. The incident at the diner had burned itself into my memory.

"You were going to say something?" Maddie asked.

"I was just thinking out loud. Is the wind dying, or is it my imagination?"

I thought it was a good save.

"Why don't we ask Emma? That sounds like her coming

up the driveway."

The huge snow clearing machine shuddered to a halt in front of the house. Blue and white warning lights flickered through the windows.

She backed up and turned around, readying for her next run.

"We got your note. If it's all right with you, we were thinking we'd travel back and forth to look after your father while you're out clearing the roads. Do you think that would be all right?"

Emma's look of relief was immediate and obvious. We were doing the right thing by making the offer.

"That would be great. The phones are still out. I wouldn't worry so much about my dad if you could do that. He's better, but he's not out of the woods. With you here it would be the next best thing to a hospital. There's no way I can get him close to one."

Huge dark circles surrounded Emma's eyes. She wasn't getting proper food or rest. Her meals at the diner were sporadic at best. She was dedicated to the road clearing. Worrying about her father and taking time to check on him was taking its toll.

"We'll do all we can to set your mind at ease. It's our way of thanking you for your hospitality. We're glad we can get away from that pair in the room beside us."

Maddie looked at Jim. "On one condition."

Emma held up her hands.

"Don't argue with me, Em." Maddie didn't know it, but Em was what her mother called her.

"You'll be taking time for rest right here. I'll make your lunches. I don't claim to be much of a cook. You can take food with you when you're on road duty, which seems to be 24 hours a day. Are you good with that?"

Emma knew better than to argue after witnessing the fierce look on Maddie's face. "No problem. I'll come see my dad and take it from there."

"Don't worry. Either Jim or I will make sure you're back on the road in a timely manner. Right, Jim? And being able to eat where you want when you want means the breaks you take at the diner are real breaks for coffee and scuttlebutt."

I didn't take time to dispute anything. I only nodded and added, Yes, dear.

Emma laughed and said something about me being all trained up. "Before I forget, I plowed a space for that wrecked car of theirs and pushed it off the highway."

"We think it was involved in a bank robbery in Denver," I said.

"Yeah, that's what I thought, too, when I saw the holes. There's nothing to do about it now. It'll have to wait until the interstate opens."

We were in agreement about that, too.

"The wind seems to be dying. What do you think, Emma?" I asked. Being local, she might know.

"It is. It's either the calm before another storm, or we're done with this one. Another half day and we'll know for sure."

"All right then. Do we need to do anything to get your dad's room ready before we move him?" Maddie asked.

"I changed the sheets and did laundry. He should be happy with that."

"When did you get time to do that? Emma, I'm telling you, you're going to have to slow down or you'll collapse from exhaustion. I swear."

Emma didn't say anything. Perhaps she knew Maddie wouldn't stand for any guff after the earlier outburst.

"Maybe Friday could stay with him, too," I said. "Boots might feel better having a friendly dog around that needs scratching from time to time."

Emma appeared to relax. "Well, dad did talk about getting a dog last summer. Thank you, Maddie. I appreciate it. It's a load off my mind."

The women hugged.

My job was done.

Chapter 33

Boots Mayberry's mood shifted to high spirits when he learned he was well enough to go home.

We helped him into the back seat and he let it be known he was eager to get back on familiar ground.

Friday jumped in beside him and the pair behaved like a couple of long-lost friends.

"I don't think Friday has ever been so spoiled with affection thanks to you, Boots. He's going to have to go on a petting and scratching diet."

"Oh, come on, he's a good old dog, even if he isn't old, are you, Friday? I enjoy the attention too, you know."

Like we hadn't noticed.

Boots was happy to be home. He looked around and checked the locked gun safe. We helped him upstairs and gave him his privacy to undress and get into bed.

Friday sniffed and snuffed his new surroundings on the ground floor. He hesitated by the kitchen stove and the fireplace in the living room and then bounded up the stairs, where he took over the bedside rug as his own.

It was only an arm's length stretch for Boots to reach down and scratch.

"I'll take Friday for his walk and bring him back. Maddie has questions about the storm."

I returned with the dog to find Maddie's eyes drooping.

Boots was reveling in demonstrating his knowledge of the worst storms that swept the valley in the recent past. His short answer was exactly what Emma told us in so many words. It looked good, but we'd have to wait and see.

The wind had died considerably, but it was still subject to fits of blowing wildly. More important, the snowfall diminished and halted. Blowing and drifting snow became the problem. Perhaps it was looking like the cavalry might be on its way sooner rather than later. If the cell towers would only activate, it would go a long way to bringing help.

"Did Janine mention anything about the people breaking into empty homes?" I asked.

Maddie snapped to attention and opened her eyes.

Boots perked up at the mention of the woman's name.

Even Friday sat up and gave Boots a look followed by a quiet woof.

"Someone is taking prescription drugs and leaving everything else."

"That makes sense. If it's Fiona and Lucky, they wouldn't be about collecting televisions and stereos. They don't have anywhere to put them."

Boots interrupted. "Who's Fiona? And Lucky?"

I didn't want to worry the man. "They're a couple who checked into the room next to ours."

"Oh. Those two. Yeah, I had to listen to their shenanigans for most of last night," Boots said. "It's one of the reasons I'm glad to be home."

"We think they're responsible for the break-ins around town. The woman was behaving suspiciously like someone in withdrawal until that started."

"You're jumping to conclusions, detective." Maddie grinned, as Boots' ears perked up.

"Yes, detective. And why would someone be

collecting prescription drugs? It's not like Fiona needs cough medicine."

Too true.

"She needs underwear, but who's looking?"

Oh, shit.

The cat and the dog were out of the bag now. I couldn't keep my big mouth shut.

"You were, obviously," Maddie said, annoyed.

Hope, like the wind, flew out the window. Maddie had somehow found out I witnessed Fiona's indiscretion behind the counter.

"Until Janine saved your bacon," she added. "How does mine compare?"

"You're actually asking me how your underwear compares to hers? Well—" I hesitated for only a split second, but it was just long enough.

"You know I have a gun now, right? And I wasn't talking about underwear, sailor."

Peals of laughter interrupted our back and forth as Boots held up his hands in surrender.

"All right, you two. I think it's time Friday and I had a little snooze."

"That sounds good to me, Boots," I said.

I turned to Maddie. "Come here, my little pussycat, and I'll disarm you."

Maddie blushed and swept out of the room.

"We'll be downstairs. Maddie already checked out your fridge. Emma must have prepared for the storm. I don't know what she'll come up with, but she's a pretty good cook. If you need one of us, send Friday down."

"I owe you two. I won't forget."

"Oh, one more thing before I forget. Janine has been asking about you. I told her to come over any time she wanted to check in person."

It was Boot's turn to blush.

Friday's ears perked up.

I couldn't figure that.

"Thanks, Jim. I really appreciate it. I never told Emma—"

The man needed to know.

"Emma is good with it too. Now get some rest."

I left before Boots he could ask questions.

Tires crunched on frozen snow and a car pulled into the spot beside us in front of the diner.

There was no need to look out the window. Fiona and Lucky's voices were carrying through the diner's frosted window the instant they got out of the car. They were in loud disagreement. The entire restaurant was about to find out about what as the door slammed shut. Realizing where they were, they quit talking and stamped the snow off their feet before looking around.

"She's checking out the sign, Jim."

The handwritten sign announced the scarcity of food. Everyone was limited to one egg and one slice of toast. It could have been worse until some locals started bringing in their surplus food.

Plenty of gossip circulated to make up for the food shortfall. The latest concerned a body.

Janine brought our plates and hovered nervously before telling us what she knew. "Fiona was the one who told me. I didn't believe her at first."

Maddie and I looked at each other. Fiona was ballsy if nothing else. "Did she say who it was?"

"No. She said the body didn't have any identification. Apparently, he was shot."

"Where's the body now?" I asked.

"It's at the highway maintenance compound. Emma says whoever found it put it in an unheated shed until the police can get to it."

Janine finished pouring our coffee before leaving to

wait on another table.

"Boots found one car. Ignition on. Car running and lights flashing. It has to be the one Fiona and Lucky are waiting for. Except, we can presume the driver is dead."

"Who else could it be, Jim? Emma has seen the body, according to Janine."

"It has to be whoever was driving the car."

"And don't forget those two are in a different car now. When did that happen?" Maddie asked.

"Exactly. They're the ones dug it out of the snowbank. They needed it to replace theirs. The body has to belong to the person bringing them the car."

"We need to warn Emma," Maddie said. "She doesn't need to be messing with those two at the compound if they turn up again."

Janine returned, this time hoping for an update on Boots' condition. It was obvious she cared for the man and was concerned for his well-being.

I pretended to check my phone to see if cell service was up. It allowed Maddie to make the invitation we talked about earlier.

"He's doing good. He's up and talking and walking slowly. It looks to me like he's going to have a full recovery.

Janine looked relieved. "Thanks, Maddie. Tell him I said hi, okay? I've been thinking about him."

"He knows. He was asking about you, too. I think you should visit him. It would be just what the doctor ordered."

Maddie couldn't make it more obvious.

While Janine circulated among the tables, we paid and departed for Emma's to check on her father.

Boots' recovery was going well.

Faithful dog Friday was babysitting the man like a pro, snorting back and forth between his mistress and Boots. His tail flailed non-stop before leading Maddie to the door.

Friday was ready for his walk in the cold.

Friday took to Emma's dad just as much as Boots took to the dog. It was comical watching Friday plop down at the man's feet, and then sit up and nuzzle him until Boots scratched or rubbed or otherwise paid attention to the dog's antics.

"Your dad is going to want to get a dog, Emma. You better be prepared."

"I haven't told him yet, but in the summer I'm off to Denver for EMT training. You might be right about getting him a companion."

"The way Janine has been asking about him, I wouldn't worry about that, Maddie said. "You should think about asking your dad if he'd like her to visit."

"Maybe you could do that? I don't want him to think—"

"To think what? That you know? He'd probably be glad to know that you don't mind. You don't mind, right?" Maddie asked.

"Of course I don't mind. It would take some of the worry away," Emma said.

"Janine gave us the third degree at the diner. It wouldn't surprise me if something was going on with those two."

Satisfied she had that settled, Maddie changed the subject. "About that body someone has in storage. What do you know about it?"

Emma surrounded her coffee cup with both hands. "Someone told me two people stranded by the blizzard brought it out. I thought it might be you and Jim."

That was something neither of us was expecting. "No, it wasn't us."

Maddie urged Emma to go on. "Could it have been Lucky and Fiona?"

That had to be where the new car came from that was parked beside ours this morning. Obviously, they needed a replacement for their own bullet-riddled car. They would need it to get out of town once the roads were clear.

"Those two were supposed to be meeting up with someone. That someone had to have become stranded in the blizzard like the rest of us. He didn't make the town before the road closed with the snow. You don't suppose it was that car, do you?"

"Let's go ask dad, Emma said. "He was the one trying to dig it out."

"One more thing, Emma."

She looked at Maddie.

"It's about Fiona and Lucky. You want to stay far away from them if they show up at the compound. There's no telling what they're capable of."

M addie was reluctant to involve Boots in the growing problem with Fiona and Lucky. She wanted him to concentrate on resting and getting better before more stress was sent his way.

"What do you think, Emma? Should we talk to your dad?"

Emma didn't hesitate. "I think we all should. We need to find out as much as we can about those two. I think they could be very dangerous."

Emma was right about the dangerous. The bullet holes in the car proved it without a doubt. Her father didn't need to know that, though.

"We'll keep the bullet holes in the car out of it, okay?"

Emma was quick to agree.

Chapter 35

Maddie approached Boots on the sofa in front of the fire. His breathing was even. Sleeping, perhaps. Reluctant to disturb him, she went ahead anyway. "You're deep in thought. Everything all right? How are you feeling?"

Boots opened his eyes and looked at Maddie before nodding. "As well as can be expected."

She sat down, clearly pleased he wanted to talk.

"I don't think I had a heart attack," Boots said. "I think it was stress and the darned energy drinks I've been pouring into my coffee."

She remembered Janine telling her his thermos hadn't smelled of alcohol, but had only reeked of energy drink leftovers.

"That's what we all think too, but we don't want you going back to work. Not until you get checked out by a doctor. Friday doesn't want you working either."

She smiled at Boots beside her on the sofa.

"That dog of yours is something else," Boots said. "You and Jim will have to start petting him more after you leave. I'm spoiling him, and he loves it."

"He's taken to you, too. Speaking of which, I talked to Janine this morning. She's worried. I suggested she come out to see your progress for herself." She waited, unsure how Boots would react.

Boots smiled. "I'm glad you did that, Maddie. I've missed seeing her, too. She's welcome any time. I wanted to tell Emma, but she's been busy clearing the roads, and—"

So the two of them were a thing. How did they manage it in a small town where everyone knows everybody's business?

Boots went on. "I think everyone knew but Emma."

"Boots, Emma knows, too," I said. "She just didn't want you to know."

With that out of the way, Maddie went on. "I need to ask some questions about the car you found."

He nodded.

"Tell me how you found it."

Boots thought for a moment. "As best I can recall. I thought I saw a blinking light through the blowing snow. I stopped the blower and turned off the headlights to see better before getting out." He shook his head. "That's not a thing we're supposed to do with the plow. I was invisible in the snow. But I needed a better look. And it turned out it was a blinking light."

Maddie nodded. "It was a car, obviously."

He went on. "Yup. I walked back and turned the blower's headlights on. I didn't want to endanger anyone if they were on the road. I got the shovel and started digging. The car was running. I freed up a door, but it was locked. Maybe there was someone inside. Maybe not."

He took a breath.

"I tried to look. I wiped at the window. It was fogged on the inside. That's when I started swinging the shovel. I wanted to break a window. That's about when I collapsed, too. I don't remember anything after that."

Maddie was convinced Boots hadn't seen anyone in the car. She was back at square one, as in, maybe there was someone in the car, alive. Why else would the flashers be on? Why would the windows be fogged on the inside. If whoever was in it was dead, they could have died from carbon monoxide poisoning.

Except for the bullet hole Emma mentioned. She wasn't going to tell Boots anything about that.

"All right. Now it's time for rest. Upstairs, the both of you."

Friday woofed his approval and followed Maddie and Boots up the stairs.

Maddie joined Jim downstairs in the kitchen. She went for the coffee pot before filling the cups.

"Were you able to learn anything new?" Jim asked.

Maddie's look wasn't encouraging. "Boots doesn't know anything. He collapsed before he could get the car door open. There might have been someone in the back seat, but the windows were fogged on the inside. He couldn't be sure."

"In that case we should head over to the maintenance compound and see what's in that shed. Whoever put the body there might have missed something."

"Emma said it could have been locals concerned about the body thawing out. They probably wouldn't have bothered going through his pockets at this stage."

"Then let's go take a look. We're detectives, aren't we?"

"Judging by the way you've been detecting Fiona—"

It was a struggle to keep from grinning. "Now look. I have no control over what she does. Just because—"

Maddie held up her hands to make her point. "Just because she goes commando doesn't mean you have to look."

"That woman caught me completely off guard, and you know it."

"Yes, she did, but I'm sure enjoying this."

Jim shook his head in disbelief. He finally got it. "Women."

"You know it, buster. Now let's get going. Don't forget we have to stop at the diner and let Janine know she can go see Boots as often as she wants."

"You think he'll be good with that?"

"Oh yeah, I have a sneaking suspicion he'd like something warm and fuzzy besides Friday. Emma's good with it, too. She knows they're a thing."

Janine blushed pink when Maddie dropped it on her, but she could tell the woman was relieved to finally get the invitation.

The two women hugged before we headed out the door to leave the welcome warmth of the diner.

"See? Told ya. Up to now she hid it well, though, didn't she?"

Chapter 36

Emma recognized the car slowing to turn into the highways compound ahead of her. She flashed the lights on the giant piece of road-clearing equipment. The small car returned the signal and she followed it into the lot. She made for the gas pumps and shut down.

She climbed down and greeted Jim and Maddie before leading them to the storage shed. Clouds of frosty breath were blown away in the wind as they made their way to the building.

Emma opened the door and flipped on the overhead lights.

The body lay stretched out on its back on an empty work bench against a wall. The man was in his twenties. Clean cut. Short hair. No beard. Blood had soaked into the clothing around a hole in his chest.

Jim worked at the frozen material to get a better look, trying to disturb as little as possible. "It could be a .38. The lab will be able to tell." He continued searching through the pockets. There was nothing. Even loose change was gone. He found a wallet. It was stripped of cash.

"Maddie. Look here."

White powder residue was scattered on the bench. Whoever dropped the body had done a couple of lines before leaving the shed. Probably not locals, given the state of the small town in its snow-bound isolation.

"It has to be Fiona and Lucky. So it wasn't only a car they were getting." It wasn't a question. "She's been remarkably subdued recently," Maddie said. "She must have got her fix in. Let's get out of here."

Emma locked the door behind Jim and Maddie.

"Maybe now she'll keep her underwear on."

Startled, Emma turned to look at Maddie. "Say what?"

Maddie grinned like she'd scored.

Jim turned beet-red and threw her into a snowbank.

She pulled him down and the pair wrestled harmlessly with too many clothes and too much snow.

"All right, you two. Get a room at least. I'm going back to work. And if you both know what's good for you, you're going to tell me about that underwear remark before I open the roads for you to make good your escape."

Maddie changed the subject. "I told Janine your dad was hoping she'd come out to visit. I hope I didn't overstep."

In the compound's dim overhead lights, Emma appeared relieved. "Of course not. It's about time. She's so worried about him I'm surprised she doesn't run us over to get there. She probably doesn't want to start any small-town rumors, I guess."

"It's been my experience that small towns are already spreading rumors, whether those mentioned like it or not. How's this blizzard looking?" Maddie asked.

A pleased expression appeared on Emma's face. "It's dissipating. We should be good by tomorrow. Maybe the interstate will be open by then, too."

Emma left the duo to climb up on the blower. She started the plow with a roar and headed off. Maddie and Jim drove to the warmth of the diner where breakfast consisted of a single egg and toast.

"Looks like Janine has the day off. I wonder what she's doing with her free time?" Jim wondered.

Maddie looked at Jim like he was nuts. "Seriously? She was worried sick about Boots. I told her he wanted to see her, and now you're wondering where she is? You don't know much about women, do you?"

Maddie was right about that. Considering how he felt about her, he wanted to be able to show her. His impromptu invitation to the ski lodge was supposed to help him do that.

Instead, they had been turned into blizzard refugees, with no relief in sight.

Chapter 37

Fiona Lubinski suspected the storm presently trapping everyone was dissipating. While she couldn't know for certain, the wind was definitely down. Visibility looked to be getting better. Most of the snow was about the wind picking up what was already on the ground. Fresh-falling snow, it definitely wasn't.

Her concern was with the roads. When would they open? When would the gate be open to the interstate? When would the giant machines clear the interstate and the back end of the highway they were stuck on? That had to be the priority since the snow had stopped.

"Lucky, we need to get ready. We have to pack."

"Pack what? I have what I'm wearing. It doesn't look to me like you have much to pack, either. Considering you stopped wearing underwear when you got a hard-on for your diner darling, I'm thinking you'll be wearing next to nothing by the time we leave this burg."

"In that case, shut up and come to bed. We can't get out of here yet. If you count your cards right, you could end up with me on a full-time basis."

Lucky didn't look convinced. And he was right not to be. She'd lose the whining asshole the first chance she got. Maybe she'd send him packing with a swift kick to his ass out the door and into a snowdrift. If she ever got out of this dump and back on the road, that is.

Fiona's eyelids closed to slits as she regarded Lucky with a critical eye. He was tall and skinny. A wrinkled shirt didn't help his image. His jeans were torn in an attempt to go for the stylish look. It wasn't succeeding.

He'd be okay for now. She'd replace him with someone more dependable when she got to civilization. Her actual boyfriend maybe, once he got out of the hospital.

Lucky hadn't pulled the trigger during the robbery. It was part of the reason they were in the predicament they found themselves in, stranded in a hick town in the middle of nowhere. In a raging blizzard with no escape.

Lucky's friend, the one who promised a car to replace the one shot up during the robbery, had become stranded in a snowbank. That he'd been partially dug out and eventually recognized by them when their own car got stranded, was a miracle. Too close for comfort, and saddled with Lucky's stupidity, she shot the man. One stupid man was enough. Together, she and Lucky dumped the body in a shed.

They kept the car.

Fiona had no problem with that. It was the car Lucky had been promised, after all. That the man was icing up like a side of beef in cold storage wasn't her problem. He'd keep. Dead or alive. She had gone through the man's pockets and discovered a little blow, so it wasn't all bad, but even that was running low.

She managed to supplant her need for drugs by scoping out a few of the houses in town. She'd done her break-ins in the dark, when no lights meant the inhabitants were most likely out of town and trapped somewhere else by the storm.

She only took the prescription drugs.

The fool Lucky wanted to load up with televisions and anything else he could carry. When she tirelessly explained they didn't have room or a place for them, he seemed disappointed.

Stupid SOB that he was, Lucky didn't get it. For sure she'd dump him at the first opportunity. All he was doing was dragging her down. Were it not for him, she'd have made it past the road closures. The bright lights of Vegas would be blinking for her.

Yeah, she'd get rid of him, all right.

She reached for the handgun in her pocket as if to reassure herself she had the means to do it.

If only her boyfriend hadn't ended up getting shot up during the robbery. They could have dumped Lucky and carried on like he'd never been a part of their scheme.

It surprised her how easily she fell into bed with Lucky. He wasn't the least bit attractive to her, yet she let him into her bed. He proved to be a good lover, better than she thought he might be. Her loud cries of passion had to have carried over to the room next door and the hottie carting around the black Lab and the woman.

She allowed Lucky to crawl all over her. Her fantasy about her neighbor brought her off, loud and hard and noisy. She hoped the man next door could hear her efforts on his behalf. She let Lucky finish and pushed him off with a vengeance.

"We should check the gas in the car. I don't want to get stuck again on our way out of here."

Lucky shrugged. "It'll be fine. We can get it down the road when we get away. What I want to know is where they're keeping all the cash from the diner."

Fiona had been thinking about that, too. It had to be a substantial amount of money by now, given the repeats cycling through the place in the last few days.

"Well, it isn't on Maddie's ass, that's for sure. The way you've been grabbing it should have told you by now. Haven't you noticed? She doesn't want anything to do with the likes of you," Fiona told him.

"Yeah, and neither did you until you got naked and

fell on your back after you jumped into the shower with me. Give it a rest, queenie. You're not the only game in town any more."

There was no doubt.

Lucky had to go.

The sooner, the better.

How, and how soon became the question.

Chapter 38

Fiona's hard-on for Lucky was only exceeded by her more recent desire for the diner's cash. Even as they filled in part-time in the restaurant, they had no idea where it was being secreted. The till was emptied three or four times a day. What Janine and Maddie did with the cash was the mystery. She never saw them stash it. And it never accumulated overnight.

She knew, because she checked the till when she came in first thing in the morning.

She kept a careful eye on Janine, now that she had returned from her time off.

It took her more than a few hours, but she finally had it figured. Near closing time, Janine carefully counted out the cash. Once satisfied, she wrapped it in an elastic and stuffed it into her purse beneath the counter. It had to be where the receipts for the day were kept, too.

Ten minutes before closing time she herded Lucky out of the diner and dumped him at the motel. She remained in the car.

"Aren't you coming in?" he asked.

"I forgot my purse. I'll be right back."

Fiona left the motel and parked the car with a clear view of the diner through the huge front window. She was in time to witness Janine lock up. She followed the woman as she turned east on the highway and passed through town toward the interstate.

Fiona wondered what kind of trailer the woman lived in. She never talked about a husband or a boyfriend. Or anything, for that matter.

Janine turned left onto a side road. Fiona slowed and stopped. Waited for the tail lights to disappear before following. Turned out her own lights. Towering snowbanks provided just enough room to keep the car on the road in the dark.

She jumped for joy when she realized a full moon was providing the light from a clear night sky. She grinned when she realized the roads would be open by tomorrow. She'd be able to get out of this dump. Encouraged, she slowed the car until the house at the end of the road came into view.

Every light in the place was on. Janine's car was parked. There was another car, too. It looked like Jim's. Then she saw him come out of the house with the dog. Walk time, obviously. She backed all the way down the driveway to the highway and made for the motel.

An impatient Lucky greeted her.

"Where the hell have you been?"

Fiona's enthusiasm knew no bounds now that she knew the roads would soon open. "Did you see the sky? It's clear. The moon is out. We'll be able to get out of here tomorrow."

"About time, bitch. I'm fed up with this dead-end dump. I can't wait to get to Vegas."

Fiona scowled at the man. Their original plan was to head for Las Vegas to relax and reap the rewards of the bank job. Maybe see some shows. Do a little gambling. Now she wasn't so sure. She missed her boyfriend. She was beginning to feel guilty about sleeping with Lucky.

If her boyfriend ever found out—

She shook her head. No way was that going to happen.

"Lucky. I have something for you." Fiona reached in her purse for the handgun.

"I have something for you, too."

Lucky unfastened his belt and pushed his pants down. He grinned and struggled to turn. His eyes flicked from Fiona's unwavering hand to the scowl on her face. "What are you doing?" In that instant, Lucky realized what was going to happen. "Fiona! No!" he screamed.

Fiona's finger tightened on the trigger.

The gun exploded in the small room.

Lucky exhaled noisily.

Arms and legs flailed.

He collapsed on the floor.

The hole in his chest filled with blood and soaked through his shirt.

His heart ceased pumping seconds later.

Fiona's grip relaxed.

The gun slipped from her hand and bumped onto the carpeted floor.

As though a switch flipped inside her, she began going through the room, opening drawers, checking the closet.

She made sure everything she found ended up stuffed into a plastic grocery bag.

Only the final task awaited.

She struggled to straighten a limp Lucky. He seemed a lot heavier than when he was on top of her in bed.

She got his arms and legs organized.

Managed to get his pants pulled up.

Didn't bother zipping or fastening.

She struggled to drag the inert body across the carpeted floor.

Eventually managed to get him close to the night table by redoubling her efforts.

It was impossible.

Sweating through the effort, she was unable to roll Lucky under the bed.

She put her back to the wall and used her legs to force the dead weight over the threadbare carpet.

She huffed and puffed and was exhausted when she finally finished.

She pulled herself up from the floor using the night table

for support and looked around, admiring her handiwork.

No one would notice.

She read about bodies discovered beneath motel beds only after the smell got so bad no one could ignore it.

She hoped that's what would happen with Lucky.

She would be long gone by then.

All she had left to do was get her boyfriend out of the hospital back in Denver and they'd be home free.

Shit. Maddie. Was she in the room next door? She had to have heard the gunshot. Shit. No. She remembered their car out in the country.

She put on her parka and picked up the gun, placing it in a pocket.

She banged hard on their door. Nothing.

She twisted the handle.

The room was empty but for their bags.

She rummaged through them and came up with nothing interesting. A few business cards. She pocketed one to look at later.

Fiona returned to her room and scanned it for giveaways.

She picked up the garbage bag containing Lucky's few belongings.

Her own grocery bag of luggage ended up in the car's truck with Lucky's.

She opened the door and checked the room one last time. No blood on the carpet. That was good.

She'd get away clean.

She was ahead of the game.

Lucky was done with.

All she needed before leaving town was the diner cash.

She'd wait until morning for that, unless the road ended up getting cleared before then.

Fiona threw her jacket over a chair, stretched out on the bed, and closed her eyes.

That Lucky lay dead beneath her didn't bother her in the slightest.

Chapter 39

Emma Mayberry tucked the cell phone back in her pocket. The towers were working, and the message from headquarters on her father's phone was clear.

She was to get the road open to the interstate by meeting up with the plow coming the other way.

She finished clearing the north-east end, hit the turnaround, and headed through town to the maintenance compound.

She finished refueling and opened the huge door on the maintenance garage. She backed the machine in and shut down. She carefully eyeballed everything her meticulous father had taught her to do on the ancient machine. She took her time checking fluid levels and greasing fittings.

With her checks completed, she ate and took a bathroom break. She'd be glad when this storm was history. She was looking forward to a couple of days to herself so she could unwind and take care of her father. She knew Jim and Maddie were doing a good job, but even so. She was grateful for the meals the duo made for her as well. And they convinced her to take breaks, which was why she was taking her break in the compound on the cot in the office.

The day had been a long one. Conditions required her to work all night. She was still worried about her dad. He had some kind of a reaction to those damned energy drinks he mixed with his coffee. She was thankful to learn it wasn't a heart attack. She was happy to learn he hadn't returned to the bottle. She thought that initially, especially after what Janine had told her in the diner.

She was grateful for the people she met during the blizzard. Jim and Maddie had been a godsend when her father needed care. Even their dog came through. Her father had finally admitted a thing for Janine, and now she was happy to have confirmed he had someone in his life besides her.

Content, Emma rolled onto her back in the dark, covered her eyes with a forearm, and managed to convince herself she'd soon be back at work.

Chapter 40

Fiona pulled up in front of the isolated stone house and parked. Waited a bit before checking the handgun tucked into the front pocket of her parka. It was cool to her touch, yet immensely satisfying knowing it was there. Knowing she had used it to rid herself of guilt over sleeping with Lucky.

Screw Lucky. It was too late for him.

It wasn't too late for her.

She opened the car door.

The interior light came on and the chime sounded.

She pulled the key out of the ignition and pocketed it. Better safe than sorry if she had to leave in a hurry.

She wished she had thought to turn the car around. She went to replace the key in the ignition, then thought better of it. Someone might hear the car start. She didn't want that. She didn't want the people in the house to know there was someone outside.

The night air was cold and crisp. With every exhale, her warm breath condensed in a cold fog. A cold white moon hovered over the horizon, illuminating the cold white snow. She shivered and involuntarily shrugged her shoulders beneath the open parka.

It had to be now or never.

Fiona wrestled the gun out of the parka's pocket.

It slipped from her hand and landed in the snow. She

bent and fumbled to pick it up. Her hand closed on icy-cold steel.

She braced for what was coming. Reviewed the plan, such as it was, on her walk to the door.

Find out where the cash was stashed.

Take a hostage if she had to.

The hostage would probably be Janine, since she was the one who ran the diner. She'd know where to find all the money.

Fiona inhaled the cold air, long and deep. Exhaled a thick fog of breath. Almost coughed before knocking too softly on the door.

The weight of the handgun dragged her arm down to her side. No one would notice it there, concealed as it would be by the thick parka.

She brought it up to knock on the door with the muzzle.

Maddie opened it.

Fiona raised the gun and pointed it at the woman, chest high. She wasn't prepared for this woman to be here, too. But where else would she be? She wasn't in the motel room.

"Back up, bitch," Fiona ordered.

A dog growled.

She forgot the damned dog.

The handgun wavered in Fiona's grip.

Her eyes nervously roamed the huge room looking for the dog.

Fiona blinked in the warm air and shook her head. "Where's the dog?"

Maddie called to him. "Friday. Stay," she ordered.

Friday's training took over. He obeyed immediately. Crouched on all fours on full alert. Every muscle tensed. The dog's eyes didn't leave the strange woman standing in the door.

Maddie backed up to the middle of the room to be

with the others. She kept her eyes on the handgun and called out to Jim. She knew better than to try anything. No way would she risk her dog by ordering him to attack. He was too far away to chance it, fast as she knew him to be.

"Jim. It's someone for you."

Maddie kept her eyes locked on the woman. She moved to keep Janine and Boots company while Jim made his way to the door.

"Who is it?" He spotted Fiona. "Thanks. I think. What do you want, Fiona?" He shifted direction to move to Maddie's side.

Maddie held up her hand to Friday.

The dog stayed where he was, out of the woman's line of sight. The woman would have to turn away from the people grouped in the middle of the room to glimpse the dog.

"The money from the diner. Where is it?"

Chapter 41

I**approached Fiona slowly,** wanting to keep between the woman and the others in the room. My eyes never wavered from the pistol until I was close enough to see into Fiona's dilated, bloodshot eyes.

"You have the cash from the Denver bank job. Isn't that enough?"

"How do you know—" She pulled the card out of a pocket. Flicked her eyes to her hand and back up. "A detective. Very good. Now where's the money?"

"It's not here," Jim said.

"Yes, it is. I saw Janine put it in her purse. It has to be here with the rest of it. I followed her from the diner."

Fiona's eyes wandered over the room. Saw the gun safe. They widened when she realized where the money was going. The handgun dropped to her side. Recognizing what she had done, she brought it back up fast. "Who's got the combination? Whose house is this? Janine? Open the safe."

She walked up to the woman. Grabbed her arm roughly. Shoved her toward the safe in the corner.

"She doesn't know it. It's my safe."

She pushed Janine out of the way and looked at the man sitting on the sofa. "Who the hell are you?"

"You're in my house."

"Well then, open the safe. Now. The roads will be clear soon and I need to get out of here."

Sweat ran down into Fiona's eyes. She shook her head to clear them. Raised a shaking hand and rubbed at bloodshot eyes.

Perspiration drained from her face to soak the front of her blouse.

The woman was suffering from withdrawal. All she needed to become a powder keg was a flame to ignite it. I didn't have options. I had to get her out of the house. But how? Where could she possibly go? She'd still be trapped like the rest of us except she'd have the diner cash and would be desperate to escape. Just how desperate would the woman be?

Could I be responsible for a woman freezing to death in the cold just outside the door?

"Where are you going to go, Fiona? There's only two ways out. East, and west. The west end of the local highway won't be open for hours. Your only option is the interstate. It'll be crawling with cops patrolling for stranded cars after the blizzard."

"I'll take my chances. Now open the damned safe."

Fiona shoved her gun into Janine's stomach and then thought better of it. Her shaking hand moved to aim at Maddie. "How do you like it, bitch? It's not looking so good now, is it?"

Boots stood up to move to the safe. "I'll open it."

Fiona smacked Boots on the side of the head to hurry him up. Blood streamed down his face. He opened the safe and grabbed the cash bag and walked with it toward the door with Fiona.

"That's far enough. I don't need your help."

She slung the bag over a shoulder, turned, and motioned with the muzzle of the handgun.

"So long, suckers. Thanks for the free room and board."

Fiona backed to the door.

Opened it with her free hand.

The last thing to disappear through it was the hand holding the gun. It wasn't soon enough.

"Friday. Now!" Maddie commanded.

Friday was prepared for the command.

He unleashed every muscle he had been holding in check.

He pushed off the floor, connected and landed hard against Fiona.

His mouth slammed shut on the woman's wrist.

The action dragged her gun hand down.

The firearm discharged in the small room, surprising Friday.

He released Fiona's wrist and the woman landed partway through the door.

The dog growled and made to grab her again.

Fiona desperately tried to hang onto the gun. She backed out the door, raised her bleeding hand, and aimed for the dog.

Friday jumped.

Landed hard on top of her.

Fiona lost her balance. Her head banged hard against the door frame.

The handgun went off a second time and she turned to escape, running for the car.

The dog made to go after her.

"Friday. Stay!" Maddie called.

He slowed but he didn't stop. Maddie gave the command a second time, louder and more insistent. "Stay! Come to me." No way was she going to allow the dog to chase after the woman in the dark. It wasn't his job. Already Jim was halfway to the door.

"Jim. No, dammit. It's not up to you, either. Get your ass back here. Now that we know she's out there, we can keep her from getting in."

"I'm not as well-trained as Friday, but I don't think she'll be coming back any time soon."

"Well then, that's a plus, isn't it? We just might make the tail end of our ski lodge vacay, won't we?"

Jim closed and locked the door before turning to Maddie.

"Where did Lucky get to? He wasn't with her. He must have been in the car."

Maddie got off an evil eye in Jim's direction before her eyes rolled shut.

She collapsed and thumped onto the floor.

Chapter 42

Jim **rushed to pick** Maddie up and carry her to the sofa. "Shit. Maddie? What the hell?"

There was no blood he could see. He ran his fingers through her hair to no avail.

"Janine? Take a look. I can't find anything."

Maddie came to and turned her head to look up at the three people hovering over her. "What did I do now?"

"You passed out. What happened?" His fingers came away wet. There it was. Blood. He gathered her hair and pulled it aside.

"Ouch! What are you doing?"

"You've been hit. Boots. Do you have any bandages?"

It wasn't a deep cut. The bullet had only grazed her. The slight bleeding had stopped, which meant that the wound was superficial. Still, he was concerned. A wound was a wound.

Janine brought a damp cloth and cleaned the cut on Maddie's head.

Maddie sat up, confused. "I've been hit? I didn't feel a thing until I woke up on the couch."

"You're so lucky I could kiss you. In fact, I'm going to do it anyway."

"Aw, shucks. That's my detective. Where's Friday? Is he all right?"

"He's fine. He's right beside you. Are you sure you're

okay?" Jim asked

Maddie looked at Janine and grinned before reaching down to Friday. "I guess that means we'll have to stay in the room once we get to the lodge. I wouldn't want to do any more damage."

Janine grinned back. "She'll be just fine, Jim. The sooner you two get out of here—"

"You have no idea. Even Friday can't hold that woman back when he's dedicated himself to applying for a job on her behalf. Right, Friday?"

The dog's ears perked up at the mention of his name.

"You leave Friday out of it. It's not his fault I was napping in my car. It was a long drive to get to where I needed to be."

"Yeah, and a couple of more blocks and it couldn't have been more obvious, woman. You're way too easy."

Janine held up her hands, smiling. "All right, you two. Get a room. Again."

Jim's eyes traveled from Janine to Maddie. "Where have we heard that before?"

"Jim. There's something you need to do for Friday. You need to wash the blood out of his mouth. Be sure you get all of it, okay? You have to be sure his teeth are clean, too. Promise me you'll do that," Maddie said, before her eyes closed again.

Chapter 43

Fiona ran down the steps to the car. She fumbled with her good hand to get the door open. The key slipped out of her fingers and fell to the floor. She searched desperately in the dim interior light. Found it. Forced it into the ignition with a bloody, shaking hand.

She wrestled one-handed with the steering wheel.

Jammed the car into gear.

Cursed herself out for not turning the car around before entering the house.

The car slammed against the frozen snowbank.

The lights flicked on and she drove the rest of the way to the main road with tires spinning and engine screaming. The car bounced off the narrow driveway's high banks.

She turned at the end of the road and sped up on the icy driveway. Laughed at her good fortune and how easy it had been.

She was on the home stretch now. Soon to be living it up in sunshine and blue sky. Half a day. Maybe a day, tops. Even California wasn't out of the question.

Fiona glued her eyes to the mirror.

Lost control of the car again.

No lights reflected.

She halted at the end of the long driveway.

Should she go back to town?

Make for the interstate?

Then she remembered Lucky and swiped at the drug-induced perspiration streaming down her face.

She tromped on the accelerator and skidded from side to side on the empty road. The need for drugs dimmed her reflexes. The headlights illuminated a huge cloud of snow churning in front of her.

What the hell? The snow had stopped. The moon was out. She'd seen it. Her grip tightened, and she leaned over the steering wheel, craning her neck to look up. The moon was still there, although it was barely visible through a cloud of some kind.

Her headlights shone through whatever was in front of her and then the car began to rock.

A deep rumbling sound accompanied the snow cloud.

Snow began tumbling onto the roadway in front of the car. It filled the roadway with more and more as it poured into the ravine created by the many passes of a snow blower. The ravine filled. The car rocked and finally halted, mired in the snow engulfing it.

Fiona turned out the lights and turned off the engine. She took deep breaths to still the shaking and her nerves before settling back to consider what happened. It had to be an avalanche. That she hadn't been tossed and turned and upside down told her she was still upright and on the highway. She'd be found when the plows came through.

Satisfied, she settled in. Gathered her gloves and the snow brush in the front seat.

She cradled her aching arm. That damned dog had given her a good bite. She should have shot it when she had the chance. She should have shot Maddie, too, just for spite.

She pressed her jacket pocket for the gun.

It was still there.

She laughed.

Next time.

Fiona stretched out on the front seat and, lacking water, struggled to swallow the last of her stash of pills.

Chapter 44

Emma **struggled to swing** her feet onto the floor from the low-slung cot. Remembering where she was, she rubbed her eyes and stretched before reaching for her phone. She jumped up in a panic, realizing she would be late for the meet-up at the junction to the interstate.

She scrambled into boots and parka and rushed to board the blower. Realizing her mistake, she climbed down to open the garage door. A cold, clear night greeted her. She smiled as she took in the moon hovering over the horizon. It was on its way to high in the night sky. It would be good going now that the snowfall was finished and the wind was down. She could look forward to home and her own bed and a well-deserved eight hours.

She started the blower, exited the garage, and climbed down to close the sliding door. In the crisp night air, her breath formed a fog in front of her. She was grateful for the two hours of sleep she had stolen. And just as well. It would be a while before she slept again. A full tank of gas ensured she'd be good for hours.

She powered out of the compound, set the blower to turning, and lowered the blade. The machine shuddered as it bit into the frozen bank. It was easy going to clear the town's main street on a single pass. The residents knew not to leave their cars on the road during a storm.

She looked toward the diner, willing it to be open for the

coffee she so desperately needed.

She smiled thinking of Janine and her dad's relationship finally out in the open. It was time he admitted his feelings for the woman. The blizzard and his reaction to the energy drinks made that happen. It was the one good thing about this storm.

She passed the closed diner and reflected on how exhausted she had been to miss the meet-up. With the upcoming main road opening, she would be forced to do a lot of clean-up before she proceeded to the town's eastern boundary. While it wasn't required, she liked to take the time to clear the driveway snowbanks that built up over multiple passes. She'd raise the blade, back up, and drop it down to slice into the hard-pack. It was a simple matter to throttle forward and carry on.

The cabin heater performed flawlessly now that the wind was diminished. The steady flow of warm air had nothing else to do but keep her warm. The windows stayed clear on their own. She removed her gloves and jacket and went to work on the highway. It was dull, boring work now that the urgency was no longer there.

Emma cleared a couple of miles, reversed into a driveway to change course, and then cleared the opposite side. It wasn't regulation, but it made sure there wouldn't be a lineup behind her on the two-lane highway. In the past, when she let that happen, people eager to get out would line up behind the blower, making it almost impossible to clear the road on the return run.

She drew even with the turnoff to her dad's driveway. She debated making a quick run down the long roadway for a quick check on him and then decided against it. If she knew anything, it was that he was in good hands with Janine and Maddie. She would have plenty of time once the highway was cleared.

She dropped the blade, pushed the snowbank out of the way, and carried on toward the interstate and the barrier and the meetup with the oncoming plow.

Chapter 45

The scuffle with Fiona hadn't injured Boots beyond a banged-up head. Perhaps it was his pride more than anything. Getting pistol-whipped in front of Janine wasn't high on his list of things to do, but it was over. The bleeding stopped and his forehead was taped. Janine was all right, too.

What aggravated him the most was opening the safe, allowing that woman to strip it of the diner's cash. She even took one of his handguns and a pocketful of ammunition. When the tail lights of the car disappeared from sight, he was inclined to chase after it.

"That's a bad idea, Boots," Jim warned him. "You don't know what's out there waiting. She might park to wait out anyone following her."

Boots had to admit it was true.

Janine didn't think it was a good idea either.

He settled down and put the coffee pot on instead. If nothing else, they could stay holed up until the police showed up.

It was Maddie who remembered Boots' daughter, Emma, was still working on clearing the road. She motioned to Jim and waved him into the kitchen. "I'm going to check in with Emma. She needs to know that Fiona is somewhere out there."

That got Boots started all over again. "I heard that."

This time, it was Janine who laid down the law.

"Emma is a grown woman operating a giant snow blower. Let her do the job you trained her to do."

Chapter 46

When Friday's jaws snapped closed on Fiona's wrist, she released the handgun and it fell to the floor. She had to have a backup. I was certain. I didn't think for a minute that she didn't. I turned out the lights and checked the window. She was at the car. I waited for the lights to disappear before turning to the others in the room.

I checked Janine's arm. It was starting to bruise, but she was fine.

Boots had a good-sized lump on his head. A bit of blood had run down the side of his face and dried. He'd be fine, too.

Fiona's threats had been well-placed toward Janine.

Boots hadn't waffled. He opened the gun safe in short order to allow Fiona to find the diner cash.

We all witnessed the evil smile take over her face when she found it.

Now Fiona was headed for the highway and no doubt on the way to a confrontation with Emma in the snow blower. How Boots' daughter would handle that was a concern.

It was Maddie's, too. "What's Emma's number? We need to let her know Fiona is headed her way."

She punched frantically at the phone's face and listened. "Dammit. She's not picking up."

A voicemail wouldn't cut it. Fiona's brutality would no doubt be transferred to Emma if the road wasn't open when she made the turnout.

Tension in the house had been set to high by Fiona's arrival. It lessened only a little following her departure.

I had to catch up to Fiona to make sure she was incapable of harming anyone else.

"Boots, I need a gun."

"Take what you need from the gun safe," he said, as he unlocked it.

I loaded up with an automatic. I filled the magazine and stuffed a handful of cartridges in a pocket, just in case. I followed up with parka and gloves and headed for the door.

"Keep trying Emma," I told Maddie. "Surely she'll pick up eventually."

In the freezing cold it was an effort to prepare the car. I hurried to clear snow from windows. I scraped at the frost and broke the wipers free. With that done, the inside of the windows continued to frost over thanks to my fog of breath.

I was learning I wouldn't be checking out of Miami for a colder climate any time soon. I should have figured it out the instant I saw Friday sitting his backside down in the snow and getting the shock of his life.

The starter growled in the cold. Nothing happened. I tried again. The engine struggled to turn over and finally caught. I fought to get the cold transmission in gear and by the end of the driveway, the heater was putting out. A dime-sized patch of clear window turned to a dollar bill's worth.

I crouched in the seat and bent over the wheel to squint into the blinding white snow-scape illuminated by the car's headlights.

Chapter 47

Emma **looked and then** looked again, staring into the giant piles of snow clogging the highway in front of her. An avalanche, caused by the weight of the snow on the smooth rock face had collapsed into the roadway. While she was unprepared for it, it wasn't the first time it happened at this location.

She halted the machine and considered her options.

More than likely, she'd meet up with the equipment coming from the opposite direction. That was the plan, at least. She had overslept though, and was hours behind. Strange that the other plow hadn't made its way through by now. The delay had to be the fault of the avalanche.

She checked her phone. Still no signal. The towers were out again.

She shrugged, engaged the swirling blades, and slowly released the clutch to move forward. The blades caught. The machine shuddered and began to power through the packed avalanche of snow blocking the highway. The long hours were starting to take their toll as the noise and vibration and the flying snow overwhelmed her senses.

She leaned over the steering wheel to see past the furious swirls of snow. The machine bogged down and she reversed and eased up. Went forward and backward again and again. She attacked the compacted snow for well over an hour. It didn't appear as though she was making progress to the turnout and the barrier.

Emma backed off and took a break. She grabbed the flashlight, climbed down, and did a quick inspection of the snow-encrusted machine as best she could. She looked for the telltale signs of hydraulic leaks. She checked for ice buildup that could cause damage when it went through the blower assembly.

So far, so good.

She looked up to admire the full moon beaming down. She recognized it as a sign the worst of the blizzard was over. From here on it would be all cleanup. Her warm breath fogged the cold air and blew away. She wanted a longer break, and had to convince herself to climb into the artificial climate created by the cabin heater.

Emma settled in the seat and looked over the gauges. She tapped at a few. Everything was in the green. She engaged the blower and accelerated slowly forward, content that the equipment was performing as it should.

While the blizzard had halted and the wind was down, the avalanche covering the road stretched in front of her. It was perhaps the fourth or fifth time she was forced to reverse while attempting to clear the road of the heavy buildup of wet snow. She re-engaged and moved forward at full throttle with roaring engine and whirring blades. Sheets of wet snow shot out the other end to cover the existing snowbanks.

Fiona woke up in the front seat of the stalled car. It took a moment to get her bearings. She was cold. Her body began to shiver uncontrollably. She recognized a growling sound. A bear. No. It was winter. No bears. She remembered. Snow collapsing. An avalanche.

She removed her gloves and rubbed the sleep from her eyes. She couldn't see anything in the dark. She turned on the interior light, revealing windows completely frosted over. Her breath was visible in the chill air.

She awoke a second time in the pitch-black interior. She sat up and pulled the hoodie over her head. Turned on the interior light. Swiped a glove-covered hand at the fogged, icy window. The action did nothing to clear it.

More growling. Louder this time. What was it? She tilted her head. As if that would help. Was the snow moving again? The car had to be upright, otherwise she'd be on the roof. It dawned on her and she grinned so hard her cold face hurt.

Road clearing equipment. Headed for the car. Her car. Soon the road would be open. Vegas. Only a heartbeat away now. She continued listening as joy slowly turned to concern.

Would the operator know her car was covered in snow? Buried, even? Hadn't there been an avalanche last night? Of course. The snow had shifted and buried her car. She was invisible.

She turned the key. Nothing but clicking. Panic began to slowly creep into the car. An image came to her of huge blades sucking the car into the guts of the blower. Spitting tin out the other end. Was that even possible? She turned on the lights and began honking the horn.

The growling grew louder. The driver wouldn't know. The car was buried. Images of Vegas flew out the ice-covered window as she pictured the snow machine destroying her dream, inch by inch. Thanks to the damned avalanche.

The growling kept on, louder. The machine was close and getting closer. The white curtain of snow began to brighten as the machine closed on her car. She could see her hand. The inside of the car became completely illuminated.

In a panic, she reached for the light switch and flashed the lights on and off, on and off.

She didn't know what else to do.

Chapter 48

Something clunked. Loud. The giant machine rocked and kept going. Emma was familiar with the noise. She had heard the same sound many times. Experienced the shudder before the machine continued on, blades whirling. The powerful engine didn't miss a beat. Chunks of ice broke free and were going through the blower mechanism.

The machine rocked a second time. Loud screeching went on for longer than Emma wanted. She pulled back the power levers. Raised the plow. Intent on reversing from the problem before getting out to investigate.

She engaged the transmission, wanting to back away. Nothing happened. Her brow furrowed. This was a new one.

A screaming, high-pitched metal-on-metal noise pierced the cabin. The huge machine rocked one more time. Halted. But for the idling engine, the sound quieted. Emma flipped levers and switches and shut down the blower. She kept the diesel engine on to illuminate the powerful bank of lights.

She forced the door open past the ice buildup. Feet slipped on the snow and ice-covered ladder. She reached in for her parka and gloves before descending the rest of the way to the ground.

Her phone vibrated. The call had to be from the

blower approaching from the opposite direction. She checked, only to see an unknown number. She ignored it and instead concentrated on the carnage illuminated by the powerful headlights.

Emma's face turned white. Shocked by what she saw, she realized what had happened. Parts of a small vehicle had been chewed up by the spinning blades. Sections of the trunk and part of the back seat were completely mangled.

Bits of paper circulated, blown away by the wind whipping down into the roadway. A strong odor of gasoline wafted up from the rear of the crushed automobile.

Her stomach churned. Shaken and unsure of how she should proceed, she took a step back and snapped a picture, as though expecting to make an insurance claim. The phone vibrated in her hand. Still shaking, she answered.

"Emma? Is that you?"

She didn't recognize the female voice.

"It's Maddie. I got your number from your dad."

Still in shock, Emma carried on as though nothing had happened. "Oh. Hi. Is everything all right? What's up?"

"No. Yes. He's fine. Your father is fine. Janine is here with him. It's Jim."

"What about him? Is he all right?" she asked, suddenly concerned again.

Maddie took a deep breath and began rushing to get the words out as fast as she could.

Fiona descended into full panic mode as the snow blower's powerful droning went on for what seemed like forever. Would the blades chew through the car? She climbed over the seat and clutched at the seat rail. She fought to push the front seat as far back as it would go. She got down on the floor and rolled into a ball.

Tears of frustration streamed down her face as it occurred to her that Vegas was out of the question now. So was Denver and her boyfriend. She sniffed. Gasoline. The smell took over the car's interior. She had to get out. Her whole body shook as she forced herself to sit up in the freezing air. She squinted through the powerful bank of lights illuminating what was left of the car.

A mass of twisted metal remained where the trunk had been. The gasoline smell grew stronger. Terrified and frozen in place, unable to move, Fiona withdrew into panic.

The racket quieted suddenly. The lights never dimmed. She remained where she was, afraid to move out of the protective metal cage provided by the car. Her lungs forced out ice-fogged breath.

The gasoline smell intensified. She tugged on the door handle. It wouldn't budge. She climbed up on the seat and rolled onto her back. Kicked the door with both feet.

Arms flailed. Feet kicked and pushed. The door gave way ever so slightly and sprung back. She pushed harder and kicked again. It squeaked and swung wide. Her body shook with the effort. She struggled out of the car on hands and knees.

She stood up and fought to make her way toward the lights. A shadow on the ground beside the machine moved. Afraid the driver might continue advancing, Fiona slipped a hand into a pocket of her parka.

She winced. It was her bad hand. The one the dog bit. She managed to get the pistol out. Switched hands. Aimed.

The muzzle swung wide and pointed everywhere but at her intended target.

Chapter 49

The buzzing phone took Emma by surprise. The cellphone towers had to be up again. She answered and recognized the sound of Maddie's voice with news of her father's condition. She was relieved to learn he was fine. She went to climb out of the cabin to escape the whine of the engine that couldn't be shut down. It quieted on its own and she stayed inside.

"I'm pretty sure I'm at the barrier. It took forever to get to it. There was a small avalanche of snow that clogged the road. I've been clearing it slowly and carefully." She wasn't sure why she was giving Maddie a progress report.

"Jim is on his way to you. Don't back up and turn around. You might run into him. I'm staying with your dad and Janine."

"I can't turn this thing around. The machine is down for good until a maintenance crew arrives," she told Maddie.

Tap tap tap on the window drew Emma's attention away from the phone. A woman she didn't recognize aimed a handgun at her. She hung up without another word.

"Get out, bitch. It's my turn."

Emma sat up in the cramped cabin. She grabbed her parka and gloves and followed the woman down the ladder. The tick-tick of cooling metal was the only sound.

The snow blower was out of service for the duration. The machine wouldn't be started again without destroying it.

Emma smelled gasoline and knew what had made the unfamiliar screeching noise. A car buried in the avalanche of snow that swept down the hillside. She had run the blower into its back end. The blower controls were jammed by the metal. If she started the machine, the blades would engage. There would be no way to shut them down now that metal had been run through the whirling blades.

The snow machine was inoperable.

Multiple sparks, even a single spark, could ignite the fumes rising from the damaged car's fuel tank.

"If you start this thing, there's a good chance you'll ignite the gasoline. You'll get trapped inside. You might not be able to get out," Emma warned her.

"Yeah, bitch, I'll take my chances."

Fiona looked up. Paper fluttered in the light wind that had come up. It was the cash from the bank robbery stashed in the trunk. Minus what she'd stuffed in an inside pocket.

She was done. It had all been for nothing. There was nothing left. There would be no going back. Even the diner cash was gone. She was broke, with nowhere to go. There would be no escape.

The woman cursed her bad luck and climbed up on the machine. A bewildering array of dials and gauges confronted her. "Show me how to start this thing, bitch, or I'll blow your brains out."

Emma's mouth opened to tell her it was too dangerous. She clamped it shut when she saw the anger in the woman's face. It was now or never. She tried the switch. Nothing.

"Listen to me. You need to start this thing. I need to get to the interstate," Fiona said.

"I can't. A spark will set off the fumes," Emma tried to explain.

"I don't care. Do it." She waved the handgun at Emma. "Get this thing moving right now."

Emma didn't move fast enough for Fiona's liking. She fired a round through the roof to make her understand. Shadows created by something coming up from behind forced her to turn in the cramped cabin.

Fiona pushed Emma across the seat and scrambled down the ladder. Her damaged hand was still bleeding. She steadied herself and fired twice into the lights.

Chapter 50

The **first round went** through the windshield. It missed by inches. I ducked, a reflex action. Realized what it was. It had to be a wild shot, the shooter blinded by the car's lights. When the second round thumped into the engine block, I knew for sure I was in trouble.

I turned off the lights and got out of the car. Slipped the action on the familiar .44 I'd removed from Boot's gun safe.

Where was Emma? If she was in the line of fire, she could be killed.

The snow machine started with a roar. Sparks flew. An explosive whoosh sounded. An orange flash of flame lit up the sky. Gasoline. Where had it come from? Fiona.

Emma must have run the snow blower into the back of her car. On purpose or by accident, it would have eaten it until the machine became jammed up with metal.

I saw them. Two people in the cabin illuminated by the flames. Emma and Fiona. Who else would it be?

I ran toward the burning machine and climbed the ladder on the back of the giant snow blower. I swung the butt of the handgun against the window. In the cramped cabin, Emma was busy frustrating Fiona's attempt to turn around.

I yelled over the screaming metal. "Drop the weapon or I'll shoot you."

The women continued wrestling in the small cabin. Emma had a grip on Fiona's bloodied arm. The hand with the gun was jammed against the dash.

Could I chance it? I had my answer when Fiona swung the pistol into Emma's jaw. She collapsed, knocked out cold.

"Fiona! Drop it or I'll shoot you."

In that split second, I knew she wouldn't do it. I had to save Emma. I squeezed the trigger. Fiona screamed over the boom of the .44 in the cramped cabin. She released her grip on the gun. It clattered to the floor.

"Shit. That hurts," she complained. "What did you do that for?"

Orange flames licked their way toward the cabin.

I shoved Fiona out of the way. She screamed and made to grab for her shoulder. I rattled the gun against what was left of the rear window to break the glass.

I yanked an unconscious Emma through the window. Her bulky parka became caught on something.

"Help me with her or I'll shoot you again," I threatened.

Using her good hand, Fiona pushed at Emma. It was enough to force her through the window.

Emma came to and together we ended up on the ground. I climbed to rescue Fiona and discovered her on the floor. She came up with a hand wrapped around the pistol.

"What did I tell you the first time?"

Fiona stared at me with a hard look.

"Drop the gun or I'll kill you."

She didn't believe me. Her look softened and she must have recognized something in my eyes. She released the gun and let it slip from her fingers. It clattered to the floor a second time.

"Smart move. Now get out."

I didn't help her. I didn't even try. Fiona groaned and

muttered and screamed and finally ended up feet-first on the ground.

Emma pulled back a fist, swung hard with her entire body, and decked the woman with a roundhouse left.

"You can be my backup in a bar fight any time, woman."

She laughed and I laughed and I knew Emma would ask.

"Would you have killed her?"

I let Emma's question go unanswered.

"Help me get her into the back seat, please. Stay with her. I don't trust the woman a bit, out cold or not." I slammed the door and started the car. "Would you do something for me?"

"Of course. You just rescued me. What do you want?" Emma asked.

"Call Maddie and let her know we're all right and on our way. Your dad and Janine will be worried sick, too."

She grinned from the back seat. "Do I tell them we're bringing a prisoner for a sleepover?"

I grinned right back. "Well, you should at least make mention of it. It'll give Maddie time to get properly annoyed."

"Yeah. She told me about that underwear deal. You've got major kissing up to do, Mr. Detective.

"Emma. Look at me," I pleaded. "There was no underwear deal. How could there be? There was no underwear."

Conversation halted while I got the car turned around.

Emma and I were grinning and snickering too hard to talk.

Chapter 51

Headlights barely reflected off the windows and already Maddie and Boots were out the door to rush the car.

It wasn't first aid Maddie was looking to do when she popped the door and attended to Fiona.

Obviously Boots hadn't wasted time telling Maddie where to find the duct tape and rope.

"I called the state police. They'll be here in about an hour. They're waiting for a road to be cleared. There's a blower working on it now."

Boots addressed his daughter, anxious that she not be caught doing his job. "Emma, you're going to let me tell them I was driving. And you better fill me in, fast. I don't want them running into anything."

Emma told her tale while Boots helped wrestle an unconscious Fiona secured by Maddie's duct tape efforts out of the back seat and up the steps to the house.

"Your daughter cold-cocked the woman. It made it easy to get her into the back of the car. Good thing it's a rental. That blood will be tough to get out."

Emma cast a nervous look from me to Fiona and I thought she was about to spill the Drop the gun or die part. She bit her lip and shook her head. It would stay our little secret for the time being. I figured she'd be all about telling her dad eventually. By then, Maddie and I would be long gone.

Janine busied herself collecting a basin and filled a kettle with water. "Put her on the floor in the kitchen," she insisted. "There's no sense dirtying up the carpet."

The women cleaned Fiona's wound and taped it as best they could.

"Tape and rope should hold her until the ambulance gets here if she doesn't struggle."

"Don't worry about a struggle. Emma will just cold-cock her again," I said.

She grinned and nodded.

Fiona wouldn't be going anywhere under her own power, secured or not, if Emma had anything to do with it.

Eventually flashing red and blues made their way behind a snow blower on the approach to the house. While Boots apprised the driver of what happened to his machine, the troopers led an ambulance in the opposite direction containing Fiona.

Lucky's name came up as an afterthought. Not one of us had seen him.

A couple of troopers were dispatched to the motel. Before long a phone call came back from a trooper. It announced Lucky's unlucky discovery beneath the bed in their room.

After a bit of head-scratching, I had to admit we were fortunate to have corralled Fiona with no harm to ourselves.

It was Emma who made the announcement. "Janine, you'll be staying in the spare bedroom tonight. It's too late to drive home."

With that out of the way, and exhausted by the events of the past few days, we collapsed in our beds.

Come morning, Emma and Maddie chased everyone out of bed first thing and we came out to the kitchen to devour a celebratory breakfast feast steeped in waffles and eggs any style and bacon and ham and cheese and sausages complete with plenty of laughter and much back-slapping.

Not to be left out, Friday traveled from chair to chair with tail wagging to receive ear scratching and petting and patting. His cold nose nuzzled hands and arms and brought forth more laughter. Please with himself, the dog wandered off to take a well-deserved break in front of the warm fire and promptly fell asleep.

Not to be outdone, Boots shortly followed, and both were off in dreamland.

We didn't get out of Boots' place until early the next morning.

By then, Emma had fussed over her dad, cooked us another breakfast, and allowed the tourists to do the dishes.

We drank too much coffee and hugged everyone too hard and too many times before we were permitted to hit the road with promises we would all stay in touch.

Chapter 52

In daylight, the huge walls of snow on either side of the highway were intimidating, but the road crews had done a good job. Driving was straightforward. I stopped a couple of times at turnouts and we got out and marveled at how we had driven through a blizzard without realizing the magnitude of keeping highways open in this part of the country.

We were exhausted by the time we made the lodge. The events of the past days took their toll. The ski lodge manager was very understanding about a couple of Miami refugees stranded by the blizzard. For goodwill he offered us a couple of extra days to make up and we accepted.

We rented equipment and took lessons and by the end of day three I was able to rest my sprained and bandaged ankle on the bar's brass rail. I told war stories about how I crashed into a tree on a tremendous downhill run, and by the fourth day, everyone was rolling their eyes and calling me a whiner.

By then they all knew I was a rank amateur. I was left to wonder who had spread that rumor.

I didn't mind, though. If no one else would, Friday always listened patiently to my stories.

In the lounge, Friday drew the women like flies. All I had to do was sit back and let him do the work. He enjoyed every minute of the ear rubbing and scratching and tail wagging. He ended up posing for selfies with several of the women.

On day five Maddie was escorted into the lounge accompanied by a laughing pair of good-looking, bronzed ski instructors. She was unconvincingly trying to tell them it was nothing through painful giggles. They unloaded her in a chair and went off in search of the lodge's medic.

Come evening, she waved off my unbelievable war story for the umpteenth time and was telling one of her own to free drinks and cheers and laughter from her male audience.

I took it all in stride. I had the advantage of the bar with Friday and a handful of women by his side. It occurred to me I could help facilitate a singles soirée if I could only encourage Friday to find his mistress.

I leaned over and whispered into his furry ear. "Friday. Find Maddie. Off you go. Good boy."

I gave him a salutary pat and he looked up at me like he needed to be told before strolling off.

A couple of the women followed after him and ended up circulating around Maddie's chair and the loitering men. In ten minutes, couples began drifting off to various parts of the lodge.

Maddie and Friday ended up left to themselves.

From my seat at the bar, I recognized my opportunity. I paid the barkeep and made for Maddie. "So then, I see you caught the ski instructor."

She grinned up at me. "No, silly. I got it running away from him. Let's go to the room and see what we can figure out without killing ourselves."

"Come on, Friday. Enough flirting with the guests and the servers for now."

The dog looked disappointed.

Come to think of it, so did Maddie as we fumbled and stumbled our way to our suite.

Chapter 53

The flight to MIA and home was long and exhausting. By the time we scrambled into an airport cab for the ride home, we were finished. Even Friday needed his bed.

We ignored the office and its phone.

"I never did get to make a snow angel. Maybe next time."

With two good legs, Maddie rushed up the stairs ahead of us.

"I'm never leaving Miami again. If I never see snow, it will be too soon."

Friday seemingly woofed his agreement, probably remembering freezing his bum off in a snowbank.

"Oh, come on, you two. Where's your spirit of adventure? You'd think you were a couple of senior citizens."

Friday collapsed on his bed.

Maddie needed help getting her blouse past her sore shoulder.

I only needed help getting my track pants off.

Maddie was experienced at that.

It wasn't long before we were snoring right along with Friday.

I only woke up once. Something had bubbled to the surface, forcing me to think about our adventure.

I nudged Maddie awake.

"What time is it? What's wrong?" Maddie asked.

"Nothing. I was just thinking."

She reached for the light. "About?"

"A puppy," I admitted.

"What? A puppy? Friday can't have puppies, silly."

"I know that. Zelda."

She regarded me suspiciously. "Who's Zelda? And do I want to know?"

"I'm going to talk to Emma. I'm going to ask if Boots might like a black Labrador from a certain Zelda that I know."

"Is that the name of a dog or a woman?"

I reached over Maddie to turn out the light.

"I'll know more tomorrow."

I struggled out of bed and donned a robe. Thumped my way like a pirate into the kitchen.

It was only nine.

I loaded up a tray and hauled it to the bedroom and we feasted in bed like a couple of newlyweds. We'd no sooner finished than Friday waited by the door.

"It looks like your one-and-only needs to take his constitutional. I'd like to volunteer, but—"

"I hope he's not in a rush. It's going to take me a while to struggle into something."

"I can help you with that," I offered.

"Judging by the look on your face, I'd say it's not help you're going to be offering, sailor."

"Talk is cheap when your dog needs a walk, your lover is incapacitated, and you want to rush out of the bedroom to take him."

Maddie slowly stretched out in the warm bed as best she could and turned toward me with an encouraging smile.

"Well, he's just going to have to wait his turn. Unlike you."

She sighed and called to her dog.

"Good boy, Friday. You're just going to have to wait until your master can get his cast on the floor."

Epilogue

It **took a while** to get it sorted.

First came the phone call to Lily. I needed to confirm that good girl Zelda would be having another litter. As luck would have it, she would be doing just that in the spring.

I explained to Lily's mom, Erica, what happened during our ski adventure. She listened patiently as I hit the high spots about Emma and Boots and Janine, and how Emma wanted to go to school in Denver.

Spring rolled around and next was convincing Lily that one of Zelda's pups should go to someone she didn't know.

Lily agreed almost immediately. It turned out all but one was spoken for. That one ended up being the runt of the litter.

Boots was tickled pink when he found out there was a pup available. Then he found out it would be a female and his joy knew no bounds. That the pup was the runt of the litter didn't make a whit of difference. He already had a name picked.

Lily agreed and named the pup immediately.

Lily would be accompanied by her mother when she brought the pup to Denver. It would be no earlier than eight weeks after she was born.

The eight weeks passed uneventfully. Emma met

mother and daughter, and the threesome bonded immediately. In no time, Erica was phoning to ask about the Mayberry family. After some back and forth, Erica was satisfied that Boots and daughter Emma and Janine weren't a family of serial dog- and people-nappers.

The pair would stay only long enough to make sure Boots and his family were a suitable family for one of Zelda's pups. Upon spotting the pile of dog books and pamphlets, Lily took on training Boots to her satisfaction with a vengeance.

The exercise took three days.

A humbled Boots took his training very seriously when all of them weren't laughing uncontrollably.

At the end of it, a satisfied Lily placed her hands on her hips for emphasis.

"You pass, Boots," Lily said solemnly. "Lady is your dog now. Zelda will be happy when I tell her the runt of her litter has a good, caring home."

When Boots and Emma and Janine called, I didn't need a picture to see their smiling faces. They sent one anyway.

Lady was on prominent display in front of everyone. Already I could tell she was a real ham.

In the background, Lilly was giving her secret Okay sign, and I knew all was well.

Jim Nash has to get to Washington, D.C. A private jet is idling on the tarmac. He's got a bag full of cash to spend, but the flight crew's hired gun has other ideas. Even Nash can't talk his way out of this one.

PX DUKE

24

JIM NASH

MEXICO TIME

Jim Nash is in Mexico looking for something he left behind years ago. All he's been able to find is a missing person. Half his problem is solved when they float into Cabo on a fast-boat. The other half will be getting out alive.

FORGET ME NOT

PX DUKE

Chapter 1

Emma Mayberry's hand slipped from the damp cloth. Her hand continued its wiping motion on the wet tabletop. Startled, she looked away from the coffee shop's plate-glass window. Her breath left her with a jolt. In a second, her gaze returned to the window and the woman across the street.

She wasn't there.

She would have the nightmare again tonight.

Emma finished with the tables and moved to the counter to wipe it down. She finished and turned to the window tables.

She looked past the glass.

Scanned in every direction.

Didn't recognize anyone.

Satisfied, she went behind the counter to take orders.

She soon forgot about the mirage and went on greeting customers with her smile and outgoing personality.

Emma used the time before the second rush of customers to reflect on her good fortune.

She realized her dream of a year ago when Boots, her father, remarried. It released her from having to care for him since her mother died.

She scrimped and saved for years to have enough for the paramedic course she always wanted to take. It meant moving a long way from the peaceful community of Escape in the Colorado mountains.

Here she was, at long last, in Blue Springs on the Florida panhandle.

Three semesters.

Twelve months.

And almost ready to graduate if she passed the exams coming up.

When she qualified, she'd be capable of serving in quite a few states where the certificate was officially recognized.

Her decision was already made. She would return to the small town where she was raised and the regional EMT base in Escape.

Her home town was isolated, the only town for mile after mile of both interstate and state highways. Few cared for such isolation; thus, a lot of paramedics came and went when they found out how boring the area was.

Recreation was limited unless you were the outdoor type.

Emma didn't care.

She liked her home town, and didn't have plans to leave. That is, until a firm in Miami headed by a graduate of her school was made aware of her marks and those of a couple of others.

The firm contacted her, offering a job upon graduation if she kept her grades up.

She was ready to accept, too.

All she needed to do before finalizing was to let her father know.

That was going to be the tough part.

Except. There was always one.

She had a boyfriend. Not her first, but not one of many, either. He, too, was in the paramedic program. They paired up for training exercises and discovered they enjoyed spending time together when they weren't in class.

She considered Danny Williams to be a kind soul. Like her, he was from a small town, albeit not so far from civilization as she was in her tiny town in the mountains. He was more fortunate in that a major city was only an hour's drive away. His parents took him on trips where they went to museums and libraries and city parks. They were things foreign to her when she was a kid growing up.

She liked her job at the coffee shop in Blue Springs. She got to know a lot of the locals and many of the construction workers who moved into town after the recent hurricane damage.

Fortunately, the coffee shop wasn't one of the buildings damaged by the storm. It became a gathering place where the locals got caught up on gossip concerning the storm and subsequent rebuilding efforts.

She was doing well, all things considered. School. A job with flexible hours after classes thanks to her boss at the coffee shop. A boyfriend who scuba-dived the local caves and convinced her to become a diver, too.

She was happy with the direction her life was taking.

Emma walked from behind the counter and stood in the open door to the coffee shop. It was another bright sunny day.

She scanned in all directions, looking and looking again. Checking. It was nothing. The woman was in prison. Wouldn't be getting out for decades.

She sighed and shook her head at her silliness and went back to work.

She checked out early and began her walk home while it was twilight.

She turned to look over her shoulder more than once, wanting to be sure. By the time she was home, Emma convinced herself.

It was an overactive imagination that kept her on edge.

Chapter 2

One of Fiona Lubinski's desires now she was on the outside was a decent cup of coffee. She hadn't had one since going to prison.

The second thing she wanted was a good lay.

The coffee she set on the night table was just okay. She forgot about it while she busied herself with desire number two.

That was going a lot better than the coffee until she was reminded of an old lover. Lucky. In that god-forsaken town. Escape. Some escape it turned out to be. Lucky was a good lover. Probably not as good as she remembered, but even so.

It was all behind her now.

Don't even ask how.

She climbed off the man and collapsed in a sweaty mess of arms and legs and a tangle of damp sheets.

She caught her breath and reflected on her good fortune.

They came for her in her cell. Told her to empty it. Shuffled her off in leg-cuffs—leg-irons, she called them. Sent her out the door where she was loaded into a van with a couple of others not as bad off as she was.

She ended up in the resort known as FCI Tallahassee. Why was beyond her.

Life was good in her new accommodations.

She kept her mouth shut.

Kept her eyes open.

Managed to keep her head down and make a few friends. That was a new one. Female friends. But the atmosphere in the minimum-security facility was good. Most she encountered were looking forward to getting out.

And now here she was, out and about and getting mediocre coffee and a good lay. Life was real good.

She reached for a cigarette on the nightstand. A breast slipped from behind the wrinkled, sweaty sheet. She didn't care. Her lover was fast asleep, more than likely not up to the task a second time, anyway.

She lit the cigarette and inhaled deeply, needing to smoke it fast to make good her getaway.

Fiona stubbed out the half-smoked cigarette and sat up on the edge of the bed. She stretched, naked, breasts exposed and upright. Didn't pull the sheet up for cover in case the one-night stand woke up.

She reached to pull the chair from beneath the desk. It slid noiselessly on the carpet.

The nameless man's jacket and pants hung on the chair.

She rustled through the pockets one-handed, searching.

Found keys and a wallet.

Stripped it of cash and credit cards and discarded the wallet on the desk.

She eased off the bed and put the cards in the bottom of her backpack.

Always be prepared.

The cards would be useful if she could find some place gullible enough that would take them.

Fiona pulled yesterday's wrinkled tee over her head. Checked herself out in the mirror before running fingers through damp blonde hair. Pinched her cheeks to get some color going.

Her stomach growled.

She considered a shower and quickly changed her mind. There was no telling when her latest conquest would wake up. Instead, she turned a tap on in the sink and splashed cold water on her face.

She dried off and tugged snug jeans past bony hips and a round ass. She slid bare feet into well-worn prison-issue slip-ons.

She was good to go.

Fiona cracked the motel-room door and squinted into the early afternoon sunlight.

The parking lot was empty but for a half-dozen cars.

She went back to the night table and retrieved the key fob. She pressed it. Lights blinked on a compact white four-door.

She collected her backpack and prepared to leave the room, then thought better of it and picked up the man's luggage, too.

She hefted the suitcase and hurried silently on her prison-issue shoes across the parking lot to the car.

Chapter 3

The phone call from Boots Mayberry was a complete surprise. Neither Jim nor Maddie had heard from him since he picked up his pup from Lily. Questions were interrupted by Boots not wanting to waste time.

"It's not like Emma. Usually, we talk on Sunday. I've tried for the past three days, Jim. It goes to voicemail every time."

"Boots, Maddie just walked in. Hang on while I put you on speaker and update her, okay?"

Maddie gave him a worried look before glancing at the phone.

"Is everything all right, Boots? How's Janine?"

"She's fine, Maddie. Lady is fine, too."

Lady was the chocolate-brown pup he and Maddie had made arrangements for Boots to adopt from Lily. The pup was from the last of Zelda's litters.

"Boots says Emma is missing, Maddie. She didn't call on Sunday and he hasn't been able to get in touch since. All his calls go straight to voicemail. She's not answering texts, either," he explained.

Maddie's look went from concern to worry. She hesitated before asking. "Does she have a boyfriend, Boots?"

"She does. Danny is his name. But I don't think—"

"They could have gone off together for a bit of a

getaway," Maddie said.

"Well Maddie, I'd like to think that, too, but end of semester exams are coming up shortly," Boots explained. "She wouldn't want to mess that up."

"You're right. I remember her telling me how much she wanted to be a paramedic. That's what she's taking, right? Where is she?" Maddie asked.

"Blue Springs."

"Florida?" Maddie looked at him and slashed a hand across her throat. He put the phone on mute.

"That's about a seven-hour drive, Jim. We can be there first thing in the morning."

Jim nodded and took the phone off mute to hear Boots talking with Janine about a ticket to Tallahassee.

"We can meet you at the airport, Boots. Let us know what time you get in," Jim told him.

Chapter 4

Trouble had caught up to Fiona Lubinski in Escape, a small-town dump in the middle of nowhere, Colorado. The town was so small and isolated a blizzard shut the place down for days, trapping her and everyone else in it. That wasn't the worst of it, though.

She was supposed to hook up with someone she didn't know. The stranger was supplying another car to replace the bullet-riddled piece of junk she and her friend Lucky used as getaway transport from the bank robbery in the city.

Long story short, that was when it all went wrong.

Lucky ended up shot dead.

Fiona rubbed at her arm where the dog bit her. She was trying to steal enough cash to get out of town when the roads opened.

The scarred shoulder from the bullet wound ached, too.

The damned roads.

And the woman driving the snow blower that ate her car and the money in the trunk.

The ex-cop and his girlfriend who ruined everything.

She would fix them all or else.

She took a final look in the curtained light of the motel room and cast a glance at her most recent conquest, still snoring in bed. She eased the door closed. Made sure it was locked.

Made for Route 90 in the stolen car.

She was careful to keep the speed to two-under. Just in case. Now that she was tasting freedom she didn't want to end up back in for stupidity.

How the hell did she ever get into that minimum security place? A mistake with her name? A wrong picture on an ID? Someone took a liking to her? She checked the boxes. It wasn't likely it was any of the above. In any case, she didn't care. All that mattered was that she was free.

Fiona had robbed and killed and ended up shipped off for twenty to thirty. Parole wouldn't be coming around until she was middle-aged. If she got lucky. Well, she got lucky—except for the bad coffee—and then she got lucky again.

Fiona snickered and stood on the gas to get her speed up to merge onto Route 90. She checked the time.

Another hour and she'd be in Blue Springs.

<h1 style="text-align:center">Chapter 5</h1>

Jim and Maddie took turns driving into the darkness of night on the way to Blue Springs. They stopped often for gas'n'go burritos. The heavy, gas-guzzling Packard needed fuel as often as they did.

Relieving and exercising an anxious Friday took time, too.

Every time one of them mentioned Boots or Emma by name, the dog's ears perked up and he whined recognition of his old fireplace-snoozing friends.

They arrived at the Tallahassee airport early. After feeding and watering and walking Friday, they caught a bit of restless shuteye in the roomy Packard with the top only partway down to provide much-needed shade.

Boots showed up with an overnight bag and a chocolate Lab.

After grinning handshakes all round, Lady took her time worrying over them, nosing Maddie and Jim.

Friday got his turn at being sniffed and snorted as he returned the unfamiliar dog's antics.

Both dogs circled and sniffed and snuffled and waggled tails and shook bodies from head to tail. When Lady and Friday finished, they sat down and looked up at master and mistress.

Boots grinned and handed over a treat to each of them.

"Lady likes all three of you, but I already knew she would."

"Yes. We had our concerns, but they look to be pretty content. Did you know they have the same mother.

A look of surprise appeared on Boots' face. "Zelda? Zelda is Friday's mother, too?"

"Yes, she is. Unfortunately, Zelda passed away."

"Well, I'm sorry to hear that," Boots said. He reached to scratch Lady's ears. "I'd like to water and exercise her. She's been in close quarters since Denver."

"Not a problem, Boots. Friday could use the same. We've got water and food in the car. It might not be what Lady is accustomed to, but if she's hungry, she'll eat."

Friday's ears perked up at the mention of food. Still, he stayed busy circling and nosing his old friend Boots remembered from the warm fireplace where they both napped away many happy hours.

"Lady isn't jealous. That's good. Friday can tend to be that way sometimes, though," Maddie told Boots.

She turned to her fussing dog. "You remember Boots, don't you? He spoiled you rotten in front of his fireplace with pats and rubs and treats."

Boots laughed, remembering their shared adventures, and addressed Friday. He was interrupted by Friday's woofs of approval. "We can get all caught up, Friday, but I can't be making Lady here jealous."

They left the airport and parked by a small park to water and exercise the dogs. They walked to a stretch of grass. The dogs got to know one another as they tossed the lime-green tennis balls back and forth. The dogs chased after them and each other as they got to know one another. They ended up drinking from the same bowl and it seemed like they would get along just fine.

Boots told them about Emma and her good marks in the paramedic course.

He covered it, but Jim could tell Boots was anxious to

get going. Hell, he would be, too.

Jim said, "Come on, everyone, we're burning daylight. We need to find a place to stay that isn't going to cost us all an arm and a leg."

He opened the passenger door on the Packard. "Climb aboard. We need to find a dog-friendly motel."

Boots sighed, and he pictured him concerned about what it was going to cost.

"Don't worry. We'll find something not too expensive. With a bit of luck, it might be near an ice cream parlor with dog-friendly ice cream."

Friday barked. He knew the sounds of those words right off.

Jim explained to Boots that his PI license was good in the entire state, if he might be concerned about it. He asked why he brought Lady.

"Well, she adores Emma so much I thought I could walk her around the college and pick up her scent." Boots held up his hands. "I know, I know. It sounds silly when I say it, but—"

Jim interrupted, wanting to reassure the man. "Not at all, Boots. It sounds like a good idea. Once we get settled in, we'll go straight to the school and make inquiries. Tell us about Emma's boyfriend." He wanted to know more about him.

What he didn't want was for Boots to suspect anything out of the ordinary. Or that he thought the boy might be responsible.

Jim had to admit he liked Maddie's idea. He, too, was pretty sure the pair were off on a weekend getaway. Maybe they decided to steal an extra day.

"I almost forgot. Janine says hi to you two. And Friday. She wanted to come, but with the diner business and all—"

"It's probably just as well, Boots."

The more bodies they had to contend with, the harder

it would be to do any real work, what with questions that would be coming and the worrying and explanations and planning out loud to make Boots feel included. Bad enough his dog was here to add to everything else they had to contend with.

Maddie busied herself with her phone and ended up exclaiming a satisfied Yes! "I found us a doggie-friendly motel next to a dog park. I booked us adjoining rooms. And it has a pool. We can all work on our tans."

Jim checked out the expression on Boots' face in the rearview. He didn't look happy to hear that.

Maddie turned to him and smiled. "I was only trying to take some of the weight off. I try to do that a lot. You'd better get used to it, Boots." As though to confirm it, Friday barked. Lady licked her master's face in sympathy.

Jim steered into the motel parking lot.

It was nice-looking. Single story. Plenty of grass surrounding the pool and lots of shade for man, woman and animals. An ice machine. A cooler for drinks. The smell of fresh paint wasn't overpowering.

So it was well-maintained, too. Bonus.

Jim said, "Come on, Boots. We'll see how much it's going to cost us."

It wasn't a terrible deal. He asked for a week.

Boots gave him a dirty look.

"We'll get the better rate," he explained. "If we have to, we can check out early and pay for a night or two if that's all it takes."

Jim hoped that was all it was going to take.

Chapter 6

Destruction. **Mile after mile.** It was all around her. Had been for the past twenty minutes, at least.

Fiona Lubinski pulled off the highway. Stopped the car. Got out and climbed up on the hood and then the roof. Everywhere she looked trees were down. Power lines. The few houses she could see were roofless or scattered like kindling.

The hurricane. She had watched news reports on the prison's TV. Hadn't realized until now the magnitude that didn't show on the small screen.

She climbed down and resumed her drive, still in awe at witnessing the disaster first-hand. She was glad she wasn't close by when it happened.

A cockeyed sign announced her arrival on the outskirts of Blue Springs. The destruction followed her all the way.

The college town was a mess. Broken buildings. Roofless homes. Collapsed walls. One after another. And then the magnitude hit her. There was almost nothing left but for an occasional entire building, somehow spared and standing proud in its untouched magnificence.

She parked the stolen car on a side street and looked around. The incredible damage brought by the recent hurricane filled her with awe. Trees knocked down. Power lines. Buildings shattered and collapsed. It seemed to be at its worst here.

She got out of the car and made for the coffee shop. It was one of the few buildings she passed on the main drag that was still intact.

She looked in through the coffee shop's plate-glass window, wondering if the building was safe. Wanting to check it out before deciding if the coffee would be any good.

She placed a hand on the window to block the light for a better view.

Did a double take.

Looked again.

What the hell? Could it be—?

Fiona hesitated at the window for only a few seconds.

She inhaled. Almost gasped.

Took time for a quick second look before backing off.

She turned and stepped casually off the curb and made to double-time it across the street. Tried to stay calm and collected. Her gait couldn't get her to the bench on the other side of the street fast enough.

The sight line from the bench wasn't direct. Still, she had a good view of the coffee shop.

She hastened through a routine she hoped made her look like a local. She draped an arm over the seat-back. Crossed her ankles. Pretended to be interested in the comings and goings on the street. Her head moved from side to side, following half-tons filled with bored teenagers as they drove back and forth.

She wasn't in a hurry. She had all the time in the world now that she was out of prison—even if she was on the run with a stolen car. She knew she would have to dump it, sooner rather than later. Not yet. It was too convenient, and besides, she wasn't a fan of walking or taking a bus.

Fiona dragged a cigarette out of a pack and lit it. She inhaled deeply and considered her options.

She turned her attention back to the coffee shop's huge window. It was difficult to make out the woman working the counter, but it sure did look like her.

Memories of the big-city bank robbery gone bad and getting trapped in a blizzard in a small mountain town in the middle of nowhere came flooding back.

Chapter 7

Maddie Spence brought the car around and backed up to two rooms on the end fronting the pool. They unloaded and Jim sat down beneath a huge umbrella with Boots and Lady.

Maddie went for drinks and ice and they all retired in the pool area with maps and notebooks and phones at the ready.

The shock at the magnitude of the devastation they drove through finally wore off and they began talking about why they were in Blue Springs.

Boots held up his phone. "I didn't tell you earlier. Emma sent me a picture after I was texting her."

"Let me see that, Boots." Jim took the phone for a quick look before handing it off to Maddie.

She looked at the picture and then at him and they both weren't happy. She handed the phone back to Boots.

"Jim? I need to talk to you about the dogs. Right now."

Boots thought he had it figured out. "Don't worry, Maddie. You don't need to worry about Friday and Lady. Lily agreed Lady could have one litter before we had her spayed."

She only nodded as Jim moved off to join her.

Content beneath the shade umbrellas, the dogs looked at them and then put them on ignore.

"You saw the hand signal, too?" he asked Maddie.

"Yes."

"The boyfriend? Or someone else?" he wondered.

"I don't know, but obviously Lily shared her hand signals with Emma," Maddie said.

"And not with Boots. What do you think?"

"I think we need to get moving right away."

They rejoined Boots and went over strategy. The discussion didn't take long. They would take Boots to the campus office right away so he could make himself known.

Maddie got busy coming up with a map of the school grounds and began sketching it out for him.

"Where was she living, Boots?" Jim asked.

He handed over a slip of paper with the address.

Maddie checked an online map. It wasn't far. "I'll walk with Friday and take a look. I think it's time Emma had an old friend visit her for a bit, right, Boots?"

It took some convincing, but Boots agreed. He needed to make himself known to the school administration anyway.

"Once I have a look at her apartment I'll meet up with you back here," Maddie said. She gathered her backpack and Friday's water bottle and headed off.

"Well, Boots and Lady—"

The chocolate lab looked from Jim to Boots. Her tail halted its wagging. She snorted and sat, waiting.

"It's time we went to college."

Boots stroked his dog's neck. "It's time for a car ride, Lady. We'll see what we can find out about Emma."

Lady's ears perked up at the sound of the familiar name and she whined.

"Yes, girl, I'm missing her, too. Let's go, Jim. It's time," Boots said, anxious to be doing something.

Jim found a spot in the school parking lot.

Boots instructed Lady to wait with him.

He powered down the old Packard's convertible roof. Lady was suitably impressed.

He called her out and they made their way beneath a tree and some shade on the grass.

As he suspected, the ancient convertible paid for itself when students walking across the lot stopped to look over the old girl.

It was his plan all along, and having Lady along for the ride didn't hurt. They soon had a small crowd surrounding them as ham-bone Lady did her thing. She was almost as bad as her mother, Zelda.

Jim used the opportunity to show Emma's picture. Some knew her as a classmate from her attendance at the EMS paramedic program she was enrolled in. Others saw her around campus, but didn't know her personally.

"She hasn't been around for a couple of days. Have any of you seen her recently?"

He learned Emma had a part-time job in a coffee shop downtown. He took the name, though it was the only one, and thought it strange she'd take off. They'd have to check with the manager.

By then Lady was having enough of the petting and scratching and was getting nervous for her master. He led her back to the Packard in time to meet up with Boots.

"Did you know Emma started working at a coffee shop downtown?"

Boots shook his head. "No, but she did mention she was looking for a part-time job. We should check it out."

"How did you make out with administration?" he wanted to know.

"The usual. They know of me from the checks I write for part of her tuition. She's been getting good grades. I casually mentioned that I hadn't heard from her for several days. They weren't surprised. Apparently, it happens from time to time when someone gets a new boy or girl friend. They take off for the occasional extended weekend and show up in a day or three."

"Yeah, that's nice and all, except Emma's not answering her phone."

"I explained that, too. It's also quite common, supposedly. They assured me it will all work out in the end."

"I'm not so sure, Boots. Did you notice Emma's hands in the photo you showed us?"

He told Boots about Lily's propensity for all safe or not-safe hand signals. He showed him the old picture the girl sent him of once-little Lady and Emma and Janine and Boots and explained what it meant.

"Emma is using both hands in her recent photo, Boots. That alone I find unusual. As you can plainly see, she's saying she's not safe times two."

Chapter 8

Emma. **That's it. The** woman's name was Emma. She was the one driving the plow. The snow blower. She drove it into the back of her car and chopped the money to shreds with the blades.

Fiona Lubinski shivered, remembering the cold. She rubbed absent-mindedly at her shot-up shoulder before picking up her belongings from the bench and making for the street. She walked back to the side street and the stolen car and settled in behind the wheel to plot her revenge.

The private detective with the black dog. She had his card somewhere. She also had his bullet-hole scar on her shoulder. It was his black dog responsible for her screwed-up arm, too. She had a nice scar to show for that.

What was the woman's name? She had the hots for the woman's boyfriend. Maddie. That was it.

Fiona pulled her backpack into her lap. Rummaged through it and found the wrinkled card. She had the card with her when she was arrested. It followed her to prison and ended up in her belongings when she was released to the resort, as she called it.

Okay. So Emma it would be.

Who else was there when she went looking for the diner and its cash? She thought back. An old man. And his girlfriend. She worked at the diner.

But it was the private dick and his dog and his damned girlfriend who did the damage.

Lucky, her bank-robbing partner was only a faint memory. She had done him in, the useless piece of crap.

Tomorrow she'd return to the bench seat across from the coffee shop and try to figure out Emma's shift hours. It was going to take time, but time was all she had now that she was free as a bird.

Fiona got out of the car and danced around it like she was doing a Chinese fire drill. She got back in and backtracked on her way out of town, intending to dump the car as fast as she could. There was no way she'd get nailed for a stolen car. Not now.

She pulled into a gas station. Parked at the pumps. Went in and purchased a five-gallon jug.

Unloading the car wouldn't be as easy as she first thought. It took an hour of driving around before she gave up and parked the car in a tangle of downed trees thanks to the hurricane.

She got out, opened the jug, and poured five gallons of high-test into the car. Waited a bit for it to soak in. Got fed up and tossed matches one at a time from as far away as she could get.

They all went out.

She ended up lighting them all at once and tossed the fireball past the open door.

A loud whump followed an orange wall of flame and the deal was done.

She shouldered her backpack and hiked back to the road to begin the trek to town.

As luck would have it, she heard a vehicle approach from behind.

Without looking back, she held out a thumb.

Chapter 9

Maddie Spence made sure she had fresh water and ice for Friday in his walk-bottle. Satisfied, she headed off with the dog to begin the hike to Emma's apartment building.

She had mapped out a direct route, one she was pretty sure Emma would take on her way back and forth.

The hurricane was still fresh, and downed trees lay everywhere. Noisy power saws and sweaty men were hard at work on the devastation left behind. The scent of freshly cut wood drifted across her path, floating on the faint breeze.

She stopped at a store and an impromptu coffee shop someone had set up. She showed Emma's picture. A few recognized her. More shook their heads. None who said they knew her had seen her recently. When asked about exams, the consensus was that maybe she went off with a boyfriend to hit the books.

"Well, Friday, for sure people know Emma. Let's go and see how we make out where she lives."

It was another ten minutes of walking before she caught sight of the two-story apartment block. It looked like the hurricane blew right past it. The building and grounds were untouched. Tall trees left standing around the building whispered in the light breeze.

The red-brick building looked impressive from a

distance. It was clean. Bright. Surrounded by a manicured lawn and trees and hedges that looked freshly trimmed. She got closer and flower beds appeared on both sides of the entrance walkway. Whoever owned it and managed it obviously cared.

Maddie halted Friday at the base of the steps leading to the front door before offloading her backpack. She was going for the trendy student look, with jeans and an untucked shirt and hair in a ponytail. She entered the building and went into full student mode when an older man appeared.

"Hello. I'm looking for Emma Mayberry. She was supposed to meet me at a coffee shop, but she wasn't there."

"You've come to the right place. I'm the building super. Name's Burt. Are you Fiona?" the super asked.

The shock of hearing Fiona's name hit Maddie hard. She hesitated, hoping she wasn't giving anything away. Unsure if she had. Surely the man would notice the look on her face.

"Yes I am. And this is my dog."

She bent to scratch Friday. She would have let him drink from the bottle but for the mess it would leave behind.

"You're a friend of Emma's, are you? How do you know her?" Burt asked.

"We're friends from back in Escape. It's a small town. Everybody knows everybody."

"Well then, Fiona. I can let you in. You're sure you're a friend?"

Maddie patted Friday and tapped his head. He looked up at Burt and snorted and woofed and wagged his tail in a fury. That got a whispered good boy compliment for his charade and a treat to go with it from Maddie.

"Follow me," Burt the superintendent said. A key chain rattled and Burt led them upstairs to the second floor. "That's a gorgeous dog. What's his name?"

Pleased that the super liked her dog, she told him. "I wasn't expecting to bring Friday, but—"

"Oh no, it's all right. We're pet-friendly here. As long as you pick up after him."

"Oh yes. I will. Thank you."

Emma's apartment was half-way down the hall.

Burt looked the dog over, eyed Maddie's backpack, and opened the door. "Here you go. It's a lot cooler inside. If you leave, lock the door behind you, Fiona."

Burt left and the door closed behind him.

Maddie rummaged through her bag for her phone and began tapping furiously. She gave up when she didn't get a response. Frustrated, she brought up Jim's number. It went right to voicemail. "Dammit, Friday. We need to get in touch with Jim."

She paged down her contacts, searching for Boots' number. She cursed out loud when she realized it wasn't in her phone. "Well, Friday, while we're here, we might as well do some detecting."

She put on a pair of gloves and pulled two plastic bags from her backpack before making for the laundry hamper. As luck would have it, she found two articles of clothing. She placed them in the bags before sealing them.

"Friday. Come." She rubbed Friday's nose in the discarded small t-shirt. "Emma. That's Emma." Friday looked up at her and barked. "Emma. Good boy, Friday. Remember. Emma."

She let him have another sniff, put the t-shirt into the bag, and zipped it. She wandered from room to room. Checked out the few photos. Discovered a phone charger still plugged in. No phone. Nodded, since it made sense. Just in case, she called Emma's phone. No phone rang in the small apartment. The call went to voicemail.

She opened the fridge. There were no leftovers, but plenty of food on the shelves. Fresh fruit was just turning in a bowl on the counter.

There was a minimum of garbage under the sink.

The place was neat and tidy. Looked like it was dusted regularly. Emma was a miss neat, with everything in place from what she could see.

She opened closet doors to find them just as organized. So were the dresser drawers and the night table in the bedroom.

Something wasn't right about the books and notebooks scattered on the kitchen table. If Emma was off for a study weekend with the boyfriend, why were her books still here? It was looking like something else was going on. She snapped a picture to show to Jim and Boots.

She tried calling Jim again. She left a message and hoped for the best. She let the water run in the kitchen sink while she searched for a spare key. She replenished Friday's bottle with cold water and turned off the tap.

Maddie placed her backpack on the counter and opened a pocket. She removed the holstered pistol. Flipped the cylinder open. Pushed the retractor to check the five-shot butterfly clip. The shells edged out. She pushed them back in, re-holstered, and clipped the handgun onto her belt in the small of her back. She adjusted her shirt to cover the concealed weapon before slipping the backpack through her arms.

Satisfied, she flipped the lock and closed the door to Emma's apartment with Friday hovering close behind her.

Chapter 10

Fiona Lubinski's **tight cutoffs** and shapely legs worked their magic. She turned to greet the vehicle coming up fast behind her.

The half-ton's screeching brakes and tires forced the truck to slow and halt. It was jacked up, sitting high and dry and spelling hillbilly while sporting dents and rust. The driver pushed the passenger door open and she climbed up.

The driver's eyes traveled from her own down to the cutoffs, halting at her thighs. They traveled all the way back up to her eyes.

She smiled and flipped her hair.

"You smell like gasoline, woman. You're not gonna catch fire if I light one, are you?"

The driver fumbled one-handed with the pack. It slipped from his fingers and fell to the floor. Fiona leaned over, rested a hand on the man's thigh, and bent to retrieve it. She squeezed and straightened and withdrew two cigarettes while leaning back against the door. She raised her hips, and, struggling, reached into a pocket on the too-tight cutoffs. Wrestled to withdraw a lighter. Lit both cigarettes and handed him one.

He took it without thanking her and inhaled deeply before exhaling a cloud of smoke that disappeared out the open window. "Where you headed?"

"Back to town. I had some car trouble. You here for the construction?" She noticed the out-of-state license plate when he slowed late and went past.

"Yeah, there's a bunch of us came over. We have a place on the edge of town. There's a barbecue tonight. You're welcome to come if you want."

Billy Denver. That was his name. Funny, that. It was the city where the bank robbery went bad.

Fiona wondered if it might be an omen, then thought no more about it.

"You can drop me off on the main drag. I'm going to look for work." It sounded good. Responsible. Like she was a regular girl who needed work and a measure of stability in her life. A man, too.

She wondered if he thought the same.

"You see that bench? I'll be there waiting for you to come pick me up later for a trip to that barbecue."

The hillbilly stopped in the middle of the street and she smiled her thanks and got out.

He never said a word. No goodbye. No see you later. No nothing. Tires screeched and he raced off.

She shouldered her backpack and made to walk around the block to case the area surrounding the coffee shop.

She noticed more now that she was forced to use her feet. There wasn't so much of anything left. Broken buildings, opened up like tin cans. Collapsed walls. Buildings wide open. Ruined businesses topped by the occasional roof that didn't blow away. And strangest of all, buildings in the middle of the destruction that weren't touched in the slightest.

Like the coffee shop.

The luck of the draw. Her good fortune once again. That, and spotting the woman before she spotted her. If she had made it inside to first in line—

She stopped thinking about it and instead circled the

area, getting familiar with the streets. The destruction was everywhere. How anyone survived was a miracle.

Finally bored by it all, Fiona made for the bench to wait for Billy. If he even showed up.

Fiona killed time with thinking.

She was barely out of prison, and here she was, smack in the middle of a hurricane disaster. Her good luck followed her so far, even if she had to over-think it. And think about it she did until she heard the roar of the truck's exhaust pipes. It halted in front of her. The door opened from the inside and she climbed in.

"Thanks. I was thinking you weren't going to show."

"Sorry about that. We had to put in some overtime to cover the building we're working on with a tarp in case it rains," he explained.

Fiona was so involved in her own predicament she didn't notice the rain clouds on the horizon. "So who'll be at this barbecue? Your friends?"

She needn't have asked. He pulled into a driveway with piles of cut wood on both sides. It was obviously cleared of downed trees.

The house was tiny. A sloped roof. Green lawn. Most of the trees that surrounded it were down and already cut and piled. The scent of fresh wood permeated the yard. Somebody had a couple of huge gray full-size tents set up in back of the house.

Half a dozen people or more circled a barbecue. Burgers cooked and orange flames jumped. A couple of lonely potatoes wrapped in tinfoil sat forlorn on the grill. A tin garbage can overflowed with ice and beer. Music from someone's phone blared through portable speakers.

Billy introduced her to everyone, but she didn't care. He was the one with the truck. She would need it eventually. \

The beer flowed. Music blared. Men and women mingled and danced and by then she had a good buzz going. She settled in while Billy took over cooking burgers on the barbecue.

It wasn't difficult to wrangle her way into Billy's bedroom and his bed. It also wasn't difficult to convince Billy she would like to stay if he would only okay it.

The disturbance in the morning as the house filled with the noises of a crew readying for work drew her out of the empty bed.

"How much time do you guys have?"

She didn't wait for the answers before opening the fridge. She hauled out milk and eggs. Cracked them into a bowl and poured in a bit of milk. She flashed up the gas stove and dropped a heavy cast-iron fry pan on it. While it was heating, she whipped the eggs and poured them in over a bit of melted grease.

"Eggs on the way, boys. Don't desert me yet."

The eggs arrived in five minutes. It took about that long for the first person to finish as the last got served.

"Leave some money for supper and I'll see what I can come up with."

Hands went into pockets and fished out wrinkled paper.

"Come on now," she admonished them. "Don't be so tight as a nail in a board."

That got laughter and more money on the counter.

It got a response from Billy, too. "You gonna need the truck to do the shopping?"

Mumbling and grumbling about walking and working and long hours didn't make the crew happy.

"Does that complaining mean I have to drive you all to work?"

Chapter 11

Maddie Spence double-timed** it to the motel on foot. Her mistaken-identity chat with Emma's super, who thought she was Fiona, had her on edge. Not finding any clues to Emma's whereabouts in the apartment didn't help matters. But calling her Fiona? How many women had that name? And how many of them claimed to know Emma?

Worried, she swiped at the sweat running down her face. By the time she reached the motel her shirt was soaked through and she was a nervous wreck. She didn't see the Packard in the lot and cursed Jim out loud.

Frustrated, she tried calling him again. In that instant, she recognized the car turning into the motel lot. She hung up and waited outside their room, tapping a foot.

Friday waited with her, impatient too.

Jim parked and got out and immediately sensed something was wrong.

"It's about damned time. I've been calling and texting you for what seems like hours."

Jim reached for his phone. "And so you have. What's got a burr up your butt?"

Exasperated, Maddie told him about Emma's building manager and the woman named Fiona he told her about.

"Are you sure?"

She sighed, exasperated and disappointed. "Jim, the building manager mentioned it. I let him think I was Fiona."

Jim steadied his eyes on her.

"The super didn't ask questions, and neither did I. I ran with it and pretended I was her. He was convinced I was a friend of Emma's from Escape, so he let me in, thinking I was Fiona. There's no sign of Emma. The place is neat and tidy but for the textbooks scattered on the kitchen table." She pulled out her phone and showed him the picture. "It hasn't been tossed. That means no thief."

Jim hesitated, thinking. "Probably. But the Fiona we know is locked up nice and tight for murder. She's in a Federal pen. There's no chance in hell she'll be out walking the streets for a very long time. Even with best behavior."

"What other Fiona would it be, Jim?" Maddie asked. "She must have called the super. It has to be her." Maddie rocked nervously from side to side.

Sensing something wrong, Friday walked slow circles around both of them.

"Look. Even Friday remembers that woman," she said.

Jim wasn't convinced. "Well, I'll give Boyle a call, but Fiona is behind so many doors—"

"Just do it, all right, Jim? Right now," she insisted.

Jim didn't need to be told twice.

Maddie reached to remove her handgun from behind her back. She placed it on the patio table.

"I need to get water for Friday. We just about ran all the way back here to find you when you wouldn't answer your phone. Come on, boy. It's time for a drink and some shade."

She waited for Jim to pick up his phone. She needed to see him do it.

He returned her gaze. Exasperated and very much

doubting that it would be Fiona, he made the call to Boyle. He was still talking when Maddie returned.

"I'm going to put you on speaker, Don. Maddie is here now."

Boyle's gruff voice penetrated the silence. "The woman in question has been out and about for a week. Someone slipped up months ago. Fiona Lubinski managed to get transferred to a minimum-security facility in Tallahassee. From there, they let her out. No one realized their error until I touched base just now. The crap is hitting the fan as we speak."

Maddie cursed her bad luck again. Neither of them took pains to explain how they knew Fiona.

Maddie said, "I think she's here, Don. We're working a missing person case for a friend. I went to Emma's apartment this afternoon. The building super thought I was Fiona. When I told him I was, he let me into her apartment. Something is going on. I don't know what yet."

She eyed Jim, wanting to make sure he knew she was disappointed with him.

"Well, you two, be careful. From what I saw on paper, she's a handful. I'll send you current intake photos after I hang up."

"Thanks, Don. We appreciate it," Maddie said.

The photos arrived. They showed a Fiona Lubinski that didn't look happy to be there. She had put on weight in prison. Her face was more filled out. At least now they had another picture to show around. Maybe someone saw Fiona and Emma together.

But that was a non-starter. They both knew Fiona and Emma wouldn't be hanging around together. They knew each other, and not in a good way after what happened in Escape.

"Jim?"

"Yes?"

"What are we going to tell Boots?" she asked.

"The truth, Maddie. He needs to know."

Maddie said, "It's about time you admitted it. You have no idea how disappointed I am in you."

Jim removed his automatic from his belt and placed it on the table beside Maddie's holstered five-shot. "I'm glad to see you were prepared when you went on your walk."

"So was I when I found out I had to pretend to be Fiona." Maddie agreed. "Emma isn't out studying with her boyfriend. Not by the look of that kitchen table and the textbooks and notebooks scattered on it."

She showed Jim the picture again.

She smiled, but it was a grim smile at best. She still wasn't happy in the slightest. "I hope Emma is all right."

"We'll find her. Here comes Boots and Lady now."

Friday took off to greet the pair

Boots' feet were dragging. He was exhausted from his meeting with the college administration. He definitely wasn't happy. "I'll tell you what. Those people need a swift kick."

He looked from Jim to Maddie, recognizing trouble when he saw it.

"What's going on? What's wrong? Is it Emma?"

Chapter 12

Fiona Lubinski was beside herself. Completely by accident, she had spotted the unsuspecting Emma. Followed her undetected. Scouted out the college where she took classes. Discarded that idea and went with the woman's apartment. It was perfect.

All she needed was a car.

Or truck.

And she had that, if she could convince Billy to loan her his.

Emma's building parking lot was unlit. It wouldn't matter what night she got her hands on the truck. It could be any night she felt comfortable.

The truck. It was all about Billy's truck.

She cursed her bad luck at setting fire to her car so soon. She told herself it was better that way, though. No chance of it being spotted by the cops and their automated license plate readers.

If they even had anything like that in the hick town she found herself in.

Maddie **allowed Jim to** take the lead with Boots. She had listened carefully to Don's assessment over the phone. She didn't want to believe it, even though she was the one who heard Fiona's name mentioned by Emma's building manager. And she was still disappointed with Jim for doubting her.

Jim said, "You better sit down, Boots. Maddie and I have something to tell you that you're not going to like."

Boots called Lady to sit beside him. A distraught Maddie could barely wait for Jim to go on.

"We just talked to a friend of mine, a detective. Wait. I'm getting ahead of it. Maddie, tell Boots what you found at Emma's apartment."

Maddie told him about Emma's building super thinking she was Fiona.

Boots was intent on interrupting, but Maddie silenced him.

"It's true," she said. "He called me by her name several times. I convinced him I was her friend Fiona from Escape. He let me into Emma's apartment. That's where I discovered this."

She showed Boots the picture of the textbooks on Emma's table.

"Emma is definitely not off studying with her boyfriend."

She hesitated before going on.

"I had a pretty good look around her place. Everything was as it should be—neat and tidy. Bed made. Dresser and closets undisturbed. I didn't find a spare key. Jim?"

"Maddie thinks Fiona is in town. She thinks she might have something to do with Emma going missing. I wasn't convinced. She's been in prison ever since our last run-in. So I called a detective I know, and he ran her. Fiona is out. Somehow, she escaped."

The statement stunned Boots. His mouth fell open and he collapsed into his chair. He didn't believe it. Finally, he spoke. "Are you sure? Fiona? Our Fiona?" He realized what he said and shook his head, as though that would change it. "That thief and murderer? She's supposed to be in prison I thought she got life. She did get life."

Jim said "Yes. She did. But something happened. According to my Miami contact, she ended up transferred to a minimum-security facility. In Tallahassee, of all places. She was released from there. According to Boyle, the authorities are still trying to figure out how that happened.

Flashing blue and red lights in the motel parking lot drew their attention away from concern about Fiona. Four uniformed officers stepped out of a pair of black and whites. They approached with weapons drawn.

"Oh shit. Make Lady sit and stay, Boots. Keep your hands on the table. Don't move them."

Jim and Maddie did the same.

Maddie commanded Friday to sit.

"We'll keep you out of it, Boots. Don't make any sudden moves."

Four policemen surrounded the table with guns drawn.

"One at a time. Stand up. Get on your knees. Put your hands behind your head."

One by one, they did as they were told.

Jim waited until the officers finished the handcuff detail.

"Officer. We're private detectives licensed by the state of Florida. We have permits for the handguns. We're in town working a case."

"Do as I say. We'll sort it out in a bit," an officer said.

It took a while once the trio was cuffed, but it was sorted on good terms. Wallets produced identification and the required permits and the contingent of police officers departed the motel.

A shaken Boots proposed they find somewhere to eat to discuss the day's progress.

"Or lack of it, Boots," Jim said.

Maddie wasn't having it. "It's not that bad, you two. We have a solid lead. All we have to do is find that woman. I'm pretty certain we'll find Emma at the same time."

But did she believe the words coming out of her mouth?

She had been to Emma's building.

Heard the manager mention Fiona's name.

Pretended to be the woman to get into Emma's apartment.

Searched and came up with nothing of consequence.

It was during dinner when Boots brought up scuba diving. Emma's boyfriend was a diver. He had convinced her to take lessons.

Maddie vaguely recalled the caves before turning to her phone. "I remember watching something on television when I was a lot younger. Or maybe it was a school project. I never paid attention. I seem to recall underwater caves around here somewhere."

Could it be something that simple? Had Emma and her boyfriend gone off on a diving weekend to spend time together and explore the caves?

"Anything is possible," Jim said. "Tomorrow is a new

day. We'll start fresh. Seven o'clock by the pool, people."

Friday barked.

"And dogs."

Maddie hoped that was it. If Emma was off cave diving, she would have missed out on a visit from Fiona.

Later, in their room, Maddie broached the subject of Boots with Jim.

"I think Boots should move into Emma's apartment."

Her reasoning was two-fold.

"I don't think they're well-off. And he'd be there if she came home from wherever the heck she's run off to."

But did she believe Emma had only run off with a new boyfriend on a temporary getaway? It was possible, of course. But if end-of-term exams were close, that wouldn't be so smart, either. She never took Emma for a fool, given her dedication to her education.

"We'll talk about it at the morning meeting. I'm going to knock on Boots' door and see if he and Lady might want to come along on a walk with Friday. You won't mind if I steal your dog, will you?"

Maddie jumped out of bed and pulled open her backpack.

"In that case, you'll need these."

She pulled out the plastic bag with Emma's shirt and her scent.

Chapter 14

J im Nash headed off first thing in the morning to pick up a fast-food breakfast for the crew.

Maddie busied herself feeding and walking Friday.

Jim passed Boots and Lady doing the same and honked. On the return he picked the pair up and made for the motel's pool patio.

They were eager to get going. Breakfast was devoured in mere minutes.

Maddie left to retrieve the plastic bags with Emma's scent on the enclosed clothing.

That alone was enough to impress Boots.

"That was a smart move. I would never have thought of it. You did good, Maddie."

She smiled at Boots. "Her place was so neat and tidy it was all I could think of to do. Now we have her scent for Friday. And Lady too, if she needs it."

Boots' positive attitude wasn't long for this world. Across the table, he was becoming increasingly despondent. He sat with shoulders forward and chest caved in, staring at the ground. "Thanks, Maddie. I appreciate everything you both are doing."

Maddie said, "We're going to find her, I promise."

Without prompting, Boots brought up the idea Maddie shared privately with Jim last night.

"I think I should move into Emma's place. Do you think the building manager would allow it?"

Jim glanced at Maddie.

She nodded agreement. "I'm pretty sure he would. After all, he let me in. Show him some ID and go for it, I'd say."

Maddie didn't let on she and Jim already discussed that very thing.

Boots said, "It would be cheaper than staying in the motel. I'm not a rich man in case you didn't notice back in Escape."

"You'd be there if she showed up unexpectedly. And I'm pretty sure it will make you feel better, too."

To change the subject, Jim brought out the map and spread it on the table. He caught Maddie's glance.

"You are so 20th century," she said.

He smiled at the reference. "Maybe, but Boots and I are old-school that way. I checked with the front desk first thing. The underwater caves are here." He pointed to the locations the desk clerk had circled on the brochure.

"If the pair took a break and went diving, chances are they're out there. Apparently, there are places you can rent. Some have a dock. Plenty of dive teams use them as a base for exploring the caves. Emma and Danny might even have gone off with a group. Some houses are big enough for a group stay and they make a holiday out of it."

Boots took one look and shook his head. "I don't know. It's not far enough away to do something like that. Why wouldn't they drive back and forth?"

Boots had a point.

"You'd do that. So would I. But I don't think the kids would. What do you think, Maddie?"

Maddie looked right at Boots and mimed chewing gum before answering. "Well, old-timers, I beg to disagree. Here's why."

Maddie grinned, and Boots looked at her like she was touched.

"Us young-uns do things differently in these modern times. We'd stay right there. Leave civilization behind. Cook. Eat. Light some candles. Make an adventure out of it for a few days before being happy to return to civilization only a few miles away."

Jim was convinced. He felt Boots was too, because he pushed back from the table and stood up.

He scooped the bags containing Emma's clothing off the table and made for the Packard. "In that case, let's get going. Come, Lady. You too, Friday."

Boots slapped his thigh twice.

Friday perked up his ears. The dog remembered Lily used that command for him, too. His mistress never commanded him that way.

"We have work to do."

Friday followed Boots without so much as a backward glance at Maddie.

A shocked expression appeared on her face.

Friday scampered after the man like he wanted to play. Halfway to the car, the dog halted and turned. He barked before scurrying off to join Boots and Lady at the car.

"You've been told, Maddie. Get with it."

She caught Boots laughing as he handed over treats to Lady and Friday and scratched at their ears for a job well done.

"Hey. Did you see that? What's happening with my dog?"

Jim shrugged and held out his hands in mock surrender. "What can I say? Friday remembers Boots. He ought to, given how the two of them used to curl up in front of the fireplace and snooze all day long. Not to mention all the petting and scratching Friday got."

"It's true. I think poor Friday had enough of frolicking in the snow and just gave up."

Maddie smiled remembering Friday's first experience with winter and snow in the mountains. The dog sat his warm bum down in cold snow and jumped up in shock as fast as he could. From then on, he went outside to do his business as quick as was doggie-possible.

Jim pushed back from the table and stood up.

"Come on, Maddie. Boots and his faithful dogs are waiting."

Chapter 15

Fiona found it easy to follow Emma, notwithstanding the woman's nervous and constant looks over her shoulder. She made sure to keep her distance. Didn't act suspicious. Never stopped to pretend to smell the flowers. Managed to keep a couple of blocks between them.

It was almost too easy with most of the trees down and buildings destroyed by the hurricane. There were no obstacles to her sightlines. Even if Emma turned to look, she was too far away to pay any attention.

Fiona made sure to keep her distance even when the woman entered the two-story apartment building.

She circled the block, checking for doors and windows on the ground floor. There were two entrances and that made for two exits. A parking lot in back fronted one of them.

She thought to check for lighting and saw the parking lot was unlit. Dark was good. She would need dark for the impromptu plan that was taking shape. She would need a vehicle. She cursed herself again for getting rid of the stolen car too soon.

Fiona didn't want to steal anything in this small town. The locals would be on the lookout. They would recognize it in a heartbeat, especially now following the hurricane, when looters would be on the prowl for anything that wasn't tied down.

It would have to be Billy's truck. There was no other. She thanked her lucky stars and her short-shorts for meeting him.

Plenty of the back roads were blocked with downed trees. She had discovered that when she went looking for a place to dump the stolen car. That wasn't good. Although it wasn't bad, either. It would mean a certain amount of privacy, especially if she could find an isolated area that wasn't well-traveled. She had the hurricane's destruction to thank for that.

She made her way around the apartment block from a distance a final time. Satisfied, she walked past one more time and then made her way to Billy's place. It would have to be his truck.

Already she was thinking about how she would play him to get it.

On the way, she stopped at the coffee shop and ordered. She took it outside. Took two sips and tossed it.

She crossed the street and sat down on the bench to wait for Billy.

Chapter 16

Emma **Mayberry exited the** college campus and began walking downtown. She hurried, not wanting to be late for her shift at the coffee shop. Miraculously, somehow the hurricane had swept past the place, leaving it undamaged. As such, it filled quickly with lines of construction workers on short breaks. Locals remained at tables, for it was a gathering place to gossip and share information about damage suffered and insurance claims. Some had it. Many didn't.

Emma felt sorry for those and commiserated with them over it.

By the end of her shift, she was exhausted. Her back ached and her feet were sore. She gathered her belongings and made for home, passing downed trees and wide-open buildings along the way that were missing roofs and sometimes walls.

She was fascinated by the storm's seeming random destruction. While it saddened her that so many people were affected and so many lives ruined, she couldn't stop thinking about how fortunate she was. Danny, her boyfriend, too. They survived unscathed but for some water damage around windows in their respective apartments.

Tired as she was, she was supposed to meet Danny later. She texted him to cancel and instead invited him over. They would hit the books at her place instead of his, since they were both in the same program.

Emma showered and dried her hair and dressed to wait for Danny.

She spread textbooks on the kitchen table and began going through her notes. She enjoyed studying with Danny. He always brought his own notes. He never once asked to share hers.

A knock on the door interrupted her studies. She put down the pen. Danny was earlier than he said he would be. She smiled as she opened the door, glad that he was. "Yes?"

It wasn't Danny.

"Emma. So good to see you. Aren't you going to invite me in?"

Emma hesitated, trying to remember.

It came to her, suddenly, as long, drawn-out realization crossed her face.

Fiona.

She panicked and heaved her body against the door.

She was too late.

It halted against Fiona's foot.

"I thought so."

The woman shouldered the door.

Emma was unprepared. The abrupt motion forced her backwards into the small kitchen. She stumbled and caught the edge of the counter.

In one motion, Fiona slammed the door closed and locked it.

She whirled to face Emma. "We have things we need to talk about, Emma. It's long overdue."

Fiona charged.

Pushed her all the way into the tiny kitchen.

Emma ended up with her back to the sink.

Fiona kept coming.

A dozen questions ran through her mind.

What was Fiona doing here?

Wasn't she in prison for life somewhere?

Emma's unbelieving eyes looked again.

How could this woman be standing in front of her?

"Yes. It's me, Emma. Did you forget about me? Did you think I was tucked away, rotting in a prison somewhere? Out of sight, out of mind, right?"

Sudden realization took over Emma's face. It was the woman she saw through the coffee shop's window. "What do you want, Fiona? Why are you here?"

"That's more like it."

Fiona's dark, evil eyes bored into hers. The woman was a fugitive. In jail for murder and bank robbery.

How did she get out?

What could she possibly want?

Fiona pulled a knife from her belt. She waved the tip and circled in front of Emma in the tiny kitchen.

She was cornered. There was nowhere to flee.

"Get down on your knees or else," Fiona ordered.

Chapter 17

Fiona slipped her backpack off and let it drop to the floor. Thinking it a mistake to leave it in front of her quarry, she used a foot to push it away before bending to dig in a pocket. She withdrew gray duct tape and tie wraps.

"Put your hands behind your head."

Emma looked up at her, not comprehending.

Fiona screamed. "Behind your head. Now!"

Scared, not knowing what was coming from the crazed woman, Emma complied.

Fiona dropped the knife on the counter.

She grabbed a wrist and forced a hand down to waist-level.

She wrapped a zip-tie around it.

She did the same with the other hand and used a third tie to force Emma's wrists together.

She grabbed a corner of the tape and ripped a length before taping her mouth.

"That should hold you for a while."

Fiona stepped back to admire her handiwork. Her eyes widened when she noticed Emma's unbound feet.

"I almost forgot."

She hummed as she unrolled a length of tape and wrapped Emma's ankles. Satisfied, she picked the knife off the counter and replaced it in her belt.

With Emma secured, she looked around the small apartment. It was neat as a pin.

Typical small-town homebody.

She ran a finger along the counter before holding it up to inspect. It came away dust-free.

A knock on the door alerted Fiona. "Are we expecting company?" She grabbed Emma's ankles and struggled to drag her down the hall and into the bedroom. She ran her fingers through her hair before opening the door.

"Hello. Who might you be?" Fiona asked.

"I'm Danny. Who are you?"

Fiona smiled sweetly. "I'm a friend of Emma's. I just got into town. It's a surprise visit." Her eyes roamed to the cast-iron frying pan on the stove-top. Who else but a country girl would have one of those?

"Have a seat, Danny." She found a mug in the cupboard and reached for the pot on the counter. "Have a coffee while you wait."

She placed the mug in front of him, and from there it was easy.

She made a grab for the frying pan.

Swung it harder than she wanted.

It connected with the back of Danny's head.

He collapsed face-first on the table.

She abandoned the zip ties and instead used tape on his wrists and ankles. "That ought to hold you."

She went back to Emma in the bedroom. "Your boyfriend is here. He's in the kitchen."

Fiona dragged Emma from the bedroom to the kitchen.

Danny was on the floor, bound and gagged.

Tears rolled down Emma's face.

Fiona stood back to survey the situation. While she was certain she'd catch Emma unaware, she had no idea about the boyfriend. She found herself with two live bodies to contend with and no means of transportation.

She opened a pamphlet on the counter. It was publicity for a cave diving adventure. The map showed an area similar to where she took the stolen car to set it on fire.

All right, then.

Billy would have to donate his truck to the cause.

She tied the bodies together, back-to-back. Emma struggled to get free. She backhanded the woman into submission.

"I'll be stepping out for a bit. Don't go away," Fiona said with a grin.

Fiona searched Emma's bag for a key.

Found it.

Laughed on her way out the door.

She made sure to lock it behind her.

Chapter 18

Jim drove Boots Mayberry to Emma's apartment and together they went to see the manager.

Maddie remained in the car, thinking it better if she wasn't seen with them. She had already showed up as Fiona. There was no sense confusing the issue.

Boots explained he was looking for his daughter. He showed the super his ID.

Jim flashed his buzzer and explained he was a private detective hired by the man to look for the girl.

The manager didn't bat an eye.

Keys jangled and they were in.

"Has anyone been looking for Emma recently?" Jim asked.

"There was a woman yesterday. She called and showed up, so I let her in. She said she was a friend from the same town back in Colorado. I didn't think anything of it. It's a college town, after all. Students are always showing up for one reason or another."

"All right, then. Thanks. Here's my card. If that woman who identified herself as Fiona shows up again or calls, let me know."

Jim made sure the door closed behind them.

"I'm going to give the place the once-over, Boots. Maddie already looked, but it never hurts to have two pairs of eyes do the looking."

"You go ahead. I'm going to unpack and check the fridge."

Lady wandered from room to room in the small apartment. She sniffed and snuffed and wagged her tail, expecting to find Emma. When the dog didn't, she sidled up to Boots and nudged his thigh.

"I know, girl. Emma isn't here. We'll find her."

That seemed to placate the dog.

Boots pulled a handgun out of his backpack and replaced the magazine.

Jim said, "You can't be out and about with that, Boots. Even if it's registered in Colorado. Florida cops frown on that sort of thing."

"Don't worry. It's not registered. It's for household defense purposes only."

Jim had a new estimation of the man standing in front of him.

"And don't ask," Boots added. "I'll never tell where I got it."

That was fine with him. "How about if we come back later and take you grocery shopping? Maddie needs some things, too." He wanted to put the man at ease, and it was the best he could summon, given the circumstances.

"That would be all right. It'll give us time to look around."

Jim waited while Boots finished unpacking.

Boots brought out a long leash for Lady. "I want to see if we can pick up Emma's scent. What do you think?"

Boots collected a shirt from the laundry for Lady to sniff. The dog busied her nose and wagged her tail at the familiar scent.

"It can't hurt. I'll see you later," Jim told him. "I'll take Maddie and we'll pick up some essentials for you. If we have any questions, we'll call, okay?"

Jim already suspected any scent of Emma outside of her apartment would be long gone.

Chapter 19

Jim walked around to the motel patio. He found Maddie beneath the shade of the umbrella. Her legs were outside, tanning in the sun.

"Boots is checking out. He's going to move into Emma's. He needs a few things. Would you like to come?"

He already knew Friday was coming. His ears were perked up and his tail wagged furiously at the mention of the man's name. "His dog is ready and waiting at the door."

He probably shouldn't have put it that way. Maddie was a little sensitive about how close Friday and Boots were becoming. He knew when he got the pouty look. "I'm sorry, sweetheart. I didn't mean it that way."

Maddie grinned.

She had me.

"Friday is my dog, gumshoe, even if I loan her to you from time to time. He knows who butters his dog food, just like you know where to find your buttered bread."

She made to squeeze his love handles, but he deftly moved out of the way and surrendered by holding up his hands. "Speaking of toast and jam, we need to go."

It didn't take them long to fill a bag with essentials for Boots. If he needed more, they were only a phone call away.

Jim stopped in front of the apartment and made for

the stairs to the second floor.

A dog barked somewhere in the building.

He knocked on Emma's door, expecting Boots to answer. When he didn't, he knocked again. Still nothing.

The barking got louder.

He twisted the doorknob on the unlocked door and walked into Emma's place.

Boots' backpack lay on the table where he left it.

He searched it for the handgun. It was missing.

So was Boots.

Jim made for the bedroom and opened the door. An angry dog growled a greeting before scrambling past him and out the open apartment door. Lady was hot on the trail of her missing master.

He hurried downstairs and called to Maddie. "Boots is gone. See if you can use Friday to corral his dog."

It took a few minutes, but they got the frantic dog into the car and hooked up to a leash.

Friday helped console her while Jim drove everyone to the motel.

"His handgun is missing, too," he said.

"He had a gun?"

"Yup. Unregistered. So he said."

Maddie shook her head. "Now the woman is armed. And even more dangerous."

"Don't be hard on Boots. No one was expecting this turn of events."

They had come here expecting an easy time locating Emma.

When Boots first touched base, he didn't envision a kidnapping. Now, with both Emma and her father missing, things were turning into something more than a missing woman and her boyfriend on a getaway.

Would he and Maddie be able to get to the bottom of it in time?

He was starting to have doubts.

Chapter 20

Fiona ran as fast as she could. Her breathing turned ragged in the humid night air. Perspiration soaked through her shirt. She considered how she would approach Billy. She needed his truck. He was a good guy but a real simpleton. She had to get the truck. She would use the direct approach.

She spotted it in the driveway. Ran past it to the house. Pushed the door open. Let it crash against the wall. Rushed into the house and found herself in the middle of a roomful of Billy's friends.

"Billy. You're here. I need help. The truck. I have to borrow your truck." She talked through labored breathing, trying to catch her breath. At least that wasn't a lie, not that she was concerned with her lies now. Or ever.

"Fiona. What's wrong? What are you running from?"

She went on, still winded. "My friend. Her boyfriend." She took deep breaths. "He's trouble. She needs help." She was only exaggerating a little now. Like that wouldn't apply to any of her women friends in a former life.

Billy stood up and fished in his pocket before pulling out the key. "I'll come with you," he volunteered.

"No. It won't help. You'd be another man she doesn't know. It would make her more upset." She made to reach for the key. "I'll be back as soon as I can."

"Are you sure?" Billy was eager. Ready to go. "I can wait outside while you do what you have to."

"No, Billy. You'll only make matters worse."

Fiona considered breaking into tears, and then changed her mind just as fast. It would only encourage Billy. She didn't want him around for what she had to do. She reached again for the key and he handed it over.

Her lips began curving upward into a smile. She bit her tongue, hard, and scowled instead. She hoped it passed for a teary thanks. "I'll make it up to you. I promise."

She marched out the door and didn't look back. She was too busy congratulating herself on how easy it was. She climbed up into the truck as fast as she could and twisted the key. She didn't want time for Billy to change his mind at the last minute.

The temperamental truck started first try. She reversed, backed out of the driveway, and shifted again. She stomped on the gas pedal. Tires squealed and she steered toward Emma's apartment building.

On a whim she parked on an off-street and made for the coffee shop. Out of habit she checked the bench across the street. She halted and did a double take.

There it was.

The dog. The black dog.

She rubbed at her arm.

Switched to her shoulder.

Son of a bitch.

She almost screamed.

Caught herself at the last second.

She didn't bother turning around. She walked backwards and in two steps she was around the corner of the building and out of sight.

It couldn't be. It was dark. The street lamp wasn't putting out a lot of light. She peeked around the corner again. The dog was between them. Licking fingers on joined hands while the pair sipped at the shitty coffee.

She must have lost track of time. What day was it? How many since she took Emma and her boyfriend? Fiona couldn't remember.

The dog's ears perked up. He got up. Looked in her direction. Woofed.

Fiona double-timed it to the truck. Cursed the damn dog and its memory. Or his sense of smell. It had to be the scent.

She almost crawled back into the truck.

She peeled rubber and took off for Emma's apartment. No way was she going to stop now.

Fiona was certain she was close to being spotted. She didn't want to chance it again. That damned dog. The one that bit her arm. The detective. His partner. He was the one that shot her.

She muttered to herself all the way to the apartment and her two prizes. If only she hadn't wasted so much time. But she knew now.

She had a bonus.

Jim and Maddie.

And the dog.

And they never saw her.

But what were they doing in town?

Blue Springs was no place for a vacation, especially after the hurricane blew through and turned it into a hellhole.

Chapter 21

Maddie looked down at Friday sitting between her and Jim.

The dog took time away from licking fingers on their linked hands and returned the look. At the same time, he tested the air, sniffing noisily. His ears perked and he got up on all fours. His tail didn't wag. He sniffed again and snorted.

"What is it, Friday? What do you smell?"

A gentle breeze swept the bench and Maddie inhaled the sweet scent of freshly cut wood in the humid night air.

Jim smelled it, too.

"I wonder what they'll do with all the wood besides using it to fill fireplaces for years to come?"

Thanks to Friday's antics, a distracted Maddie changed the subject. "There was no scuba gear in Emma's apartment. I would have seen it."

"We'll look again anyway. She might have a storage area in the basement. You said there was a brochure for a diving place. If they're shacked up—"

"I don't think they're shacked up, Jim. Emma never appeared to me as the shacking-up type."

"Why not? They're young. They think they're in love. What's not to shack up about that?"

Maddie remained doubtful. "Is that the way you

spent time with your girlfriends when you were younger?"

"Pretty much. Why wouldn't Emma and Danny?"

Maddie resigned herself to a day of checking out spots in the boondocks for the missing pair. We'll pick up Boots and Lady first thing, before the heat and the humidity get too intense. Now come on. It's time for bed."

"Bed? It's barely nine." Jim grinned.

"Yes, well. You need your rest. So does Friday."

"Somehow, I doubt it's rest either of us will be getting."

"Yeah, but Friday—"

Friday chose that instant to test the air with his nose again. He tugged at his leash and tried to head off in the direction opposite the car his mistress was leading him toward.

"What's with him? He's been skittish for the last ten minutes."

Maddie still wasn't convinced the scuba thing was worth wasting their time, and she let Jim know.

"What else do we have, Mads?" he asked.

She let out an exasperated sigh. "We have someone named Fiona looking for Emma, that's what we have. You know she's out. Boyle confirmed it."

"But what would have brought her here? To this devastation? She wouldn't have known Emma was anywhere near here. I don't believe it for a minute," Jim insisted.

"What if she was passing through and spotted Emma? That's possible, isn't it?"

Jim considered before answering.

"I suppose it's possible. If she wanted a coffee. If she spotted Emma in the coffee shop. If she put together a plan on the spur of the moment. If she somehow got hold of Emma's apartment manager. That's a lot of ifs."

It was true. Maddie knew it. The chance was slim to

none Fiona was a part of this. Except. Except that bit about the manager thinking she was Fiona when she showed up at Emma's apartment. Fiona, a friend of Emma's. From her home town of Escape.

She was so certain, she had hauled out her revolver and tucked it into her back. And she was still certain, even if Jim wasn't.

"All right, gumshoe. I'm convinced," she admitted. "Tomorrow we'll do the scuba thing out in the boondocks."

If nothing else, it would eliminate another possibility.

Chapter 22

Except they didn't do the scuba thing out in the boondocks. Dealing with the missing Boots was taking up valuable time. Now they were stuck with another dog that needed wrangling.

"We should have done this last night," Maddie said.

They were on the way to the apartment with Friday and Lady, intending to walk Boot's dog around the grounds of the building.

"We'll be lucky if Lady picks up anything" she continued.

"You were just as shocked as I was to discover Boots missing. It's no wonder we completely blew it."

Maddie wanted to say I told you so, but she knew better. It wouldn't help matters. Jim had to be feeling just as bad as she was.

"I still think we need to check out the scuba places." He was still hot for the diving shacks on the lake.

"Jim—" Maddie gave up, exasperated, too disappointed to say so, then changed her mind. "We're wasting time on that. We've got three people missing. I really don't think romantic diving with a boyfriend takes precedence now, do you?"

It took them two long, hot hours beneath a cloudless sky to maneuver the car past downed trees and power poles. Jim ended up putting the convertible top up on the old Packard and turning on the air conditioner. By the time they arrived at the first scuba shop, no one wanted to get out. A sign at the end of the first driveway announced Closed until further notice.

Maddie opened her door and quickly closed it. Even Friday and Lady didn't want to get out. "Well, that's that, wouldn't you say?"

Jim wouldn't say, and so they headed north to the second diver's roost. The driving was just as difficult. He was forced to maneuver the car past the burned-out hulk of a car on the edge of the road.

"I wonder if someone wanted an insurance claim?"

Maddie ignored him. She was still upset that they were wasting time. "Can we just get this over with?"

At the second dive house, they set the dogs free. They ran and jumped and chased down nothing but butterflies.

Maddie couldn't resist rubbing it in. "See? Told ya. Now let's get back to civilization, all right?"

She made Jim stop on the return and loosed the dogs, wanting him to believe they needed a pee break. Instead, she chased them around the grounds of the first dive house. Convinced no one was there, she loaded the dogs into the Packard.

"All right. Let's go. I'm satisfied now."

Chapter 23

They had wasted hours on a useless search that turned up nothing. Even the dogs seemed disheartened. They were listless in the back, sitting, barely looking outside. Which, come to think of it, Maddie appeared to be doing the same thing.

Jim said "I'm sorry. You were right. I should have listened to you."

He slowed, passing trailers parked in a huge paved parking lot that must have been a giant department store's lot before the hurricane tore it apart. A bulldozer was busy leveling what was left. Trucks were laying down piles of sand to be leveled by a grader.

"What are those?" Maddie powered down her window to get a better look at the white structures.

"Probably those federal trailers. What's it called? Emergency something or other."

He took a better look. The few cars probably belonged to workers. The trailers appeared unoccupied. "I don't think I'd like to live in one of those."

"When your home is gone and there's no place to go for shelter, I'd want one."

The devastation was horrible, with downed trees and destroyed buildings everywhere. Construction was slow. Workers were few. He wondered who was paying them. Were they living in the trailers?

"Who gets one of those trailers, Maddie? Do you know?"

"No idea. I'll look it up later. Are we going back to Emma's for another look?"

Hope was slim, and they knew it, but now, with Boots missing too, he was starting to believe it was all Fiona's doing. It had to be. Who else could it be?

"Somehow, that woman stumbled onto Emma. She must have been passing through. Stopped at the coffee shop and saw her. Decided on the spur of the moment to have her revenge for what went down in Escape," he said.

Maddie turned to the dogs in the back. "Finally, boys and girls. He comes around to our way of thinking."

Friday woofed. Lady yelped and nudged the back of Maddie's neck. She laughed and scolded the dog. "Lady. Your nose is freezing."

"Now you know how I feel when Friday does that. They're both Zelda's offspring, aren't they?"

Not to be outdone, Friday did exactly the same thing to the back of Jim's neck with a cold nose and a sloppy tongue.

"Two peas in a pod, both of them."

He suspected Friday was disappointed that he didn't admonish him as he usually did, because seconds later, the dog did it again.

Chapter 24

The local PD recognized them the instant they walked into the building. Following the confrontation with drawn weapons at the motel, they were happy to see them.

Jim suspected they were exhausted by events caused by the hurricane, and welcomed visitors who didn't have complaints.

They were sympathetic to our problem with the missing people. He told them about Fiona Lubinski, and showed her photo.

They showed them the bulletin and let them know they were on the lookout. It was unfortunate, but everything they were dealing with due to the hurricane was taking precedence.

Looters. Flim-flam artists. Phony construction companies. Workers who promised to do work, took money up front, and then disappeared without a trace. It was overwhelming for everyone, both citizens and the police department alike.

"You two have no idea how happy I was to learn you were licensed private detectives when we did the firearms call."

"You and your men handled it professionally, Chief. My partner and I appreciated it, too."

"I'll have my men keep an eye out, but we can't

promise much more, given the circumstances," the chief said.

"I understand. We'll be sticking around until we locate our friends." Jim got up to leave. "Oh. One more thing. Those trailers on the edge of town."

"What about them?"

"We noticed them on the drive. Are they occupied?"

The chief shook his head. "Unfortunately, no. Apparently, there's some problem between the feds and the state. The town has been told we can't occupy until the paperwork is completed. When that will be, nobody seems to know."

"I'm sorry to hear that. I'd bet that a lot of people would rather be in them than in a tent on their front lawn beside a destroyed home."

"You're right about that, although some only desert their property as a last resort. There are plenty of firearms around, too. We're hoping nothing happens to cause us to take drastic action against any of them."

"Well, I guess that's it. Thanks again, chief."

Jim returned to Maddie out front in the car.

"Well? How did it go?"

"As we suspected. The department is overwhelmed by the aftermath of the hurricane. The chief was sympathetic, and he'll see they do what they can, but don't expect much."

"More than they can handle."

"No doubt about it. We're on our own."

It was near dark. Jim drove to the motel with Maddie and two dogs.

"We're going to need another set of dog dishes, Maddie."

"No, we won't. Two bowls are enough. We can feed them at the same time. I'll rinse the bowls and they can have all the water they need after that."

Friday and Lady had become friends, thankfully.

There was no rivalry. He was tickled that Lady had taken a shine to him in Boots' absence. Even Maddie noticed it.

"Boots better not find out Lady is following you around like you're the puppy."

"Ah, puppy-love. She's no puppy now."

"Neither are you," Maddie added and smiled.

Chapter 25

Dim light filtered through the curtained motel window.

Jim appeared to be fast asleep.

Maddie nudged him, wanting to make sure. Satisfied, she crawled out of bed and donned her jogging outfit. She halted at the foot of the bed. The dogs lay back-to-back, gently snoring almost in unison.

She checked the table for the room key and pocketed it before exiting. She eased the door closed. The latch clicked and she put an ear to the door and listened. Satisfied she had disturbed neither man nor dogs, she made for the street. She picked up her pace and headed off toward the trailers.

It took ten minutes beneath the few functioning street lights. Broken branches and small trees presented obstacles in her path. She narrowly missed tripping over them in the dark. She slowed as a result, but running was still treacherous. She jogged through several blocks with no lights to finally reach the trailers. Huffing and puffing, she slowed to a walk to catch her breath. Sweat rolled down her face and soaked through her top.

There were no lights in any of the buildings in the complex. So the chief was right. She didn't doubt, but only wanted to reassure herself—which was probably doubting.

Maddie scoped out the trailers as best she could. She walked the gravel avenues, hesitating, trying a few of the doors. Felt for the latches. The ones she checked were all secured with padlocks. She cursed silently for not bringing a light.

The sound of an approaching vehicle forced her to halt. She took shelter out of sight behind a trailer. A half-ton turned into the complex. It slowed before the driver dimmed and then turned out the headlights.

What's it doing here?

Was it making use of an empty trailer until finding a place to stay, perhaps?

The truck halted beside a trailer. Its sole occupant got out. The interior light didn't turn on. A man, probably. Wearing a ball cap. Dark clothes. It was difficult to keep him in sight. He had to be checking trailers for locked doors.

A watchman.

That settled it, then. Obviously a security guard. And no doubt needed, given permission wasn't granted to occupy the trailers.

She headed back to the street. Halted and took shelter from prying eyes when the truck started up. Waited impatiently for it to pass before heading back to the motel.

She ran all the way.

Maddie slipped the key in the door and entered the room. No one was up. She breathed a sigh of relief until a light flicked on.

Jim and both dogs were in bed, one on each side of him. Flustered, she said the only thing that came to mind.

"The dogs aren't allowed to be on the bed, Jim."

"No shit, Sherlock. The dogs are with me to make sure you didn't come home and slip into bed without waking us up."

Caught out, she stammered. "Well, I—I-I-"

"Well, nothing. They woke me up, all worried you weren't here. I told them you went for a walk, like they could understand. So they jumped on the bed and waited with me since I wasn't in panic mode."

"Aww. You're all too sweet."

"Sure. I'll buy that. Now, are you going to tell me about it, or do we have to sweat it out of you?"

The dogs were busy keeping an eye on both of them, like they were trying to decide who to believe.

Maddie called to them.

They refused to budge from the bed.

That was when she knew she was in real trouble.

"You're right. I went for a jog."

"I'm a detective, remember? You were sweating and huffing and puffing when you sneaked into our room. Where did you go?"

"I jogged out to the trailers. The chief was right. There's no one in them. Not a light to be seen. And there's a security guard, too. He came on the lot. I waited him out before leaving."

The dogs kept looking from Jim to Maddie. Seemingly satisfied, they jumped off the bed and settled at the foot, back-to-back so they could keep a wary eye on the door.

"Thank goodness. I was starting to think I was going to have to rent a room of my own."

Jim's smiling face looked up at Maddie.

She wasn't happy she'd been caught.

"You still might if you take off by yourself like that again, woman. We have enough to worry about, don't we, dogs?"

Jim turned out the light.

Maddie undressed in the dark, happy that man and dogs forgave her transgressions.

Chapter 26

Maddie Spence made sure she was out of bed early. She dressed in a hurry. Fed and watered the dogs before Jim was even awake.

She sat on the edge of the bed.

The huge dogs jumped up and fussed with the covers, trying to burrow beneath them.

Annoyed, Jim tossed the sheet aside.

"Good dogs. Now what, my people? Is our woman trying to make good another escape?"

The fussing halted. Both dogs were satisfied the male was awake.

"No, silly. I fed and watered the dogs. I thought I'd take them for a walk. We wanted to be sure you were awake before we left."

"Yeah, and that guilty look on your face is no make-up for last night's folly, dear."

"Folly-schmolly. It's walk time, boys and girls. Let's go. I'll expect you out of the shower by the time we get back."

She closed the door and led the dogs toward the trailers. It couldn't hurt, could it? Friday was obedient, but Lady put up a struggle, straining at her leash as she led the dogs down the now-familiar sidewalk.

"What is it, girl?"

A half-ton passed them and then slowed and turned

down a side street. Maddie ignored it and continued on with the dogs. At the last minute, she turned off the main road and headed back to the motel on another street.

"Our man better be ready, boys and girls."

She struggled to handle the dogs. Lady wanted to keep going. Friday pulled her toward the motel. Frustrated, Maddie called to the chocolate Lab. "Come, Lady. Heel. We're going back to see Jim."

Reluctantly, the dog obeyed, but not without announcing her displeasure with a loud, solitary bark.

"What is it with you today, Lady? Are you still mad I didn't take you with me last night?"

Lady didn't answer, of course.

Maddie slapped her thigh twice in rapid succession. Lady followed her all the way to the motel without complaint. She has been well-trained by her master, Boots.

So that's the secret.

Lily must have taught the signal to Lady and to Friday, both.

Chapter 27

Fiona Lubinski couldn't believe her luck. She recognized the brown dog right away. It belonged to the man in Emma's apartment. The dog she locked in the bedroom. The man, Emma's father, was instrumental in her capture in snowbound Escape.

She had him with the other two. She spared no expense. Each in a trailer of their own. Bound up as they were, she wasn't concerned they would go anywhere.

She pulled the cap down over her eyes before turning the truck around. She drove past the woman. Recognized her. Maddie. It was her dog that tore apart her wrist. And lo and behold, woman and dog were walking down the street. Right here in beautiful downtown Blue Springs.

She turned off the main drag, parked, and got out to follow them on foot. It was plain they were headed to the motel. Where else would they be staying?

Now what?

How would she get that damned woman into the trailer complex without alerting the woman's partner?

And once she had them all there, what would she do with them?

Certainly, they were all responsible for her imprisonment. Okay, so maybe the credit union armed robbery had something to do with it. Losing her boyfriend hadn't helped matters. He was shot during the robbery attempt. And killing one of the partners in the robbery in that snow-covered hick town got her a long time in prison.

The more Fiona thought about it, the angrier and more frustrated she became. By the time she returned to the truck, she was ready to kick rocks down the street.

She headed back to Billy to thank him for letting her use the truck the only way she knew how.

F iona finished with Billy and crawled off on top of the tangled, sweaty sheets.

"One of the guys with a van wants to take us all fishing tomorrow. You want to come?" Billy asked.

Fiona pretended to consider for only a few seconds before blurting out a response. "I'd like to, but I have things to do tomorrow. If I could use your truck again, it would be perfect, sweetie."

The word passed her lips and she almost grimaced. She forced a quick smile before swallowing hard, barely managing not to choke.

With that out of the way, she headed off to the shower.

Chapter 28

Stubborn as she was, Maddie knew better than to go off on her own. She knew, but still, it didn't seem right. She knew Emma and her father, Boots. Both were instrumental in Fiona's capture.

Even Friday played a part when he attacked the woman and bit her in the arm holding the gun.

It came to her, out of the blue.

Friday bit Fiona.

She was certain the security guard in the trailer park was cradling the right arm. Favoring it, maybe. As best she could tell recalling the inky darkness of last night.

Of course it was Fiona. Who else would it be?

She tied the dogs to the Packard's driver-side door handle and took off running. She made for the trailer park as fast as her legs would take her. She recalled how the guard had only checked the door handles of three of the dozens of trailers parked in the lot.

Three people missing. Three trailers. One for each. How did it not occur to her last night?

She cursed her misfortune for not recognizing the woman. She cursed again for being stupid and not telling Jim. She cursed a third time and then gave up.

In her haste she left her phone behind. And her pistol. Both were in the night table by her side of the bed.

Jim would be sure to kick her butt when he caught up.

If he caught up.

She stopped wasting time and energy thinking and increased her pace. She kept to the road and avoided the sidewalks. Except. She couldn't banish thinking. If she could find the exact trailers in daylight. If she could get them open. She would need a pry-bar. An old lug-nut wrench. There was one in the back of the Packard. Sharp on one end. Jim had to explain what it was.

She cursed her stupidity again.

She knew she should turn back. Make for the Packard. Surely Jim would be showered and changed by now. Handguns. She could get her handgun in the night table. Jim would be there to help. Friday, too. Lady.

Dammit but why didn't I think first before taking off like a teenager?

The trailers. There they were, right in front of her.

The half-ton, too.

She halted. Almost tripped over a log half on the sidewalk that she'd somehow missed last night.

Exhausted, she bent over.

Put her hands on her knees to keep from collapsing.

Straightened and wiped sweat out of her eyes.

Bent over again.

Dammit dammit dammit.

Fiona **knew Maddie would** come. The woman would have figured it out by now. It was only a matter of time.

She made sure she was prepared. With the gun she found in Emma's apartment when she took Boots. The ugly brown dog made such a fuss she had to force Boots to close it in the bedroom. Even then it wouldn't shut up. She had considered shooting it, then changed her mind. The gun would make even more noise.

She took her time preparing. She checked the locks on her trailers. She made sure to open a fourth, just for Maddie. She climbed in and sat with her back to a wall. Stretched out her legs. Faced the door at a ninety-degree angle. It might give her an advantage. If there was gun-play, she'd be out of the direct line of fire. Temporarily, at least.

She didn't fare so well the last time there was gun-play with this crowd. She rubbed at her shoulder with her bad arm, remembering. Jim Nash. The private eye. The one who shot her. Maybe it was her fault for not listening. But he was the one who pulled pulled the trigger.

Gravel crunched, alerting her to a presence outside the trailer. She tensed. Remembered to pick up the handgun and grip it with her good hand and arm. She allowed it to rest against her thigh. Her arm didn't have the same strength since getting shot in the shoulder. At least it was warm here. Hot and humid. Not like that hillbilly town in the mountains.

Footsteps sounded on the iron stairs leading to the door. It opened

Bright sunlight flooded the trailer, blinding Fiona. She blinked. Blinked again. Twisted to see out the door.

A shadow crossed her face and blocked the scalding bright sunlight streaming into the trailer.

"Fiona? What the—"

Chapter 30

Maddie **took a step** back. Panicked and frightened, she reached behind her back before remembering the handgun she left in the room. She brought both hands in front of her. Held them out to show Fiona there was nothing in them.

"Well well well. We finally get to meet once again. Get your ass in here. Where's your dog?"

Fiona leaned to get a look out the door, wary of the dog.

The handgun wavered in Fiona's left hand. Her good hand. She was forced to use her scarred right to help steady the gun.

"Get on your knees."

Maddie complied. She knew by instinct and experience Fiona meant business. She suspected the woman already had three people locked away in the tin-can trailers.

Before she could say a word, Fiona bashed the side of her head with the pistol. Maddie collapsed on the floor and stayed there, eyes closed, pretending to be unconscious.

Fiona stepped away and Maddie opened one eye to assess. Her assailant held the pistol in her left hand while she rummaged through a bag. She pulled out a couple of zip ties and placed them on the counter. Her hand went back in and came out with a roll of gray tape.

The woman returned and bent over her. In seconds,

her wrists ended up behind her back.

Maddie tested them anyway, to be sure.

They were zip-tied too tight to move.

A strip of tape ripped and ended up covering her mouth. No gag. A small comfort that she'd be able to breathe easily and not end up choking.

She inhaled, in and out, taking deep breaths. Tried to stay calm. Succeeded, mostly.

Except.

Fiona paced back and forth.

Ranted.

Raved.

Babbled incoherently.

Something about not enough time. Or too much time. Or it was time for something.

She cursed.

Yelled.

Jumped up and down.

The woman appeared suddenly pleased about something.

Maddie was pretty certain she knew what it was, since she was the one bound with mouth taped on the floor of an empty government trailer on the fringes of a town destroyed by a hurricane.

She closed her eyes and let the woman rage on. And on. And on.

Finally, Fiona halted and kicked her.

She opened her eyes.

"That man of yours is next. And the dog. I'm going to get you all, bitch."

Maddie looked up at the crazy lady and rolled her eyes. It might not have been the smartest move, but it sure felt good.

For her troubles, Fiona delivered another kick.

Maddie blacked out.

Chapter 31

Jim **Nash parted the** curtains and looked out of his motel window more than once. Not that he was anxious. Maddie had the dogs with her. Sure, two of them might be a handful, especially Boots' Lady, but even so. She was experienced. And Friday would certainly look out for her if it came to it.

He checked the nightstand on Maddie's side of the bed. Her revolver was there.

He flipped it open. Empty. The butterfly must be in her backpack. Now he was concerned, until he figured that if she was off looking for Fiona, she would have taken her handgun.

Satisfied, he headed for the shower, expecting Maddie and the dogs to return any minute.

Shaved, showered, scrubbed and shampooed, he dressed and opened the curtains wide.

His eyes went just as wide.

Friday and Lady were tethered to the Packard's driver door handle. They were waiting patiently for Maddie to return—unlike him, now impatient and angry to know what the hell was going on with that woman.

He cursed and took it back.

He cursed again and ran water to fill the dog bowls.

They were more than glad to see him, as evidenced by the whining.

He shut them up with the water and the grateful sounds of slurping dogs.

Maddie wouldn't be so grateful when he put her over his knee.

Like that would ever happen.

Jim retrieved Friday's long leash and swapped it out for the short one tied to the Packard's door handle.

He left Lady with her short leash. She would be easier to control that way.

Now that they were organized, where to begin? It was obvious Maddie hadn't run off to pick up coffee. Yet she left the dogs. Why? Maybe she was after coffee after all. Coffee and donuts in one of those trays wouldn't be all that manageable with two dogs dragging her down the street. They were trained to be better than that, though.

He left the worst for last and somehow knew it had to be. She must have spotted Fiona. Or worse. Fiona spotted her. Was the woman following her? Or was it the other way around? Was Maddie following Fiona?

That would make the most sense. She couldn't very well traipse after someone with unruly dogs in tow. Thus, she dropped them. Why didn't she knock on the door to let him know?

He went back into the room and picked up a shirt with Maddie's scent.

Friday picked up on it right away.

He had to convince Lady to stick her nose in it. Once she did, the dog took off like a shot. He knew right away he should have put her on a long leash, too.

Friday was no slouch. He picked up his feet like he was headed for ice cream.

All he could do was try to keep up. It was a struggle. Those wasted office snoozes with Friday when they were supposed to be working off their love handles didn't do a whit of good.

He'd be fixing that when they got home.

In the meantime, Maddie was missing and two dogs were leading him down what he hoped would be the one-way garden path to finding her.

He cursed for not picking up his handgun when he had the chance, but trying to convince the dogs to backtrack wouldn't be the best idea.

Not when the dogs were certain they were hot on Maddie's trail.

Chapter 32

Jim was busy wheezing. Trying to keep up with the dogs. Looking down at feet and sidewalk to dodge the branches. Trying not to stumble. The farther they got from town, the more downed trees interfered with progress.

He slowed and led the dogs to the cleared street and stopped huffing and puffing. The lot full of white trailers was coming up.

He called the dogs to heel.

Lady obeyed instantly. Friday, not so much.

He was sure he thought he was on Maddie's trail. Nothing was going to stop him.

"Friday. Heel. Sit."

The dog knew by the tone. He sat down beside Lady and woofed a complaint. Lady agreed with her own woof.

They nosed thighs and thumped tails, but there was no way he was giving them the lead. With Boots' handgun missing, he wasn't taking chances that a desperate and crazed Fiona would end up emptying it on the dogs.

If it was Fiona.

Why was he still doubting Maddie's suspicions? With four missing people and no one else in the hot seat, Jim finally had to admit she was right.

Didn't he?

To add to the confusion in the impromptu trailer

park, a convoy of trucks was there to greet them. Roaring diesel engines and wailing back-up beepers sounded the alarm. Dump gates crashed against raised truck boxes.

A grader busied itself grading the piles of sand left behind by the trucks. Men in orange vests waved arms to direct traffic. Surveyors laid out lines they marked with rattle-can paint.

"Well, boys and girls, it looks like we have our work cut out for us. Come on now."

He slapped his thigh and the dogs agreed to heel. They patiently followed him into the maelstrom of exhaust and engine noise and dust coupled with wailing back-up alarms.

He approached a flag man. He told him more trailers started arriving just before sunrise. He thanked the man and allowed the dogs to pull him toward the rows of trailers.

The dogs marched up and down rows of blinding white buildings. They arrived at the beginning of a new row, and tails ceased wagging. Sniffing noses and nervous back-and-forth movements replaced the motions.

He called softly for the dogs to heel. They obeyed, given they must have Maddie's scent. And probably that of Boots and Emma, too.

"All right, you two. Those doors are all padlocked. I need a tire iron."

Except, they weren't all padlocked. The dogs halted and wouldn't go beyond one that wasn't. They kept silent, too, forcing him to pay even more attention.

He had struck gold, thanks to Friday and Lady.

"Come along, Lady. Heel. You too, Friday. Heel. We need to pause and regroup."

He considered himself fortunate neither dog started their barking. Hell, even he knew Maddie was here. And most likely Fiona, too. Why the woman didn't keep watch was weird until he considered the noise of the trucks and the dust they kicked up. The strong wind and blowing sand wouldn't be a help for her, either.

"We have to have a plan, dogs. And I need a crowbar. Let's go find one."

Jim walked to a bleating semi backing up to position its load. The driver exited to unhitch, and he approached.

Jim explained he lost some keys to the padlocked doors. That his supervisor would kick his ass when he found out he wasn't able to do the inspections. He begged a tire iron. A crowbar. Anything. He allowed the driver to fuss over the dogs and he obliged by opening a compartment. He rummaged through it and came up with a crowbar.

Jim said his thanks and led the dogs around the front of the semi. He knew he'd be finding more trouble than any of them needed.

Friday and Lady had better be prepared to pull their weight.

He cursed one more time at his bad luck for not bringing his handgun.

He still wasn't thoroughly convinced he'd find anything.

No matter what Maddie thought.

Chapter 33

Dust flew past the flapping door into Fiona's trailer. The door thundered against the frame and bounced back to slam against the aluminum siding wall. She made a grab for the handle. It slipped from the fingers of her bad hand. The door bounced. She cursed, made another grab, caught it and closed and latched it.

The heavy equipment noise quieted and immediately she bent to finish taping Maddie. She sat her up against the kitchen counter. Her head banged and she groaned.

"That should hold you for a while. How long do you think it's going to take your partner to twig that I've got you?"

Fiona ripped the tape from Maddie's mouth. The woman's head banged against the cabinet a second time in an effort to escape the pain.

Maddie grimaced and licked her lips before speaking.

"When Jim shows up, you're going to be in dire straits, Fiona. You better count the rounds left in that handgun and save one for yourself."

Fiona grinned an evil smile. An expression of hatred took over her entire face. "I already counted. I've got enough for your dog, too. That black devil ruined my hand back in Escape. He's not getting another chance to do more damage to anyone if I have anything to say about it."

Maddie smiled noticing Fiona absent-mindedly rubbing at her shoulder.

"I see where Jim left his mark on you, too."

Fiona's backhander slammed Maddie's head against the cabinet.

The force of the blow aggravated Fiona's hand. She dropped it to her lap and rubbed at her shoulder. "He'll pay, too. You're all going to pay. Every last one of you."

Fiona sat down across from Maddie and leaned against the wall.

"I couldn't believe my luck when I spotted Emma in that coffee shop. I almost didn't believe it at first. Luckily, I didn't walk in. I followed her for a bit and found out where she lived, and look at me now."

She placed the gun on the floor and held out her hands. "I should buy a lottery ticket when this is over."

"You won't be in any position to buy anything, Fiona. You'll be dead." The words came out unfiltered and faster than Maddie intended.

Fiona looked across at her with a deadly smile. "I don't think so. You're the one that will be dead. I'll be just kind enough to make sure I bury you with that dog—if I can find a shovel, that is."

Fiona had enough. She taped Maddie's mouth before standing up and opening the door. The wind grabbed it again, yanking it out of her damaged weak hand. It slapped against the trailer's outside wall with a loud bang. More dust drifted into the trailer. She made a grab for the door and slammed it closed.

Chapter 34

Jim tuned an ear in the direction of the sound. Was it a door slamming? He couldn't be certain with the noisy trucks and the wind. If it was, it could only mean one thing. It was the trailer that was unlocked. Why, and what was inside that it needed to be?

He grabbed the crowbar and made for the last trailer in the line. It was the fourth one from the trailer he recognized as unlatched.

"Come Lady. Come Friday. We have work to do."

He pried the latch, using the noisy trucks to mask his work with the crowbar. Aluminum ripped and separated from the wall. He opened the door and peeked in. Someone he didn't recognize stared up from the floor.

"Danny?"

It had to be. He bent over and cut wrists and legs free before tearing off the tape covering the boy's mouth. "I'm sorry I don't have water for you. The dogs brought me here in too much of a hurry."

Danny only nodded and rubbed at his throat. He swallowed, dry, and in a faint voice said thanks. He managed to wheeze out a name. "Emma."

He helped the boy stand and was forced to catch him when he collapsed.

"Don't worry. I'll find Emma. You need to stay here. You're too weak to help. I don't want you getting in the way. Understand?"

Danny nodded weakly, and he helped him slide to the floor.

He left him and went outside to find Lady in front of one trailer and Friday in front of another. He slapped his thigh and both dogs rushed to his side.

"Good girl, Lady. Good boy, Friday. Heel. Stay with me."

He busied both hands with patting and head rubbing, and reluctantly, they heeled.

Together, they proceeded to the second trailer.

Jim popped the latch and Lady rushed up the steps and through the open door. She greeted Emma with a wet nose and a severe tongue licking.

It was all he could do to get Emma's arms and legs free as both dogs fussed over her. Lady even growled at him for getting in the way of her celebration.

"Am I glad to see you, Emma. Your father is going to be thrilled. Judging by how excited Lady is to see you, she's about ready to burst."

Emma's arms went around Lady and she looked up. "Jim. That monster—"

"Fiona. I know. She has your father and Maddie, too. The dogs found you all. Danny is free in the next trailer. I want you to go to him. I want both of you to stay there. You're too weak to help."

He helped Emma up and half carried her under Lady's watchful eye to a grateful Danny. "Remember what I said, Danny. Emma, you too. Stay here and stay safe."

He nodded and the young lovers hugged.

Lady worried over Emma, fussing and licking.

The dog wasn't so sure how to take Danny.

Danny got a nervous, soft nudge from Lady before he was forced to call the dog to follow out the door.

"Good girl, Lady. Heel."

Chapter 35

The construction noise was too much for Fiona. Trucks backed up. Warning beepers screamed. Wind whipped dust into a frenzy of blowing sand. Trucks pulled away. A grader engine groaned and leveled dirt. Diesel engines revved, releasing fumes. Doors banged.

Maddie stirred.

Fiona went on full alert. Was he here? That, or it was the wind again. She already had too many false alarms. She was edgy for some action. If only the damned construction brigade she found herself in the middle of would quit.

She checked Maddie's bindings. Satisfied, she went to the door. Looked out the window. Couldn't see anything but trucks and blowing dirt and dust. She waited, anxious. Told herself it had to be the wind.

Nervous and on edge, Fiona returned to the kitchen and Maddie.

"Don't get your hopes up. It was only wind. A false alarm. A truck door slamming."

Maddie couldn't speak past the tape over her mouth. She held still. She couldn't do much but keep her eyes on Fiona.

"You're not so happy now, are you? Not since you found out I have all your friends. I even have one you don't know about. Emma's boyfriend. He's in one of the trailers, too."

Fiona laughed and strutted back and forth in the small kitchen. She was proud of her abilities. Emma and the boyfriend and the old man. And the queen bee of them all. Maddie.

She had pulled it off all by herself on the spur of the moment.

She started to wonder if she forgot anything. Started to doubt. Went to the door again. This time she opened it. The wind caught it and it flew open. It banged loud against the aluminum and slammed shut in her face.

"That was close."

She might as well be talking to herself.

She looked over at Maddie. The woman wasn't listening. Her eyes were closed, feigning disinterest. Fiona suspected the woman's ears would be tuned to the sounds outside of her aluminum prison.

It's where hers were tuned, too.

Chapter 36

Maddie **was almost certain** she heard a familiar sound. She tensed. Listened with every fiber in her body. There it was again. A dog. Maybe. The wind howled, and the sound drifted away. Surely Jim would control them. Friday would obey. She wasn't so sure about Lady. Would Lady be the one to give Jim away?

Had Jim and the dogs found the others? Were they in one trailer? Separate? Were they still alive? She refused to think otherwise. She shook her head, drawing Fiona's attention.

"You might as well resign yourself to it, loser. You're going down hard. And so is your partner," Fiona insisted.

Did that mean the others were already dead?

Maddie's eyes shifted to Fiona and looked away. She thought back to the hotel room in Escape and the body of Fiona's dead boyfriend under the bed. A sound caught in her throat.

"Your dog is toast, too. I owe him one for the useless hand."

Maddie opened her eyes to the sound of Fiona slipping the magazine from the automatic. Watched her check it.

"Emma's father was nice enough to bring me a present. Don't worry. It's full."

Fiona slammed the magazine into the grip. A grin crossed her face, but it wasn't friendly. It was anything but.

"I ought to get a medal for all of this. Who would have known I'd trip over one of the people responsible for my misfortune in Escape? That she'd be working in a coffee shop in this hillbilly heaven?"

Fiona sat down beside Maddie and joined her leaning back against the counter.

"The boyfriend was a bonus. You should have seen the look on his face when he saw that cast-iron fry pan coming his way."

She placed the handgun on the floor between them, tempting but for the hands tied behind her prisoner's back.

Maddie's eyes shifted to the gun and she looked away. It was too much to be so close yet so far.

"Yeah, go ahead and look. It's all you can do now. Just like you're going to watch me take out the big fancy private eye and the dog." Fiona's lips parted. A crazed laugh escaped the woman's mouth.

"After all these years. Manna from heaven. Who could have known? Who could have known?"

Fiona stood up and jumped for joy.

Lady followed **Jim and** they joined up with an upset and worried Friday. The dog sensed Maddie was close. He looked at me, and then at the next trailer. "All right, dog. I was wrong. Maddie was right. I should have listened to her sooner."

He called to Friday. Reluctantly, he came, but not before running to the suspect trailer. His nose would not be fooled. Finally, he snorted and settled in beside Lady. His ears perked and his tail halted.

"I know, dog. Maddie is close. But we have one more thing to do. We have to help Lady, okay? Help Lady."

Jim jammed the crowbar against the latch. It slipped past. He pried gently, not wanting the noise to alert Fiona. The latch separated from the aluminum wall and popped off. He opened the door and the dogs scrambled through his legs in their haste to get in.

Lady was ecstatic at the sight of her master.

Boots was taped and laid out on the floor.

She snorted and nudged and stuck a cold nose against the back of Boots' neck.

Friday was no slouch either when he recognized the man. No doubt he remembered all the times they spent snoozing in front of the man's fireplace.

Jim cut Boots free while explaining that his daughter and her boyfriend were safe in the first trailer. He nodded acknowledgment.

"I'll help you get to her. You have to stay there, Boots. You're too weak to be any help."

He nodded again, determined to stand up by himself. He couldn't do it.

Jim helped him straighten. "See what I mean? I need Lady, too. Is that all right?"

Boots nodded and he helped the man limp to the trailer and his daughter. It was old home week with both dogs and Emma and her boyfriend as introductions were made.

"Jim?"

I looked at Emma. "Danny is going to try to get to a truck and get one of the men to call for help."

It was obvious they had already discussed it. He wouldn't talk them out of it. "If that's all he's going to do. We don't need more help."

"We?" she asked.

"Lady and Friday and me. I already asked your dad if it was all right."

Boots nodded. He still couldn't talk.

"I'm sorry I don't have water for you. Maybe Danny can get some from one of the truckers."

Boots tapped his thigh to summon Lady. Reluctantly, she left Emma, but settled in front of the man. His voice wheezed.

"Lady."

The chocolate lab sat on her haunches. Her ears straightened as best they could. Dark brown eyes looked intently at Boots.

"Go with Jim. Help Jim. Stay with Jim. Help Jim."

The dog looked over at Jim and snorted.

He couldn't tell if it was one of derision for taking her away from her family.

She stood up and approached him.

Boots called softly to her.

"Good girl, Lady. Go with Jim," he encouraged.

Jim had a last word for Danny before he left.

"Try to get to the truckers. Get your hands on a phone and call the police. Get some water, and get back to Emma and Boots. Okay?"

The boy nodded and touched Emma's hand and then walked away on unsteady legs.

It was time.

Lady's tail stopped wagging and straightened.

Two dogs accompanied him out the door and down the steel steps.

Chapter 38

The door caught in the wind. Jim made a grab for it and missed. It slammed hard behind Danny, and he figured they were cooked. Surely Fiona must have heard the metal-on-metal thundering against the aluminum echo chamber.

"That tears it. She knows now."

Boots sat up and mumbled something he couldn't hear.

He tried again. "I'll come with you, Jim. Two of us—"

He interrupted, careful not to make the man feel like a third wheel. "No, Boots. I can do it with the dogs."

"What if she has my gun?"

As far as he knew, that wasn't a what if. It was a definite yes. She had the gun. How could she not?

"It's too late now, Boots. Danny will get help. I need you and Emma to stay here and stay safe. Keep Danny here when he gets back, all right?"

Jim looked at Emma.

She nodded.

The determined look on her face told him she'd do his bidding.

Danny's bindings had been the loosest, thus he'd sent him for help.

Emma and her father were still struggling to massage ankles and wrists.

But for that, he would have sent them off to walk as far away as they could get.

"All right. Well, it's not getting done if I sit here jaw-jacking."

He looked over at the dogs. They were still fussing over Emma and Boots.

"Friday. Lady. Come. We have work to do."

They heeled immediately.

Lily had trained them well, and Boots used the opportunity to remind him.

"Our girl Lily did a good job, didn't she? With both of them."

His face beamed with pride in his dog.

Jim couldn't disagree. How good, he was about to find out.

"Wish us luck."

He didn't wait for a reply.

Neither did the dogs.

They followed him out the door and took up the scent leading to Maddie. They slow-trotted, being sure to wait for him.

Like he had a plan.

Were they in for a surprise.

Chapter 39

Adoor slammed. **Fiona** halted and listened. It had to be caught in the wind. A trailer. Immediately, she knew something was up. As far as she knew, they were all locked.

"He's here," she announced.

Nash.

Who else would it be?

The noise she filtered out returned and she remembered they were setting up new trailers on the lot.

Was it really him?

She stood over Maddie, prone on the floor. Took out the knife. Slipped the blade through the tape to free her feet. She would need the woman to stand when it was time.

"Don't get up on your own or you're dead," Fiona told her.

Or maybe not.

Fiona cursed silently at her indecision.

A dead Maddie wouldn't give the detective a reason to save her, to come looking. She thought better of it and instead left the tape over Maddie's mouth so the woman couldn't scream a warning.

Fiona returned to the front window and peeked out.

Spotted the black dog.

Waited impatiently for Nash to come into view.

He was only two steps behind.

His lips moved.

Probably talking to the dog.

Trying to keep it calm.

The dog most likely had the woman's scent by now. Maddie's scent. That's what dogs did. If he thought his mistress was in danger, he'd probably be uncontrollable. Like he had once before.

Fiona thought back to that godforsaken, frozen town in the middle of nowhere buried under a mountain of snow. Remembered how the dog attacked her, even as she was retreating out the door.

She rubbed her right hand at the memory. The dog had rendered it almost useless.

She cursed out loud and went to the window to check on Nash's progress.

"All right. It's time. Get up."

Fiona struggled to get her prisoner upright. With one bad arm and Boots' handgun in the other, it was a near impossibility. She had to let go of the gun to get the woman on her feet. She placed it on the counter.

"Listen to me, bitch." She slapped Maddie, making sure the woman's eyes locked onto hers before she went on.

"You're going to stay in front of me. I'm going to open the door. Then we're going to go outside. You will stay in front of me or it's curtains. Do you understand?"

Maddie nodded.

"Good. I'm glad you see it my way."

Fiona almost thanked her for helping.

Chapter 40

Jim edged up to the trailer door, wondering. Was this the one? There was no lock on the hasp, unlike the other three.

He threw caution to the howling wind and sand, and forced Friday to go prone to the right of the door. Lady took up a position on the other side, mimicking Friday. Both dogs were at attention. Tails erect. Ears facing forward and up. Two pairs of brown eyes concentrated on the door in front of them and slightly off center.

"Good girl, Lady. Good boy, Friday. Wait for my command."

If they heard him, the dogs didn't make a sound. It was as good as it was going to get.

"Fiona!"

Nothing.

He called again.

A voice filtered past the wind and dust whipping through the rows of trailers.

The door opened.

Maddie appeared. Hands and arms taped. She was proving to be a handful.

Fiona struggled not to lose her grip. Fiona's other hand held the handgun. It wavered. She struggled to keep it steady.

Maddie kept moving forward on the small landing at

the top of the stairs. Her feet reached the edge. She halted, leaning back and forth. Would she stop? Was she going to keep going?

Too late, Fiona tried to halt the movement.

Maddie stepped off the landing.

A gust of wind caught the door.

It banged against the wall.

Distracted by the sound, Fiona was too late. She made a grab for Maddie and came up with an empty hand.

Maddie's feet slipped off the top step and she tumbled out of Fiona's grip.

The handgun went off. A boom echoed down the row of trailers. If Emma and Boots heard it, they'd be on their way, crawling or walking.

There was no time left.

Jim yelled. "Now! Go!"

Two hundred pounds of silent black and brown dogs launched themselves into the air. Only a disappearing cloud of dust remained in their wake. Neither dog made as much as a sound.

Maddie fell.

Landed against him. Together, they tumbled to the ground.

He rolled and made a grab for her belt.

Connected.

Dragged her away.

In that instant, the dogs hit their mark, center-mass. The unstoppable force slammed into Fiona.

She was forced hard against the closed door. Her head connected with a bang and she slowly slid down onto the top step. She only halted when she ran out of door and fell onto the steel landing.

Both dogs recovered and stood over her. They didn't make a sound. Bare teeth showed.

He wouldn't want to be Fiona if the woman planned on putting up a fight.

"Good girl, Lady. Good boy, Friday. Stay on Fiona."

He found his knife and slit the tape on Maddie's wrists. He yanked the tape off her mouth and she gave him a dirty look.

"Sorry, baby, but I had to do it that way. You can spank me later after I'm done with you."

He helped her stand. She leaned against him to allow feeling to return to her limbs.

In the background, wailing sirens sounded.

"Lady." She looked up at me. "Good girl. Find Boots. Find Emma. Go."

The dog trotted off to find her master.

"I hope Danny called an ambulance. It doesn't look like Fiona is going to move any time soon."

The woman hadn't moved. She was still on her back. Her neck was at an odd angle against the bottom of the door. He walked up to her and reached. He wanted her in a more comfortable position if she was seriously injured.

"Don't touch her, Jim."

Emma.

"I told you to stay in the trailer with your father."

Okay, so maybe he was being a bit harsh. But you could never tell with Fiona. "She could be faking it."

That got a dirty look from Emma and she went into full paramedic mode. She took the woman's pulse. Checked her breathing. She didn't move Fiona.

"She'll need a neck brace. If her neck is broken—" She didn't finish.

He didn't say word one. If Fiona's neck was broken, as far as he was concerned, she'd be out of business for the rest of her life.

He picked up the handgun, slipped it into the small of his back, and concealed it with his shirt. The police were arriving, and he had plans for the unregistered handgun he wouldn't be revealing to Maddie. Or to anyone.

Not yet, anyway.

Chapter 41

Friday and Lady were badly shaken when they slammed into Fiona. The sudden stop caused them to land on the steps in disarray. Breathless and gasping for air, they struggled to stand and stay close to Fiona in the confined area.

Convinced that Fiona was finally out of action, Jim sent Lady off to find her master. She returned with Boots and Emma and Danny.

The dogs did an admirable job. After much petting and stroking and words of encouragement, they eventually settled down and began prancing around everyone. Sniffing and snorting and tails held high. Happy dog expressions on their faces told the story. They made the rounds more than once. They even bumped their own noses together and snuffled at each another.

The ambulance departed with a still-comatose Fiona.

Emma wanted to go with her, but we soon disabused her of that. She remained behind with Danny and the rest of us.

It was Boots who mentioned the gunshot.

"We heard a shot, Jim. What happened to the gun?" he asked.

Jim didn't mention it was tucked into the small of his back. "I didn't find it. You're certain it can't be traced, Boots?"

Just to be sure. He had to know.

"Not a chance, I promise you that. I'm from a small town in the wilderness, remember?"

That was good enough for him.

Following the on-site police interviews, they were herded into the back seats for a ride to the motel.

From there, Jim loaded everyone into the Packard and proceeded to make for Emma's. He even put the top down for the short trip.

Danny said his thanks and goodbyes and was about to depart. "I'll see you later, Emma."

He hugged her and shook everyone's hands, and then knelt to pet and pat the dogs.

Friday and Lady lapped up the attention, snuffling and sniffing and licking and sticking cold noses against bare skin.

Peals of laughter echoed in Emma's apartment as Danny almost tumbled on top of them.

"A good girl and a good boy. It doesn't get better than this."

The dogs separated and pranced around Danny with tongues hanging out and tails held high as he fought his way past the dogs to the door.

"Don't say any more, Danny. We have to get those dogs home eventually."

Jim and Boots headed for the grocery store for steaks and the fixings to grill on the super's borrowed barbecue.

They thanked their lucky stars no one was hurt.

They praised the dogs, and they started all over again with the prancing and tail-wagging and snorting and snuffling.

Jim was pretty sure both would be sore come morning if they weren't already. If so, they were doing a pretty good job of hiding it to get all the praise they deserved. Exhausted, they eventually wandered off to curl up together in the relative isolation of Emma's bedroom.

They left Boots to stay with his daughter after making arrangements to get him to Tallahassee and on a plane for home.

Jim and Maddie headed off to the motel. After a quick swim, they hit the sheets and passed out, exhausted from the heat and the wind and the dust and the day's events.

Jim was so tired he forgot to put Maddie over his knee and spank her for running off on her own.

It was probably a good thing.

Chapter 42

"Dad, when you get** to the airport, text me. Don't forget," Emma said.

Maddie smiled at Emma's concern for her father, especially after what they had all been through. "You know he will."

"And dad, when you get home—" Emma began.

Boots interrupted her before she could finish. "Text, text. Everything is text these days. These new-fangled phones—"

"No, dad."

Boots looked at his daughter and waited, a bemused expression on his face.

"When you get home, call me. It's still a phone, you know."

He grinned. "Yes, daughter. I'll call."

Emma escorted the crowd of people and dogs out the door. She locked it before following them down the steps to the small lobby and outside.

Warm sunshine bathed everyone. The humidity was down. It would be a pleasant day.

"Do you have your ticket, dad? And your driver's license?"

Boots sighed. "Yes, daughter of mine. I have everything right here." He held up the airline ticket, took out his wallet, and waved the license. I'd wave the bag, too, but it's so heavy I can barely wheel it."

"That reminds me," Emma said. "Don't forget you have to check your bag this time. They won't let you through with all those glass jars."

Emma had packed her father's bag with some of his favorite preserves she had put up weeks ago. They were the same ones her mother used to make for him.

"I made up a sampler for you, Jim. If you like them, I'll send Maddie the recipes. You're going to have to be the one to convince her to dedicate her life to cooking and baking for you."

Jim wouldn't look in Maddie's direction. He knew the grin on his face said everything. "Yeah, no. I don't think that'll be happening any time soon. Good try though. You better send those recipes to me."

Maddie exaggerated making a fist and drove Jim a good one in the arm.

"Ouch. That smarts, woman."

"Maybe she could send you an apron too, sweetie," Maddie told him.

He made a face and began rubbing the spot. "There'll be a bruise there for a week. See what you've started, Emma?" He shook his head. "The things I have to put up with."

Boots reluctantly called to the dogs. Come, Lady. You too, Friday. It's time to go."

The dogs pranced after Boots, following him to the huge Packard. Friday didn't look back.

Boots opened the door and leaned the seat-back forward. Both dogs jumped in the back and waited. Boots climbed in, and they scrambled to rearrange themselves on either side of him.

"What has that man done to my dog?" Maddie asked. "Boots? You can't take Friday home with you. I won't allow it."

Boots handed over treats and the dogs settled in beside

him. He looked at Maddie and grinned as she called him out.

"I saw what you did, Boots."

Emma leaned into the Packard and hugged her father, admonishing him a final time. "Call when you get home. Did you call Janine to let her know when your flight gets into the city?"

Boots rolled his eyes. "Yes, daughter dear. I did. Twice."

"In that case, I've asked Maddie to stay with me for a bit. I hope you don't mind, Jim."

"She's right. She needs the company," Boots said.

Jim couldn't argue with that. It only made sense.

"And don't you dare let Friday get on that airplane with Boots, gumshoe." She smiled sweetly at him.

"I would never do anything like that and you know it."

Good-byes said, Jim made for the highway, and in an hour he had them all at the airport.

"So long and thank you for everything. You too, Friday. Thank you for keeping my daughter safe. And me. And Lady."

Tears welled up in Boots' eyes.

Friday barked.

Lady sat and waited patiently for Jim to open the trunk to retrieve the luggage.

"Holy mackerel, Boots. You were right. This thing weighs a ton."

Jim tied a bandanna around Lady's neck.

The dog licked his hand.

Boots grinned at his dog's antics. "I was lucky to get one of Zelda's pups. You're a good girl, aren't you, Lady?"

Boots made for the entrance to the airport. Lady pranced along beside him, tail held high. He halted and pulled out his phone and began tapping. The dog stopped beside him and turned and barked.

Friday barked back at her before she followed Boots through the door.

"It's going to be a long drive home, Friday. Once we collect Maddie maybe we can stop somewhere along the way and make a holiday out of it now that everyone is safe."

Then he remembered he had somewhere he needed to be. He mumbled something about talking to a dog.

Friday's cold, wet nose touched the back of his neck.

"Zelda! I mean, Friday. Stop that. Bad boy."

The dog did it again for spite. For good measure he licked an ear.

Jim broke out laughing.

"That's my good boy."

Chapter 43

It would be a short drive to visit Warren and Allie. Jim was pretty sure Lily and James would want to see Friday, too. He had little trouble convincing Maddie. She must have noticed Friday's ears perk up when he mentioned Lily's name. She willingly allowed Friday to go along for a visit.

Emma appeared happy Maddie would stay a little longer. He couldn't blame her after the nightmare she experienced, thanks to Fiona.

"We'll be back in no time. You two be safe, okay?"

He felt guilty as hell, but he averted his eyes and loaded Friday into the Packard. "See you in a couple."

Friday plopped down beside him.

Maddie reached in to pet him.

Friday stuck his head out to bark his goodbyes and they were off.

Only a couple of hours later, he was pulling into the marina parking lot in Panama Crossing.

Friday recognized his surroundings and began barking the instant he got out of the car.

Zoe wandered over to investigate the fuss in the parking lot.

Friday trotted off to greet the dog, and the barking intensified.

Finally, Lily and James wandered out of a building.

Lily recognized the car and screamed.

Together, the dogs pranced off to investigate further.

"Max Friday. How's my dog? Are you still my good boy?"

Friday knew where his dog food was buttered in Panama Crossing. He pranced and snuffled and nudged and fussed over Lily and James.

Zoe did the same with Jim, and it was like old home week.

He didn't have time to waste. He went off to find Warren and Hank before the rest of the women came out to see what the fuss was about.

He spotted the men at the end of the pier tying off a boat. He figured they just returned from a charter. He got the pleasantries over with and got right to it.

"I have to take a trip. Can one of you take the car and the dog back to Maddie in Blue Springs?"

Warren wasn't having it, of course.

Jim knew he wouldn't, but after an explanation, he went along.

He didn't tell him the real reason. He had no choice. Allie would be on him like a wet blanket.

"I'll need to take Allie, Jim. Maddie isn't going to like knowing you're off somewhere without her."

Warren was stating the obvious.

Jim only mumbled thanks. He must have sounded guilty as hell. He purposefully hadn't told them where he was headed.

He didn't mention why, either.

Chapter 44

Warren and Allie discussed what they would tell Maddie on the drive to Blue Springs to return Friday and the Packard. They weren't happy with the way Jim dropped it all on them. Even so, they swallowed hard and knocked on the door to Emma's apartment.

Maddie answered the door and Friday scrambled past three pairs of legs. His nose hovered over the kitchen floor and he completely ignored Emma sitting at the table. He sniffed and snuffled and zig-zagged his way through the kitchen and down the short hallway to the bedroom where he doubled down on the search.

Maddie greeted the couple before moving past them to check the hallway in both directions. She regarded Warren and Allie with a raised eyebrow. "Where is he?"

Friday chose that instant to scramble back to Maddie's side where he promptly sat down. He woofed once, as though to emphasize the question.

Warren looked from Allie back to Maddie.

"We don't know."

"You two better come in if you know what's good for the both of you."

Emma looked up from the table. "I think I'll go for a run."

Maddie used the opportunity to go to the kitchen window and look out.

The Packard was parked in the street. The marina van was behind it.

"Give me a minute. I'll be right back."

She took the Packard's keys and opened the trunk. Jim's handgun and the oversize magazines were in their hiding place. She checked a couple of empty stash spaces in the front before returning to the apartment.

"Well, his hardware is there. The magazines, too. Are you sure he didn't say where he was off to?"

She looked at Warren, but the question was really for Allie.

"No, Maddie. He wouldn't tell us anything. Believe me, we tried. In fact, he said so little he didn't even swear us to secrecy.

"I tried, too, Maddie. He wouldn't say a word to either of us," Warren said.

Maddie knew Warren was Jim's best friend at one time. If Jim hadn't said a word to the man, it had to be something pretty bad.

"Well dammit to hell. That man is going to be the death of me yet."

She put the coffee on and they sat around the table.

Pleasantries over with, Maddie announced her decision.

"I'll be staying here with Emma until she's finished with exams. She has a job offer in the city. She'll be coming back with us."

She looked down at Friday and scratched an ear.

The dog whined, making known his disappointment.

"If you happen to hear from that Nash desperado, you can tell him we're waiting."

She reached to slap Friday's side.

"Oh, and one more thing."

Friday snuffled and nudged Maddie's thigh, as though to remind her he wanted to know where Jim was, too.

"If he gets in touch, you better make sure to let him know the story better be a good one, or else."

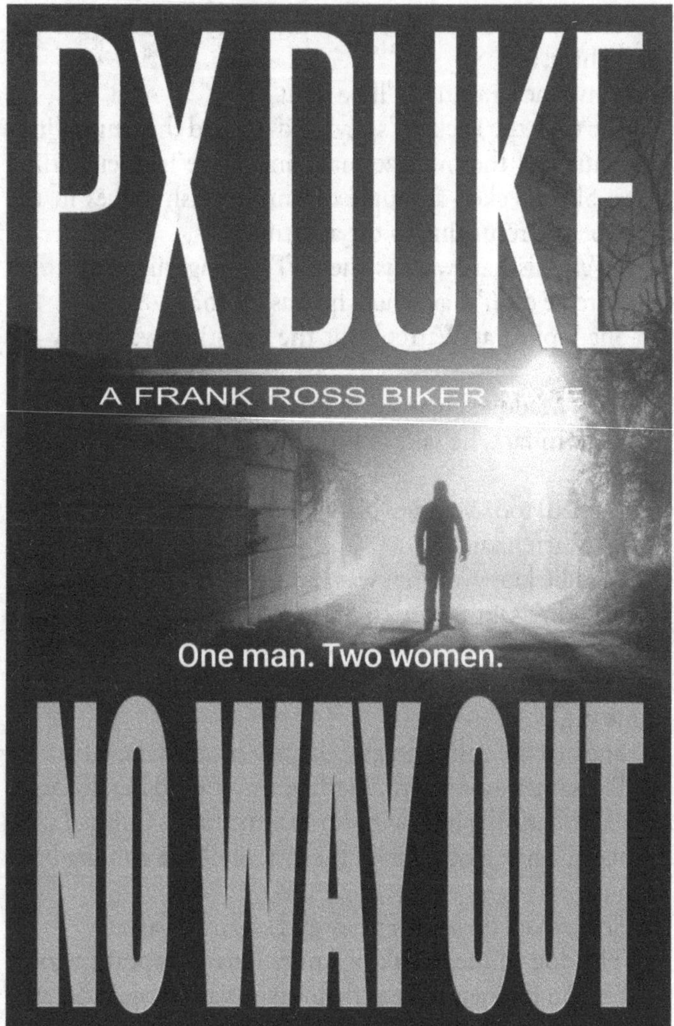

Frank Ross is out of Mexico riding north. He's just across la línea, looking for shade and water. He finds it, and a lot more than he bargained for when he breaks down at a casino by the Salton Sea.

About the author

Peter Duke is a Canadian author. He resides and writes in a small college town in the Province of Ontario, Canada.

Aviator. Motorcycle rider. Vagabond. Drifter. Trouble-maker. Jack of all trades and master of none. Peter Duke has been riding and writing about the places he's been and the people he's seen for quite a few years. Some of his writing is factual; some of it isn't. He likes to leave it up to readers to decide which lies might be the truth.

pxduke.com

peterxduke@gmail.com

Print books

Jim Nash
Jim Nash The Beginning
Gun Crazy
Gun Crazy 2
Gun Crazy 3
Fallen Angels
Last Stop to Nowhere
Revenge is Justice
Escape / Forget Me Not
Wedding Bell Blues / Breakdown
Mexico Time
No Free Ride / Gone
LOBO
Stealing America
Blame It on Djibouti
No Escape
Trouble in Paradise
Nash & Delaney Collide

Harry Delaney Adventures
Dead Reckoning
Lie Cheat Steal
Uncharted
Go-Around
Sand Storm
Harry Delaney Collection

Frank Ross Biker Tales
No Way Out
Bad Girls
Bank Robber Dames

Other
The Last President

9 781928 161615